ACKNOWLED

I am indebted to many people in the [...]
some of them are innocent bystanders, others were writing, generous with their expertise. Special thanks to Sergeant Sheila Maloney of Ottawa Police Services, Professional Standards, for her time and insight. Once again, I am happy to report my friend, Janet MacEachen, has kept me out of legal quicksand. John Merchant's eagle eye and lightning speed are excellent traits in a brother and most appreciated. The Ladies' Killing Circle: Linda Wiken, Sue Pike, Joan Boswell and Vicki Cameron offered their unique observations followed by no-holds-barred recommendations and, as usual, made things better. I am thankful that my husband, Giulio Maffini, has the strength of character to cope with dangerous writerly emotions and I thank Barbara Fradkin, Lyn Hamilton, Mary MacKay-Smith and Lois O'Neill for their friendship, support and laughter. As usual, the redoubtable Cheryl Freedman of Crime Writers of Canada ensured that Alvin Ferguson got airtime. And of course, without my long-suffering publisher, Sylvia McConnell, music-making editor, Allister Thompson, and agent, Leona Trainer, there would be no book.

Any errors in the text are entirely my own. At the time this book was written, the path behind the Supreme Court of Canada was open and unobstructed, although that just goes to show you that dangerous things can happen in beautiful places. As usual, some restaurants, streets, intersections and private homes in Ottawa and elsewhere are figments of my imagination. Unfortunately, this means there is no Maisie's Eatery featuring white and dark chocolate cheesecake with raspberry cognac coulis and caramelized pecans on the dessert menu. Deal with it.

Now and Forever

She no longer flinches when his hand strokes her cheek, long fingers gentle but powerful, tracing her jaw line. She reaches deep and brings forth her best smile. Why should she shrink from him? He is the protector. They are powerful with him in charge. They are safe. She wills herself to forget the past, memory brings only weakness. Her parents, a blurred mental image. The others: white faces twisted with terror, howling amid the shriek of gunshots, white flames from the Molotov cocktails, the silver spikes of cascading glass. And Kimmy, dark blood pooling around her perforated body, surprise on her small face.

They know the price to be paid for a new world. Her past is gone. The future belongs to the Settlers. The right names are on the lists. When the time comes, the oppressors and their lackeys will be eliminated. The world will be put right.

He will see to that.

The van rumbles along the rough backcountry road, lurching through potholes, swaying wildly, flinging bodies against the sides. Every five minutes, someone pitches over, the sound of bone slamming into metal reverberates. No one laughs.

He moves slowly on cushioned soles, from one to another in random order, whispering to each one, stroking a forearm, an earlobe, a chin. Handing out round white mints. Keeping each girl calm, reminding them of the job they had done and the tasks that lie ahead of them. Special words and touches for those who had let down their guard. You did not want to be responsible for a setback. You did not want a special touch.

There is sweat in the air she breathes.

He reaches her at last, in the corner where she has pressed herself, trying for balance. Her heart near to exploding. He says, "But you will be careful."

"Yes."

"Now and forever." These days he uses his soft voice. The voice that makes you focus totally, completely, absolutely, on him. To listen is to forget you are in a stolen van, driving without lights on dirt tracks leading to nowhere, anything to evade the state troopers. The soft voice reminds her why she is fighting, what she has lost and what she will gain. What she stands for. The voice binds her to him.

She is careful. Always.

His words, so light, she has to lean forward to hear. "Do you believe it?"

"Now and forever."

"The future is ours."

"The future is ours."

"What do we believe?"

"Those who represent evil will die. Those who are deserving will live in harmony."

"Who will make the difference?"

"The Settlers will make the difference."

"Some of the others were not so careful. You see what happens when you let your guard down."

"Yes." Six girls are left. She wills herself to be strong, to have a full voice, the voice of the powerful. She pushes away thoughts of Kimmy, left alone in her lake of blood.

The smell of urine fills the van. Behind her, somewhere in the dark, one of the careless ones has wet her pants.

Please, let her be strong enough to survive.

One

It was the dog end of a wasted summer. As a fitting finale, a Crown Prosecutor had dropped the ball in the case against the con artist who'd swindled my seventy-five-year-old client.

The creep who had wiped out her retirement savings reacted to his "not guilty" verdict with a smirk. By now, he'd be in his Porsche Boxster heading for a golf foursome. My client was still in shock from the vicious grilling by his lawyer. No golf club for her. She'd be lucky to afford Kraft Dinner in her one-room apartment. And she could forget the satisfaction of seeing that shit-heel go to jail. I'd given her a hug and cab fare home. My goddam car was on the fritz again.

Sometimes the life of a victim's rights activist is just plain crap. You care too much about your clients. You long to give the prosecution a kick in the pants. You take the defence tactics personally.

I wasn't happy when I found myself nose-to-nose with the swindling scumbag's lawyer. Sheldon Romanek stood like he owned the place on the wide stone steps of the Elgin Street Court House. He breathed deeply, filling his lungs with the Friday afternoon traffic fumes and the swirling, end-of-August dust and grit. I marvelled. Such a dumpling. So harmless looking with his dirt-green suit, gunky tie and dangling shoelaces. Sheldon was forty-five, but on a good day he could pass for sixty. A jury member might easily imagine him bumbling through the park with his beloved grandchildren. But Sheldon was single, without friend or family as far as anyone knew. A persistent rumour around Court had it that his heart belonged to a collection of arachnids he kept in his bed. That might have been the mutterings of the defeated.

He grinned at me.

I said, "Hey, Sheldon, if I hadn't seen it with my own eyes, I'd never guess you were the embodiment of evil."

"You win some, you lose some, MacPhee," he said, adjusting his comb-over.

"As long as you can sleep nights."

"I sleep like a baby."

"You know about babies?"

He leaned forward. "You want some advice?"

"From you? Hell, no."

"No charge for the insight. Here's my secret: I win my cases." His grin showed nicely greying teeth. Whatever Sheldon spent his money on, it sure wasn't dentists.

"You mean let the bastards walk."

"Rule of law in this country, MacPhee. Innocent until proven guilty."

"Sure. Let the fraud artists and drug dealers run free and happy."

"By all means, fall back on to your knee-jerk, left-leaning conspiracy theories, if it makes you feel better."

"You know what I fall back on, Sheldon? Principles. You might consider picking up a six-pack of them for the weekend."

"My principle is called victory."

"At any cost."

He chortled. "At least I don't have the shame of letting my clients down. Give that a try."

"Give this a try," I said, raising my middle finger.

"Funny. You used to be a smart girl, MacPhee. You did some gutsy defence work a few years back. Forget the lost causes. Get back to the law."

I didn't dignify that with a response. I don't dismiss running an advocacy agency for victims of crime as a lost cause. Even if that pretty much summed up every one of my recent files. On the other hand, I was getting sick of steering some poor soul through the justice system, only to watch the Crown cut a deal.

Maybe I was just spoiling for a fight.

Sheldon turned as a pair of Assistant Crown Prosecutors scurried down the stairs, avoiding eye contact with him.

The evil gnome actually winked at me.

"If you bottom out, you could always work with them," he said.

For historical reasons, I am *persona non grata* at the Office of the Crown Prosecutor, so that wouldn't be happening. I'd had enough of Sheldon. I adjusted my backpack and headed down the Courthouse steps.

"I might be able to find a place for you," he shouted after me.

"Not a chance."

"Call me if you want a real job, MacPhee."

"You kidding? I love what I'm doing."

No longer quite the truth, but damned if I'd admit that to Sheldon Romanek.

* * *

The *Devil's* in the Details

A Camilla MacPhee
Mystery

by Mary Jane Maffini

RENDEZVOUS
PRESS

Cover art: Christopher Chuckry

LE CONSEIL DES ARTS DU CANADA DEPUIS 1957 | THE CANADA COUNCIL FOR THE ARTS SINCE 1957

We acknowledge the support of the Canada Council for the Arts for our publishing program.

Napoleon Publishing/RendezVous Press
Toronto, Ontario, Canada

Printed in Canada

08 07 06 05 04   5 4 3 2 1

Library and Archives Canada Cataloguing in Publication

Maffini, Mary Jane, date-
        The devil's in the details / Mary Jane Maffini.

(A Camilla MacPhee mystery)
ISBN 1-894917-12-X

        I. Title. II. Series: Maffini, Mary Jane. Camilla MacPhee mystery.

PS8576.A3385D48 2004   C813'.54   C2004-903128-7

I was still smouldering as I approached my office a few blocks down Elgin Street. I'd stopped long enough to get a late afternoon caffeine fix at the Second Cup. Despite the fall nip in the air, I'd chosen an iced latte. I had stuff in my life that required a clear head. For instance, finding a new office location, since our landlord had decided to renovate the building and given us notice to quit the premises, such as they were. And more to the point, figuring out if I was wasting my time trying to hold Justice For Victims together. Period. No one seemed to believe my services to crime victims did much good. Not that I care about the opinions of others. Still, our contributions from private benefactors had shrivelled to zero, our clients were rarely in a position to pay for services, and government funding was harder to come by at every level. Alvin Ferguson, my so-called office assistant, was supposed to handle grants and fundraising. But Alvin had not been a peak performer in recent months. At least he used to come into the office occasionally to lick stamps and make long distance calls to his extensive family in Sydney, Nova Scotia. That was before he and my neighbour, Mrs. Violet Parnell, discovered hot air balloons.

Who was I to criticize? My latest client was out of cash, out of luck, out of hope. Having a victim's advocate hadn't done her a scrap of good. She hadn't blamed me. But I blamed myself. Maybe I'd lost my way in this whole advocacy process.

My family was pressuring me to get back to the practice of law, where you could make a dollar and not get shot at. And they didn't know I'd dug into my own limited savings to keep JFV going.

Still, nothing could entice me into a corporate practice. Not even the copy of *Litigation For Fun and Profit* which my sister Edwina had presented me for my thirty-sixth birthday. And I had no intention of turning to family law. Family law gives me hives. Before my husband Paul died, I'd spent a few years doing criminal law, mostly legal aid cases. I'd enjoyed it. But how could I return to defence after working with victims? Maybe that creep Romanek was a reminder from above to continue with the good fight.

I was so deep in thought I almost mowed down a young couple on the sidewalk. I did the kind of double-take you see in second-rate comedies. I'd almost knocked over Bunny Mayhew, my all-time favourite legal aid client.

"Wow, Camilla. I haven't seen you since your Legal Aid days. Boy, do we miss you."

"Bunny." I couldn't keep the grin from racing across my face. "You look terrific."

But then Bunny always looked great. He couldn't help it. Part of it was his crooked little boy smile, the stray lock of sandy blonde hair falling over his hazel eyes. His air of utter inept vulnerability was like an aphrodisiac for most women. I was aware of this effect and not totally immune.

"You remember Tonya?"

"How could I forget?" Bunny's long-time girlfriend Tonya also looked good. Why wouldn't she? She was five ten, with curves out to here. Her tan looked real. Her legs and arms were nicely defined, and currently she sported copper, auburn and burgundy highlights in her shoulder length dark bob.

Tonya had been in court for each of Bunny's hearings: Bail Court, Plea Court, Trial. Radiating hope, trust and undying love. Tonya was a solid citizen. She had a good income from her small hair salon, The Cutting Remarque, and a recent college diploma in Business Admin. Tonya kept her figure trim, her customers happy, and paid her taxes, or at least some of them. Traditionally, Tonya posted bail for Bunny.

Tonya was part of the reason Bunny never got convicted. But

only part. Mainly, it was Bunny himself. The child of an alcoholic mother, father unknown, he'd been cursed with dyslexia, ADHD and a tendency toward unauthorized borrowing. He'd dropped out of school in Grade Ten. So what? He was still the best damn client ever. He lacked the anger and sense of entitlement of so many petty criminals. Plus he was the only guy I'd ever met who looked good in an orange jumpsuit from the Regional Detention Centre. Sure, over the years, he'd been charged with 138 burglaries, but no one's perfect.

Judges liked Bunny too. Next to him, the burgled homeowners and other witnesses appeared sleazy and capable of insurance fraud. Honourable police officers looked like bullies. In my opinion, Bunny Mayhew represented the best the Canadian criminal classes had to offer.

Bunny squeezed Tonya's hand. "Guess what, Camilla?"

I hate guessing. "What?"

"I'm going straight."

"Get away."

"It's true," said Tonya.

"That's great news. Quite a surprise. What brought this on?"

Bunny looked shyly down at his feet.

I said, "It seems like a major career change."

Bunny patted Tonya's flat belly. "Gonna be a family soon, Camilla."

"Not that soon," Tonya said.

I didn't ask how Bunny was going to get over his compulsion to liberate paintings and original bronzes. It would have seemed rude to mention it. I hoped Bunny and Tonya had a plan.

"Show her your ring, babe."

Tonya lifted her finger and flashed a spectacular marquise diamond.

My eyebrows lifted.

Tonya frowned. "Bought and paid for. With after-tax money."

"Amazing." Especially the bought and paid for and after-tax parts. "This is the best news I've had all week."

"Thanks, Camilla." Bunny said.

"I wish all three of you well."

Bunny blushed. "We're thinking about getting married. Maybe next year. Right, babe?"

"We owe you a lot," Tonya said. "For keeping Bunny out of prison."

"But that was years ago."

"We never forgot what you did, Camilla," Bunny said.

Tonya said, "Come by the shop some time, and I'll fix your hair."

Bunny gave Tonya an affectionate nuzzle. "She's an artist. Aren't you, babe? Tonya can do miracles."

As the short, dark, dumpy sister of three tall, elegant blondes, I take such comments in stride.

Tonya glanced at her Gucci watch, possibly bought and paid for. "We're going to be late."

"Coming, babe."

"Good luck," I said.

My black mood had lifted. I was still beaming when I opened the door to the office.

Oh, did I say office? I must have meant voice mail hell.

Two

BEEP

"Camilla? It's Alvin. You're probably in court, but when you get in, call. You have to change your mind and come with me and Violet. You don't know what you're missing. Watching the sun across the river. Looking down on the trees. Peace, tranquillity. There's nothing else like this in the world. We're saving a place for you for the dawn take-off tomorrow. By the way, I won't be in the office today. I'm a bit under the weather."

BEEP

"Ms. MacPhee? Violet Parnell here. Young Ferguson tells me you have misgivings about our most excellent outing. The lad deserves a bit of excitement to help him recover from his wretched summer. People don't get over such grave problems quickly. You yourself are overworked of late, and long hours are taking a toll. Join us tomorrow. *Carpe diem*, Ms. MacPhee. You have nothing to fear but fear itself."

BEEP

"Camilla? It's Edwina, your sister, in case you have forgotten. Pick up. I said pick up, Missy. Don't think you can get away with skipping the Labour Day activities at the lake again. This is a family tradition, and we expect you to attend. Alexa and Donalda feel exactly the same way. If Stan can forgive you for what happened to his Buick and Conn can overlook your stunts, which we all know caused him a huge amount of embarrassment with his fellow officers, the least you can do is show up and be civil. Need I add Daddy will be disappointed if you don't come? We're setting off at noon sharp. Today. Friday. We expect you for dinner at the cottage. Bring your manners."

BEEP

"Camilla? Alvin again. Use your imagination! 150 hot air balloons rising together and floating across the river and over the city. It's going to be awesome. Like a dream. We're still holding on to a place for you. The balloon is a spectacular shade of candy-apple red. We need to confirm that you're coming."

BEEP

"Ms. MacPhee? Violet Parnell here. Would you be kind enough to come to my apartment, on the double? It's a matter of some urgency."

BEEP

"It's Alvin. Holy shit, get over to Violet's place. Fast."

*   *   *

I shouted into Mrs. Parnell's voice mail. "Mrs. P.? Is something wrong? Alvin? Are you there? What's happening? I'll get there as soon as I can."

After I left the message at Mrs. Parnell's, I tried her cellphone. Nada. I tried Alvin's. Ditto. The apartment super didn't pick up. His voice mailbox was full. I tried calling a cab. The dispatcher snickered. Fifty minutes to an hour wait. Holiday weekend.

*   *   *

Bad scenarios played in my head. Mrs. Parnell was coming up to her eightieth birthday and had been using a walker for a couple of years for balance. She's had a few shocks to her system and at least one trip to the ICU since she got to know me. Even though I knew she had the smarts to dial 911, I figured I'd better hustle. It's a fifty-minute hike from downtown to our apartment building near the Champlain Bridge. That's at the best of times, which this wasn't.

I hustled up toward Wellington, keeping an eye out for a cab. No joy. I figured it would be faster to walk. Of course, that was before I discovered my regular walking route home, the path along the Ottawa River, had been disrupted by some emergency behind the Parliament Buildings. Mounties redirected foot traffic on the path, and I had to push though a flock of confused tourists. The detour cost me an extra fifteen minutes.

I was in a lather by the time I reached our building. Mrs. Parnell's apartment is the second unit down from mine. I shot out of the elevator on the sixteenth floor and headed straight to her open door. I took a deep breath, wiped the sweat from my forehead, strode into her living room and swore.

Mrs. Parnell was positioned in front of her oversized black leather club chair, holding a tumbler of Harvey's Bristol Cream in her left hand and with her right, tracing a pattern in the air. As far as I could make out, she was in the middle of a dramatic re-enactment involving a crippled Allied reconnaissance plane and a nest of German snipers somewhere

13

in the mountains of Northern Italy in late 1944. The smoke from her smouldering Benson & Hedges was part of the story. Lester and Pierre, Mrs. Parnell's evil little lovebirds, shrieked in the background. Her custom-made titanium walker lay idle on the far side of the room.

Alvin Ferguson perched on the matching leather sofa, leaning forward, listening. His entire bony body was caught up in the drama, eyes wide behind his cat's-eye glasses. His beaky nose tracked the spiral of the imaginary plane, his ponytail flipped as he followed the arc of the snipers' bullets. The sun glinting off his nine visible earrings added to the magic of the moment.

"Against all the odds," Mrs. Parnell said, "with only his pistol, the major fought his way through and single-handedly wiped out the entire nest of snipers. Of course, there was no dealing with him afterwards. Still, he reminds me a bit of you in a pinch, dear boy."

"Lord thundering Jesus, Violet, that's one wicked story," Alvin said.

Mrs. Parnell nodded modestly.

I cleared my throat.

"Ms. MacPhee! We thought you'd never get here."

I narrowed my eyes. "What's the emergency?"

"Emergency?"

"Yes. You both know goddam well you left me a message."

"I don't believe we actually said it was an emergency," Mrs. Parnell said after a long sip of Harvey's.

"You used the word urgency."

"Urgency, yes, but we had no desire to alarm you."

"No? Mind telling me why you didn't answer your phone?"

Mrs. Parnell turned to Alvin. "Did you hear the telephone, dear boy?"

Alvin shook his head.

I said, "Since you are sitting less than two feet from it, I find that hard to believe."

Mrs. Parnell made a conciliatory gesture with her sherry glass. "Perhaps you called while we were on the balcony observing some of our fellow balloonists."

Alvin said, "Yeah. I bet that was it."

Mrs. Parnell has a panoramic view of the Ottawa River and the Quebec shore on the other side. Even so, I wasn't falling for the balcony bullshit. Ditto for their innocent looks. "Let's see if I have this straight: there's no emergency. Nor was there an emergency at the time you called. Would that be correct?" I used my courtroom manner, usually reserved for cross-examining sleazy witnesses.

Alvin may be the bane of my work existence, but at least he had the grace to look abashed. That didn't last long.

"Sorry, Camilla. It's been hard to get your attention lately. You've been so preoccupied."

"Really. That's because I am up to my ass in alligators. You will remember, Alvin, the name of our enterprise is Justice for Victims. The way to ensure our clients have a hope of seeing justice is to be there when they need us. In court, if they're facing a vicious cross-examination, such as happened today when you were, I believe you said, under the weather."

"Sheesh, Camilla. You don't have to get your knickers in a twist."

"Not only are my knickers in a serious twist, but I am damp and sweaty and mad as hell. That would be because I raced, yes, that's right, raced, from downtown Ottawa, because I was under the mistaken impression you had an emergency."

Alvin, cool and collected in his summer leathers, was prepared to brazen it out.

Mrs. Parnell, on the other hand, showed her diplomatic side. "It slipped my mind that your troublesome vehicle was in the shop again, Ms. MacPhee. I regret the oversight. We wished to convey that time was of the essence. Muster the troops. Even more urgent, since it took you so long to get here. Young Ferguson and I must be at the field by seventeen hundred hours."

"If this was a trick to get me to go on that lunatic balloon ride, you can forget it."

"You wound me, Ms. MacPhee. We would never resort to such underhanded behaviour, would we, dear boy? But we do want to discuss something. Please sit down."

"I don't feel like sitting down. I feel like taking a shower."

Mrs. Parnell picked up the sherry glass again. "Join us in a toast. Here's to adventure!"

I didn't like the sound of that.

"And comradeship," she added. "One for all and all for one!"

"Depends," I said.

Alvin said, sitting back, "We respect the fact that you're afraid to go up in the balloon."

"I'm not afraid."

"We pass this way but once, Ms. MacPhee. Our days are fleeting. Courage."

"Courage has nothing to do with it. The balloon experience just doesn't interest me. And why do you need courage if it's so safe?"

"We all have our demons, Ms. MacPhee."

"I don't have demons. And if I did, I wouldn't be doing a goddam thing about them on the Labour Day weekend. I'm spending the next couple of days relaxing, getting the kinks out, and realizing I missed the best of the summer. So no relatives. No forced marches. No balloons."

"Understood. This won't tie up much of your weekend, Ms. MacPhee."

"Look, if the two of you want to float hundreds of feet over bodies of water, clinging to a tiny wicker basket held up by an inflated piece of canvas and an open flame, you have my blessing."

"If you'd just listen, Camilla," Alvin said.

"I have been listening." I sounded more peevish than usual, even to my own ears.

"I understand your concern, Ms. MacPhee, but consider this. Three years ago, I rarely left this apartment. I was old and alone. I had come to believe my days of adventure were finished. My friends and colleagues were dead, my old pins unsteady, the days were long and the nights endless. I was safe but of no use to anyone. Then I met you and Young Ferguson, and now life is full of adventure. I wouldn't retreat to my miserable former existence for anything."

I smiled noncommittally.

"Ms. MacPhee. This will be a magnificent moment for Young Ferguson and for me as well. I do not know if I will get another chance such as this. I feel rejuvenated being airborne again. Even if you keep your feet on the ground, your participation would contribute greatly to the esprit de corps."

"Violet has never let you down, Camilla," Alvin said.

"I know that."

"Even when she ended up in intensive care."

I hate it when they turn up the guilt burner.

"I get the point."

"Young Ferguson has always been there for you." Mrs. P. inhaled deeply.

"Frequently getting arrested while following your instructions," Alvin said.

"Yes, dear boy, that is true. Injured as well. And there was the loss of your home last summer."

"Hold on," I said. "You can't blame that on me. It wasn't my family member whose life was in danger. I was the one helping out."

"Not a question of blame, Ms. MacPhee. Merely making the point one can count on Young Ferguson, regardless."

I sank onto the other end of the leather sofa. Lester and Pierre ruffled their feathers and shrieked in triumph. "No balloons," I said.

"Accepted," Mrs. Parnell said. "There is one other thing."

I closed my eyes and rubbed my temples. "What?"

Mrs. Parnell said, "We want you to be our official photographer. To record the adventure, from the ground. I'll get the aerial shots."

A couple of photos didn't sound too demanding, although there were a few stumbling blocks. "I don't have a camera."

"You can use one of mine, Ms. MacPhee. I have an auto focus digital. Nikon. You'll have no trouble with it."

"We're asking you to take pictures, not donate a kidney," Alvin said. "You don't have to invent excuses."

Mrs. Parnell laid a hand on his bony shoulder. "She needs time to reflect."

"She needs a certain cop from Sydney to call her soon, so she can stop being miserable."

Unfair! First of all, Sgt. Ray Deveau, of the Cape Breton Regional Police, was on a three-week intensive course somewhere else in Nova Scotia, away from his base in Sydney and apparently out of phone communication. Second, I did not need Ray Deveau or anyone else to call me. Third, it was none of their beeswax.

"Onward and upward, Ms. MacPhee?"

"Onward anyway," I said. "Then will you leave me in peace for the rest of the weekend?"

Mrs. Parnell said. "We'd better synchronize our watches. The first mass launch is this evening."

"Wait a minute. I still have to shower and eat and walk the dog, which Alvin should really be looking after, and feed the cat, which I believe is yours, Mrs. Parnell."

"You know my new landlord won't let me keep Gussie," Alvin said.

I figured Gussie's habit of stealing food and non-food objects, such as carrots, candles, smoked salmon, chewing gum and the subsequent impact on the dog's digestion had figured into the landlord's decision.

Mrs. Parnell seemed ready for any objection. "The initial launch is going to be spectacular. We'd like a record of that. And as you are aware, the feline terrifies poor Lester and Pierre."

I heard a small but evil shriek of agreement from the lovebirds' cage.

"Whatever. The weekend traffic to Gatineau is going to be hellish."

"We'll head over now," Mrs. Parnell said. "As long as you're there by seventeen hundred and thirty hours."

Oops. "I don't have a car."

"Take mine. I'll go with Young Ferguson."

"Your new Volvo?" Mrs. Parnell's 1974 LTD had been handed down to Alvin.

"Of course."

"You know the kind of bad vehicle karma I have. Remember Stan's Buick? I'd feel better if it was something that couldn't get wrecked."

"I insist, I shall ride ahead with Young Ferguson."

"But why don't I take the LTD?"

Alvin's head jerked. "That's my car now. You can't just commandeer it without consultation."

"Ms. MacPhee, I fail to see your concern."

Alvin said, "It's not like any of this is going to kill you."

Three

Like so many things in life, it was a matter of split-second timing. But I had it all worked out. Sure, there'd been setbacks. For instance, dodging my po-faced new neighbour and his endless complaints about noise from my apartment. Closing the door in his face had put an end to that.

I had to check my phone messages. Might be something urgent. I had a couple of "blocked number" calls. They might be from Ray Deveau, not that it mattered. But wouldn't Ray have left a message?

Okay, forget him. I had to feed Mrs. Parnell's little calico cat and Gussie, my purely temporary dog, then take Gussie for a bit of quick relief in the park.

Next, a shower and change of clothes were called for. I had a small box of Godiva chocolates left over from my birthday. They'd make a nice dinner. After that, take the camera and drive like hell for the Quebec side of the Ottawa River and the Festival des Montgolfières, as the balloon festival is officially called. First, I'd have to figure out which of the five bridges would be the least congested. Then snag a parking spot, figure out the French signs, track down the goddam candy-apple red balloon, snap a few shots and head home.

I hadn't counted on a couple of strangers hammering on

my door as I dished out the Miss Meow and Waltham's Geriatric Canine mix. People don't just bang on the doors of sixteenth floor apartments. They're supposed to be buzzed into the building. Gussie howled at every knock. I was steamed as I squinted through the peephole.

Two unfamiliar uniformed police officers stood in front of my door. I wouldn't win a popularity contest with the Ottawa cops, so what was this about?

It's hard to see through the peephole, so I attached the chain and opened the door a crack. They seemed nervous and unhappy. In my experience, cops are almost always unhappy and almost never nervous, so maybe it was wishful thinking.

Working as a victim's advocate, you learn it's best not to let strange men into your home when you're alone. Mind you, they wore uniforms, and they appeared clean-cut and apparently well-intentioned. Judging by their precise haircuts, bullet-proof vests and crisp shoulders, they were cops all right. Never mind. I'd had plenty of fuel for my distrust of humanity. A lot of badass types look respectable enough to take home to meet the folks. And how hard could it be to get your mitts on a couple of uniforms?

"Camilla MacPhee?" the shorter officer said.

"Yes."

"We'd like to speak to you."

I admit I was curious. "Why?"

Gussie barked all through the answer.

"We'd like to come in, ma'am." At least that's what I think he said.

"Quiet, Gussie. What?"

The tall one raised his voice. "It's better if we come in."

"I'd like to know why."

Traffic ticket? Fund-raising? I had no idea.

The shorter one rubbed his upper lip. "We need to speak to you in person."

"Speak," I said. That set Gussie off again. "Not you, Gussie."

"It will be better if you let us in, ma'am."

"All right. Show me your ID."

"Can't hear you with the dog barking."

"Be quiet, Gussie. Show me your ID cards."

The tall one flushed. He'd have to control that if he planned to move up in the police force.

"It's really hard to hear you. Can we please come in? It will make it easier."

The po-faced neighbour pounded on the wall. This gave Gussie a new focus.

"Be quiet, Gussie. Your ID, please."

ID cards were pressed forward. Constable Mario Zaccotto and Constable Jason Yee. Looked official. Still, I could think of no reason for the police to seek me out. Whatever it was, given my history, I knew it would irritate the crap out of me. "Sorry, can you come back later? I'm in a rush."

"I'm afraid it's important, ma'am."

I sighed. "Okay, give me five minutes. I need to get dressed."

You must comply reasonably with police requests if you want to hold on to your license to practice law. Anyway, I was mildly curious.

My brother-in-law, Detective Sergeant Conn McCracken, answered his cell, even at the cottage. I was grateful he didn't hang up, since he is still not speaking to me.

"No lectures," I said. "Just tell me why two uniforms are standing in front of my door. Constables Yee and Zaccotto respectively."

"How would I know? It's officially the Labour Day weekend here at the lake."

"What a coincidence," I said. "It is here too. That's one reason I'm wondering about these guys. I figure it's not about the dog tags."

"Why don't you ask them?"

"I'm ahead of you there, Conn. They'll tell me why I need to let them in after I let them in. Is this some kind of harassment to do with Mombourquette?"

"You're a fine one to talk about harassment. If it wasn't for you and your crazy schemes, Lennie, who is one of the most dedicated officers, twenty-nine years on the force, coming up on retirement, wouldn't be getting put through the SIU meat grinder."

"It wasn't my fault, and you know it. Anyway, he did the right thing, and he had no choice."

McCracken said, "I'm hanging up now."

"I know you're pissed about Mombourquette, but is that any reason not to answer a simple question?"

"You're a pain in the ass, Camilla. Call the station."

"Oh, sure. Press One to get lost. Press Two to sit on hold forever."

"Goodbye, Camilla."

I played the wife card. "Alexa will find out for me. Put her on the phone."

He caved. "I'll get back to you."

At least I knew Yee and Zaccotto weren't there to give me bad news about the family. No one had drowned in the outhouse or blown the gas barbecue sky high. That was good.

Why else would the cops want to talk to me?

Four

I hate being dusty and sweaty. I calculated I had time to have a speedy shower and hop into clean clothes before McCracken called me back. I was still damp but dressed when the phone rang.

"Better let them in," he said. "They'll talk. You listen."

I was surprised to find them still in the hallway when I opened the door. Zaccotto shifted from foot to foot. Yee gave him a look.

"Sorry it took a while," I said. They didn't waste time. I closed the door behind them and heard the lock click into place. "It's been a bit crazy here."

Zaccotto looked around the living room. "I can see that," he said.

Yee shot him another look.

"You officers on some kind of housekeeping inspection?"

If they had been, I would have been ticketed for sure. It's a beige, basic and functional apartment at the best of times. The best of times was before Gussie. Today he had scattered a couple of blankets, pushed his food and water around and tossed grubby, saliva-covered squeaky toys far and wide. He'd also eaten through most of the Yellow Pages. He'd knocked over my prickly cactus but didn't appear to have eaten that. Not bad for a day's work. Mrs. Parnell's calico cat could be charged with leaving excessive hair in three colours on my old Ikea sofa.

I could be cited for leaving two weeks worth of unread newspapers in piles around the living room. I might get away with the stacks of case files. They stood in neat towers at one end of the dining table. On the other hand, the documents from several other dossiers were sprawled at the far end. Through the open door of my bedroom you could see the overflowing hamper and the unmade bed. My three sisters would have had synchronized cardiac arrests.

Except for coffee cups in the sink, the kitchen would pass inspection, since I hadn't had much time to eat that week.

Of course, they were there on police business. I didn't think uniforms would be involved in the SIU investigation into Mombourquette, and although it was possible I was being called back for another interview, this seemed a peculiar way to make the request. I had a sudden thought. "It's nothing to do with theft of library books, is it? I'm not taking the heat for that. You can talk to Mr. Alvin Ferguson."

God help them, they blinked.

"Please sit down, ma'am. This is important," Yee said. Zaccotto smiled sadly.

I plunked myself in the middle of the sofa to discourage company. They each reoriented a dining room chair and sat.

Gussie and Mrs. Parnell's cat took up defensive positions.

Yee had a piece of paper in his hand and a bead of sweat on his downy upper lip. Zaccotto looked more relaxed, but then he wasn't in charge of talking. I broke first. "So what can I do for you?"

Yee said, "I am afraid we have some bad news." Even from where I sat, I could see the beads of sweat had spread to his forehead.

26

Yee tried again. "I'm afraid there's been an accident."

The little calico cat went flying as I jumped to my feet. "I told them to stay out of those goddam balloons."

Yee said, "What?"

"Is Mrs. Parnell okay?"

Yee said, "Who?"

"Violet Parnell, my neighbour."

He frowned. "I don't know anything about a Mrs. Parnell."

"Alvin! I knew that LTD was a deathtrap."

"Alvin?" Zaccotto said.

"Alvin Ferguson. My office assistant. Has something happened to him?" I found myself standing, despite the tremor in my knees. Things always happen to Mrs. Parnell and Alvin.

"Please let us finish," Yee said. "Ma'am."

Gussie barked. The new neighbour thumped on the wall.

Yee took a deep breath. "I am sorry to inform you that Laura Brown died today."

It was my turn to say, "Who?"

Yee blinked. Zaccotto blinked too. I imagine I blinked along with them.

"Laura Lynette Brown."

"Laura Lynette Brown?"

Zaccotto raised his chin. "Yes, ma'am."

"Dead?"

"Yes. Sorry, ma'am."

I thought hard. Laura Lynette Brown. Not a friend. Not a relative. Not a client. I knew a Laura Brown from my Carleton University years. A pleasant and attractive woman with a luminous smile. I ran into her several times a year. She'd flash the smile. We'd make vague remarks about getting together for lunch. Lunch never happened. Maybe that's who they meant. But why tell me?

"That's terrible, but I hardly know Laura Brown. I didn't even know her middle name was Lynette. If it's even the same Laura Brown."

Again with the looks. Yee glanced down at his sheet of paper, looked up again and said, "We have you as next-of-kin."

"Next-of-kin? Oh, I get it. Must be some other Camilla MacPhee."

"No mistake, ma'am. Yours is the address given. Is this your telephone number?" He held out the sheet of paper.

I stared at my telephone number. Because of the nature of my work, I do not give out my address, even to clients. My telephone's unlisted. Clients get my cell number but not my home number.

"Well, it doesn't matter what your papers say. It's still a mistake."

"Doesn't look like a mistake, ma'am."

"If Laura's dead, her family needs to know."

"We have no information about them, ma'am. Do you have an address?"

"No. I don't know them."

"But we have you listed as…"

"I am not the right person. I run into Laura every couple of months, tops. We're not even friends, just old acquaintances from university. So you see, you've got me mixed up with someone else."

Yee's lips were just the tiniest bit pursed. He wouldn't have been long out of university himself. "Do you know where her family might be?"

"No clue. Wait. She used to make a joke about being from a small town in the middle of nowhere."

"So you don't recall the name of the town?"

"Somewhere in Ontario, I'm pretty sure. We took classes together in 1986, so I can't recall details. I'm surprised I remember about the small town. Started with C, I believe."

Yee wrote down something. C perhaps.

Zaccotto was unable to contain himself. "Carleton Place?"

"I don't think so."

"Caledon?"

"No."

"Collingwood?"

"Maybe it started with G. I'll let you know if it comes back to me."

"G?" said Zaccotto. "Georgian Bay?"

Yee said, "If she put your name as next-of-kin, it could mean her relatives are all dead."

"Still must be someone closer than me."

"Apparently not, ma'am."

"Okay, I guess we'll get to the bottom of it. How did Laura die?"

"We don't have the full results. But our information is that she slipped down the escarpment behind the Supreme Court Building."

"Behind the Supreme Court? She fell? What a terrible thing to happen."

"Yes, ma'am."

"Was that this afternoon? There was a lot of disruption on the bike path about an hour ago."

"Yes. It takes a while for them to get the scene processed."

"I didn't know you could go right to the edge of the escarpment there. I always thought it was fenced."

"According to witnesses, Ms. Brown climbed over the fence."

"What a strange thing to do. It doesn't make sense."

"No, ma'am."

"Laura Brown was sensible." I tried to block out the image of how she would look after bouncing off rocks for a hundred feet.

"Our information is that she may have lost consciousness once she got behind the fence."

"Do you know why?"

Zaccotto said, "I don't want to say anything until the autopsy. They'll let you know the results. As next-of-kin."

"You're sitting here telling me she's dead, that she climbed over a restrictive fence and then passed out."

Yee said. "She was diabetic. Possibly that would account for it."

"Really?" I sank back onto the sofa.

Yee watched me carefully. "You must have known she was diabetic."

"No. I didn't."

Zaccotto's brow furrowed. "But you were her next-of-kin."

I may have raised my voice at this point. "I was not her next-of-kin. I don't care what it says. I am not related to her. I don't even know where she lives. I only ran into her in this one restaurant every couple of months. Really, that's it."

Zaccotto cleared his throat.

"Hold on," I said. "How do you know she was diabetic?"

Zaccotto said, "She had a MedicAlert bracelet."

Yee said. "We called them. They had your name too."

"What?"

"Yes, ma'am. You were listed as Personal Emergency Contact," Zaccotto said, giving Yee a break. "This address and telephone number plus one for your office. Justice for Victims, right?"

"Wait a minute, you said my name too. You mean there's someone else?"

"No. I meant you were also listed on the information card

in her wallet. It said next-of-kin there. We can show you," Yee said.

I said, "This will turn out to be a clerical error."

"One more item," Zaccotto said.

I was ahead of them. "Oh, no."

Yee said, "We will need you to identify the body."

Five

I'm not that crazy about the morgue. I made the point again. "It should be a member of her family."

Yee stuck to his guns. "You are listed as the contact in case of…"

"I hear you. My point is that Laura must have some family members who will be pretty upset if someone else IDs her. You have to make every effort to contact them."

"We'll work with you on that," said Yee, cagily. "But before we contact them, we need the body identified. It will speed things up."

"Come on, guys. Maybe it's not even Laura Brown. This is all so bizarre, I wouldn't be surprised."

"Then you would inform us the individual was not Laura Brown, and we would pursue her identity through the proper channels."

I felt a new throb in my temples. Whatever the circumstances, there was something horrible about leaving a person in the morgue waiting for ID because of a clerical screw-up.

And if the person wasn't Laura, at least some other family would be informed early rather than late.

"Fine. I'll do it. But we have to walk the dog first."

I took Mrs. Parnell's Volvo to the hospital. I didn't like the idea of sitting in the back seat of a cruiser. Too many of my former legal aid clients had been there. Yee and Zaccotto stopped the cruiser in the entryway. I found a parking spot and walked back. They waited for me to catch up. As we headed into the bowels of the hospital, they walked slowly but, even so, I found myself lagging on the endless stretch of corridor. My heart had already started to thud. Once you've identified your husband on a stainless steel tray, even six years later, the route to the morgue will be intensely disturbing. In recent months, I thought I'd come to grips with Paul's death, but in front of the door to the morgue, I struggled with old images.

Any emotional upheaval triggers my father's voice in my head. A lifetime of aphorisms and advice. "MacPhees are not afraid to do the right thing. No matter what the cost."

I took a deep breath. I had forgotten about the chemical smell and how it can kick-start memories. Images flooded my brain, shattered bone, jagged slash against a pale lifeless cheek, hands that could never hold or be held again.

"Are you okay, ma'am?" Yee said.

"Fine." I wasn't fine, but that was none of their goddam business. I wanted to run like hell for home, crawl into the unmade bed and wail.

Yee and Zaccotto waited.

"You're awful white. You aren't going to pass out, are you?" Zaccotto said.

My father's voice said, "When faced with a hard task, get it over with."

I braced my shoulders and instructed myself not to think of Paul. I followed the officers through the door.

I hated the harsh lighting, I didn't find the stainless stylish, and I didn't even wish to speculate about the background noises.

Two minutes later, the attendant slid the body toward me. The attendant lifted the sheet. Her hair was out of sight, her right cheek bruised and scratched.

I nodded. "Yes."

Laura Brown's luminous smile was gone.

*　　*　　*

I don't know what felt stranger, the contrast of the bright sun after the morgue, or the fact I was walking out holding a small stack of Laura Lynette Brown's possessions. Of my few memories of Laura, she was usually sitting in the sun. Now she'd never see it again.

Her fanny pack contained a house key and wallet. A few pieces of ID, no credit cards. Nothing else. I saw for myself where Laura had carefully hand-printed my name and address, in green ink, right down to the apartment number and postal code. Why would she specify next-of-kin anyway? I didn't have my next-of-kin noted anywhere. Even your passport just asks for emergency contact. It was too weird for words.

The two constables were still walking with me.

I said, "May I ask you not to release her name until I locate her family? I wouldn't want them to hear it on the news."

Not a problem, apparently. They promised to follow up on that.

As Zaccotto and Yee sped off in their cruiser, I headed for the Volvo. The sight of it, still unscathed, was at least a relief. I climbed in and turned on my cellphone.

It rang immediately.

I was actually hoping it would be a "blocked number" call, but no such luck. Instead it was Alvin, calling from the balloon.

I held the phone away from my ear, but not far enough to drown out his words.

When the tirade died down, I said, "Are you finished, Alvin? Because contrary to your suggestion, I had a good reason for missing the launch, and it was not just to make people miserable. I was identifying a friend at the morgue.

"Come on, Alvin, I am not making that up. Why are you acting like such a jerk lately?

"No, I don't believe I am the most self-centred person ever born. Nor is it true I don't have a friend left in the entire world because no one can count on me. Is Mrs. Parnell there? I'd like to talk to her, if you're quite finished raving.

"Well, the same to you, Alvin."

I turned off the cellphone after that.

Even if Ray Deveau did manage to call, who had time to talk? I needed to track down a goddam candy-apple red balloon.

*   *   *

There wasn't a single balloon in the evening sky at eight-thirty when I finally gave up. I couldn't figure out where Alvin and Mrs. Parnell had drifted. They could have been miles down the Rideau River or half-way up the Ottawa. Or in the Gatineau Hills. Even back in Mrs. Parnell's living room swilling sherry.

Plus, I still wasn't any closer to understanding the Laura Brown situation.

Life was definitely not a bowl of cherries. On the other hand, since I did have Mrs. Parnell's Volvo at my disposal, since I was tense and jumpy after my visit to the morgue, and since I had pretty well lost my appetite, I figured I might as well check out Laura's place. It was bound to shed some light on her life. Something would point to her parents or friends. I could hand over the fanny pack, the ID and keys along with the responsibility of being next-of-kin.

Laura Brown had lived in the Glebe. No surprise there. She would have fit perfectly in this affluent, tree-lined neighbourhood, home to professionals, coffee shops and quirky boutiques. The area was still sprinkled with enough students, artists and musicians to keep it interesting and funky. And it was close enough to walk to Parliament Hill but far enough not to notice.

Laura's address was a few blocks from Bank Street on Third Avenue. I found a small, attractive infill single with the distinctive touches of a local architect. I glanced around the street, hoping to find someone to talk to.

It was before nine on a Friday night. In the Glebe, I would have expected lots of neighbours puttering in gardens, strolling slowly along the sidewalk, chatting in small groups. But I saw no one.

The key opened the front door, no problem. The problem arrived with the shriek of the alarm. Within a minute, a telephone rang nearby. Lucky for me, the phone was close to the foyer. Thank God, someone was calling Laura.

"Yes?" I was slightly out of breath as I shot into the living room to pick up the receiver.

"Pronto Security. We have a report of an alarm going off in your residence."

"Thank you. Can you turn it off?"

"Are you the homeowner?"

I said. "Not exactly."

"Do you know your code?"

"Can't say that I do."

"Do you have an access card?"

"An access card?"

"Are you listed as having access to the house?"

I raised my voice. "Probably not. It's hard to hear with the noise."

"Where is the homeowner?"

"She's dead."

"Dead? Are you the police?"

"No. Turn off the alarm."

"Do you know her mother's maiden name?"

"Of course not. Please turn this thing off."

"Sorry, can't do that."

"Look, I'm a lawyer." Well, I'm still a lawyer when it suits me, which it did at that moment. "Laura Brown has died, and I can't waste time."

"Nice try," he said. "Are the police there yet, or do you want to make a run for it?"

"I think that's them now."

I stepped back out to the front porch, carrying the portable receiver. The alarm was a loud one, very effective, the type that gets folks in an upscale area engaged. The previously invisible neighbours were already gathering. A cluster of people were actually advancing toward the house.

"I didn't see a sign that said premises protected by anybody," I said, peevishly.

"That's the idea," the dispatcher said. "The element of surprise."

"Well, I'm surprised. Hang on," I said and waited for a chance to explain to the police how I was the next-of-kin but didn't know about the alarm, the alarm code, the homeowner's mother's maiden name or anything else.

As the first squad cars converged on the house, roof lights flashing, I stepped toward them. Two young officers, a male and a female, got out, leaving the doors open.

"Hi," I said. "You're not going to believe this."

I was right.

After a longish time, they reached Yee and Zaccotto on the radio and confirmed my right to enter Laura Brown's home.

My inner lawyer knew this was not as clear-cut as Yee and Zaccotto thought, but I kept that to myself.

The officers entered the house.

"Maybe you should talk to the security company," I said, as yet another cruiser pulled onto the street. Neighbours continued to spill from their houses. We now had an audience three deep.

The female officer was young, black and brisk. She dealt with the security company, spelling out my name among other things.

"They need to know your birthday," she said.

"August 10th," I said. I'd turned thirty-six, and the less said about that the better.

"August 10th. Good. And your mother's maiden name?"

"Are you kidding me?"

"Do I look like the kidding type?" she said.

"MacDonald," I said. "M-A-C."

"MacDonald," she repeated. "M-A-C."

Three seconds later, she punched in a code and finally, blessedly, the alarm stopped.

"Thank you," I said.

"No problem. They had your details on file."

"What?"

"They have you listed as an authorized person. But you should have had your access card on you. Could have saved all this trouble."

"No one ever sent me an access card for the security system." Of course, compared to not mentioning I was next-of-kin, it seemed a minor oversight.

"Not our problem. Better arrange to get your card from them," the cop said, handing me the receiver.

I gave my particulars to the dispatcher.

"That it?" he said.

"How about a new code? Can you give me one?"

"You just select a four digit number and key it in."

"You don't give it to me?"

"No. You're the only one who knows it. That's why you have to remember it. Four numbers. Something you won't forget. Not 1111, and not your birthday either. Key it in now."

"That's all?"

"You key it in once. You key it in again to make sure it's the same. I'll confirm. Then all you got to do is use it when you leave, then you key it in again when you come back. Easy."

I picked 1986. The year I'd met Laura Brown. I was troubled. How and why had Laura gone to the trouble to find out my mother's maiden name?

"We'll send you an access card. Call the 1-800-number on the alarm box. Write it down and keep it with you."

The cop waited until I finished.

"This call's going to cost you sixty bucks for a false alarm. You'll get a bill."

That was truly the least of my problems.

Six

Laura Brown's place was cosy and well-ordered. It was full of suede cushions, silky throws and the kind of upholstery you sink into with a book. Laura must have done that often. I found four historical novels scattered around, each with a bookmark, indicating she hadn't finished. A couple of recent CanLit bestsellers in hardcover editions were stacked on the coffee table.

Laura's colours: copper, warm yellow, woodsy brown, dominated the decor. Every room had potpourri with a pleasant green apple scent. I'd become more aware of these important details since my sister, Alexa, had started dragging me through model homes.

That's how I knew the kitchen was a showpiece. The Chinese red accent wall warmed the room, and black granite counters screamed big bucks. The stainless steel appliances might have been chic, but they still creeped me out. I kept my mind off the morgue and headed upstairs. In the linen closet, I found Egyptian cotton sheets, including some still in their packaging, next to stacks of white towels.

Laura's home had everything. Flat screen television, air-conditioning, central vac. Some lovely moody watercolours on the walls. Originals.

No sign of a home computer though, and I'd thought I was the last person without one. Even Alvin had his laptop. Mrs. Parnell had a computer system and two laptops.

Speaking of Mrs. P., she would have approved of the high-end sound system. She loves Bose. Laura's taste ran to light classical, jazz and easy listening. I found a half-finished knitting project in a covered basket near the sound system.

But I didn't find a single photo, not even one of herself. No diplomas. Not a letter or memento. Not a message held by a fridge magnet.

After a serious search, I found bank statements in a portable file box in the upstairs den closet. The monthly statements from her broker were included. She had one hell of a portfolio. I now had the name of her bank and her account numbers for chequing and savings. There was nothing much of interest in the statement. Debit purchases at clothing stores and restaurants, mostly Maisie's Eatery, the popular new spot where I'd run into her the last few times.

Most of her bills were on direct debit. Hydro, phone and gas records had been neatly placed in labelled household files. There was not one long distance call on any phone bill.

I went through the small file box hoping to find her passport and with it her place of birth. No deal.

I did find two envelopes. The first, marked "Emergency", held three new-looking one hundred dollar bills. The second was in a legal-sized envelope from Barkhow, Delaney and Zolf. It held Laura Brown's will. Good news. If you don't mention your relatives and friends in your will, where do you mention them?

Laura's will was crisp and to the point.

She left all of her worldly belongings to Camilla MacPhee. Frederick Delaney was named as the executor. It goes without saying that the office of Barkhow, Delaney and Zolf was closed for the weekend. I dialled the number anyway and left a message for Delaney, leaving my name, home and cell numbers.

That was all I needed. To be the sole heir of someone I hardly knew. To make matters worse, Laura had made no bequests, no mention of anyone else, and no charitable donations. Nothing.

I stuck the small envelope with the cash into my canvas backpack for safekeeping. I rolled the envelope containing the will to make it fit and shoved that in too.

Next stop was the master bedroom closet. A nice selection of flowing summer dresses in copper, yellow and apple green. A collection of linen separates that I could never afford. Two halter dresses. And the regular assortment of slacks, jeans, cotton sweaters, plus two pairs of Birkenstocks, the footwear of choice in the Glebe.

What had I expected? It was an elegant yet practical wardrobe for any fortyish successful woman. Nothing unusual. I kept going. The bed was made, although not to my sisters' standards. I dropped to all fours and peered under it. Waste of time.

I straightened up and asked myself why I spent so much time looking under other people's beds. My sisters were always saying I needed a hobby. I hoped this wasn't going to be it. I flicked on the clock radio and found it set to Oldies 1310. "Stand By Me" was playing.

Laura had been neat but not compulsive. Her home was comfortable and welcoming, even if something seemed missing. It was several grown-up housekeeping steps ahead of mine.

Laura's reading taste ran to popular magazines. She had baskets full of those and a shelf lined with mass market editions of historical novels. Her bedside table held a hardcover copy of

One Man's Justice by Thomas R. Berger, and three more historical novels. I'd been meaning to pick up a copy of the Berger book, since I was an admirer of the man. I figured Laura wouldn't mind if I took it, being next-of-kin and all.

There's no way to check out someone's medicine cabinet without feeling sleazy. The cabinet yielded nothing of interest, unless you count high-end moisturizer and an apricot face masque. No over the counter medications. I was looking for prescriptions. Something with the name of her pharmacist and doctor. Anything that might get us a step closer to knowing something, anything about Laura Brown. There were no prescriptions. Not a single outdated antibiotic container, nothing for allergies or migraines. No birth control.

The rest of the bathroom was equally unremarkable. A damp towel hung slightly askew on the towel rack. The sink was clean but not sparkling, same for the tub and shower. A couple of strawberry-scented bath-bombs waited on the side of the tub. An electric toothbrush sat on the vanity. A hair dryer with a big diffuser hung from a hook. Could have been anyone's bathroom.

I'd learned nothing about Laura's friends and family when I headed back to the kitchen.

I forced myself to open the stainless steel door of the fridge. As I expected, I found food—a half-filled bag of skim milk, a container of orange juice, a chunk of cheese repackaged in a Ziploc bag, some leftover roast chicken. All neatly arranged. A large supply of condiments, including three kinds of Dijon mustard, and two jars of fiery salsa, plus salmon fillets, asparagus, a salad that looked like arugula, a tub of mascarpone cheese and an array of other cheeses. And honey. No chocolate anywhere.

Lots of ice cubes in the freezer.

The pantry held canned soups, jars of red peppers, a few dietetic jams and no sweets whatsoever, except for a large package of Splenda.

She had a serious collection of cookbooks, including several on cooking for one. Two Lucy Waverman cookbooks that I recognized from my sister's kitchen sat next to *Bon Appetit Weekend Entertaining*. A couple of pieces of paper marked recipes. I opened them to see if anything interesting fell out. Nothing did.

A list on the counter said:

Salmon Fillets
Asparagus
Arugula
Chunk Parmigiano Reggiano
Balsamic Vinegar
Mascarpone
Figs

Every item on the list had a check mark next to it. Laura already had a nice selection of moderate to high-priced wines, nothing flashy. Heavy on the Australian Shiraz, but with some Italian and French pinot noir too. A bottle of Fat Bastard stood on the glass bistro table, with a stainless steel bartender style corkscrew lying next to it.

Looked to me like Laura had picked up the ingredients for a special dinner. But for whom? She obviously hadn't had it at the time of her death, because the ingredients were all still in the fridge.

With luck, if I persevered and learned the name of her guest, I might find out something more about her. I just hoped it wasn't some new acquaintance.

The basement was down a fairly steep set of plain wooden stairs. On the side ledge, Laura had organized her cleaning supplies, easy access, yet out of sight. The vacuum hose was wound around a hook on a pegboard and hung alongside a broom, mop and a long-handled feather duster. Neat but not prissy.

A quick peek in the basement storage area revealed cross-country skis, solid but not top of the line. No skates. A rack with a bicycle. One swimming noodle. A pair of flippers. A pair of well broken-in hiking boots. A tennis racquet and a squash racquet.

She had obviously liked sports. But she must have biked with someone, skied with someone, hiked with someone. Who would have only one swimming noodle?

The basement storage connected to a neat, empty garage.

I headed back upstairs.

The magazines were ordinary enough. *Maclean's, Canadian House and Home, Style at Home, Walrus.* The previous week's *New York Times Magazine.*

I found no clue about where Laura worked. Everything about her lifestyle indicated she was some kind of professional. But everyone has something from their place of business. A Health Insurance form. A T-shirt. A mug. Or some kind of a file. I chugged back to the second floor to recheck her T-shirts. None of them had logos.

Back downstairs to hunt for mugs.

At least I was getting some exercise.

The dining area had a fashionable dark wood streamlined table and a Zen-looking sideboard. The table was set for two with fashionable pale green china and sleek silverware on cream linen placemats with contrasting napkins. A trio of creamy orchids sat in the middle as a centrepiece. Slender wine and water glasses flanked each place-setting, confirming my special dinner theory.

Back in the kitchen, the cupboards held dishes for four, in a pumpkin colour, with matching cups and mugs. I peered in the depths of the cupboard. Not a single mug with a letter or graphic on it. I pulled one of the bistro chairs over and climbed up on it. I squinted at the far corners of the top cabinets, the place I always hide junk, such as undesirable Christmas presents. The corner looked empty. I stuck my hand in anyway. I netted two mugs. One said Ottawa printed over an image of the Canadian flag. The other said Toronto, printed over an image of the CN tower.

Okay, forget that.

I climbed down and decided to have a look at the phone. Laura had a couple of the high-end ones, the type that showed your last ninety-nine callers if you pressed the down arrow. Except for the security company call, only six calls were recorded. The date for three was July 14th. More than six weeks earlier. One on July 13th and two on the 15th. As far as I could tell, no one else had called Laura Brown.

The six calls had come from "Unknown name. Unknown number". Was that the guest she'd invited? Someone from out of town? No way to know.

Of course, I realized the unknown name thing was no more mysterious than a cellphone not on the Bell system. Maybe someone choosing to block calls. Maybe a telemarketer. A glance at the times of the calls made me reconsider that. Telemarketers favour dinner hour. These calls had come during the day and evening.

I had nothing left to check but the garbage. Upstairs to the bathroom, the smart little mesh wastebasket was empty.

Fine.

While I was up there, I checked the small den on the same floor. Nothing.

Laura had a stacked washer and dryer. Front loading, Energy Star. I peered through the glass. Both machines were empty. The wastepaper basket held two dryer sheets.

On the main floor, the only garbage can was in the kitchen. It was empty too; a pristine white kitchen garbage bag lined the can. Nice fresh lemony smell too. No paper of any kind. No container or wrapper that gave out any information.

I tried the back entrance, where a large garbage can and both blue and black recycling containers stood. All empty. I lifted them, just in case something had slipped underneath.

Nothing had.

What were the chances that the garbage and recycling were collected on Friday morning in this neighbourhood, and Laura hadn't been home since?

I'd just have to find out.

Feeling rather foolish, I checked in each of the stainless canisters on the counter. The flour and sugar contained flour and sugar. The tea and coffee contained tea and coffee. I found that irritating.

As a last resort, I opened the drawer in the hall console. I picked up the telephone book and flipped to the Bs.

No listing for Brown, Laura, L. or L.L. at that address. Or any other address.

I took one last look around Laura Brown's lovely home. It stood in sharp contrast to the dwellings of most of my clients. As far as I could tell, Laura Brown had everything she could have wanted until she took that last walk.

I collected my new book, set the alarm with my access code and slunk off toward the Volvo.

I didn't get far.

Seven

It was nearly eleven and, although it was Friday night, the street was empty once again, except for Laura's neighbour to the left. He was standing alone, clearly visible in the glow of the street light. He was an attractive man, late forties, early fifties, with close-cropped salt and pepper hair, blue eyes behind pricey looking rimless glasses. He wore a short-sleeved taupe golf shirt, although the temperature had fallen, and there was enough of a nip in the air to make me wish I'd worn a sweater. He stood on the sidewalk, staring at his immaculate front garden, scratching his head. The head-scratching seemed to be brought on by a selection of mums in nursery pots.

His garden had the look of a professional design, profuse, yet precisely planned, with just the teensiest suggestion of goose-stepping storm troopers. I could hear a woman's voice from inside the three-storey brick house. "Stop obsessing, plant your wretched mums on Sunday. We have to get up early tomorrow, in case you've forgotten."

"You know I like to do things right," he said. I caught the implication that others came up short in the doing things right department. He didn't make that comment loud enough to be heard more than two feet away.

"Hello," I said, fishing out my best smile.

"I'm trying for a lively, jaunty mood this fall," he said. "I can't just have them stuck in straight lines. Can I?"

Like I cared. "Good point," I said.

"Gardening's an art form, really. The harmony of the whole." I assumed he was seeking support for his position.

"You bet," I said.

"I don't want to be up all night," the woman inside the house said. She had a voice that carried.

"My name is Camilla MacPhee," I said. "Did you know your neighbour, Laura Brown, well?"

"Laura Brown?" he said.

"Yes, the woman in this house right there." I pointed to the house he had just watched me leave.

He shook his head.

"She's your next-door neighbour."

"Brown," he said. "Is that her name?"

"Has she been here long?"

He shrugged. "A couple of years, I guess. My wife might know."

A silver-haired woman with amazing cheek bones stuck her head out the door. "Now," she said. She looked like she meant business.

"The woman next door, dear, have you met her yet?" he asked.

"Why?" she said.

He turned to me. "What did you say her name was?"

"Laura Brown." These people had a BMW parked in their driveway. You'd think they could have purchased a few brains.

"This…um…person was asking." He turned back to the tricky matter of arranging the mums.

His wife stepped out onto the veranda.

"I am inquiring," I said, pleasantly, "whether you had met

Laura Brown, your next-door neighbour."

"And you are?"

"Camilla MacPhee." That didn't seem to be enough. "I'm a lawyer," I said, stepping up to the veranda and extending my hand. "Mrs...?"

She didn't volunteer her name. "May I ask what your interest is in my neighbour?"

"She's had an accident."

"Oh." That took her by surprise. I wondered what she'd been expecting.

"Do you know her well?"

"Hardly at all. Sometimes make a remark about the weather, that kind of thing. I don't think we'd ever introduced ourselves."

"But you saw her?"

"Yes, I see her coming and going. Is she all right?"

"I'm afraid not. This seems like a friendly neighbourhood, and I'm hoping someone can help us find her relatives."

"That sounds serious."

"She was killed in a fall today." I figured this woman could take it on the chin.

Her hand shot to her mouth. "That's dreadful."

"Yes," I said.

"I don't think I can help you much."

"Did she know anyone else on the street, do you think?"

"She kept to herself. Wasn't one to socialize. I don't think she really was friendly with anyone, you know, beyond a smile and a hello." She paused. "But, of course, I don't know that for sure. You'd probably be better off to ask around. Although, it's a bit late now." She glanced at a small watch. I thought I spotted the flash of diamonds.

"Right. I'll try tomorrow."

"And it's Labour Day weekend. Lots going on, people are at their cottages."

"Did you ever see people coming and going? Friends? Boyfriends?"

"We have better things to do than spy on our neighbours."

I said, "I'm sure you do, but the houses on this street are quite close. Did you notice if she had regular visitors?"

"I don't believe I ever saw anyone come or go. Just her. Laura Brown, you said?"

"Do you have any idea where Laura worked?"

"None. As I said, we never spoke about anything. I used to see her walking back from downtown in the evenings. I assume she was returning from work, because she'd have on a nice suit and pair of running shoes. That's such an awful look, don't you think? It always sticks in my mind. And usually people who are dressed like that are coming back from offices. I can't imagine what they're thinking."

As someone who regularly walked to work in business clothes and running shoes, I bit back my comment.

"What about seeing regular delivery people at her house? Anyone like that? Cars parked in front?"

She shook her head. "We're not home all that much. We're busy. Concerts and community commitments. And the garden, lest I forget."

"Did you ever see her outside the neighbourhood? At a concert or anything?"

She paused, apparently thinking. "No. Not that I recall. It's a shame, isn't it? Such a nice-looking woman. Obviously doing well for herself, they don't give these houses away. Or those cars."

"What cars?" I said.

"Well, her car. She drove an Acura Integra. Brand new. Black."

"Where did she park it?"

She flashed me a look calculated to reset my self-esteem to a lower level. "In her garage. Where else?"

There was no car parked in the garage now. I hadn't noticed any car payments in the bank statement, but then I hadn't been looking for them. There hadn't been a car registration or insurance certificate in her fanny pack, but lots of people kept those in the glove compartment. But now I had something concrete to speak to the police about. Wherever Laura's car was, it shouldn't take them long to track it down.

I dug into my shoulder bag and fished out a business card. "If you remember seeing her or seeing anyone here, give me a call."

"But surely you'll be able to track down her family without too much trouble?"

"Not so far," I said.

"There must be information in the house."

"Nope. One more thing, what day is your garbage collected?"

"I don't see what difference it makes, but they pick it up on Tuesday mornings. James. In the house. Now."

By the time I made it back to the sidewalk, she had separated her reluctant husband from his mums, and they'd vanished through the door. And I had something else to think about.

Aside from the missing car, the fact that Laura had created no garbage for three days and the creepy lack of personal information, there was something else wrong in Laura's house, something out of whack, but damned if I could figure out what it was.

Eight

I was ready to drop when I got home. And I still had a purely temporary dog requiring recreation. The routine went like this: take the elevator down sixteen floors, walk to the park, poop, scoop, walk back from the park, elevator up, repeat as needed. I might have been bushed, but Mrs. Parnell was ready to party. She whipped open the door of her apartment as I dragged myself past with Gussie on the way to the park. There was no sign of Alvin, which was good news.

"Ms. MacPhee," she said. "There you are!"

Apologies don't come naturally to me, and many people have suggested I need a bit of practice.

"Sorry I let you down about the pictures of the take-off, Mrs. P., but I didn't have much choice. I had to identify the body of an old school friend. Apparently she named me next-of-kin. I'm not sure if Alvin passed on that information. I was glad to have the Volvo. I drove around trying to spot your red balloon, but all the balloons were gone by then."

"Of course, you did what you had to do. When duty calls, one must obey."

That was a relief. Or it was up to the point where she headed down the hall to my place. By the time I'd returned with Gussie, Mrs. Parnell had settled in for a chat. She made

53

a production of filling two juice glasses to the brim with Harvey's Bristol Cream. She handed one to me.

I supposed a little sherry couldn't hurt.

"Give me a minute," I said. I wanted to leave a message for Constable Yee and a matching one for Constable Zaccotto to see if Laura's Acura had shown up anywhere. I knew they'd probably gone off duty at eleven, but they'd get on it when they could.

Mrs. Parnell waited cheerfully. As soon as I put down the phone, she raised her glass in a salute and settled onto my sofa to light a Benson & Hedges. "Death is never easy. But when you have seen as many bodies as I have, Ms. MacPhee, you develop a certain sang-froid."

I couldn't imagine my *sang* getting any more *froid,* and I sure didn't need a couple of hours reliving Mrs. Parnell's World War II adventures.

I tossed back a bit of the sherry. "I'm glad you understand."

"And don't worry about Young Ferguson. Don't take his outburst to heart. He is young and sometimes hot-headed."

"Right. I hope you had fun."

"An altogether first-rate experience. We found ourselves well down the Rideau in record time. Left some of those other chaps in the dust, so to speak. Excellent pilot."

"I'll take some shots tomorrow."

"Splendid. I think the dawn launch will be even more dramatic," she said.

I put the drink down with a splash. "The dawn launch?"

"0600 hours. I think we'll be fine if we get to the field by 0530. We'll pick up Young Ferguson first. If you decide to come along for the ride with us, we'll dragoon someone else into taking the photos."

"Thanks. I'll just stay on the ground," I said.

"As you wish. But to return to your problem, was this a close friend? Something unexpected?"

"Not a close friend. I'm not sure what's going on. But I have to locate her family quickly so they can arrange the services and all of that. Otherwise, I'll have to make decisions about what to do with her body after the autopsy. She can't stay in the morgue. I don't think funeral homes can just put you in storage either. I have to do something."

"Indeed, highest priority," Mrs. P. said, raising her glass again. "Bottoms up."

"Right."

Mrs. Parnell paused. "Did you have an address for her?"

"Yes, and the keys to her house. She lived on Third Avenue in the Glebe. I spent the evening searching, but I haven't found anything that might lead me to a member of her family. Or even friends. I have to keep hunting."

"That's the spirit, Ms. MacPhee. By the way, I am sure Young Ferguson will send his condolences on your loss."

"I liked her well enough, but it's not really my loss. Even so, I can't say I'm looking forward to telling people that she's dead."

"I don't blame you. There will be people who cared about her deeply."

"For sure," I said. "Somewhere."

Mrs. Parnell's eyes gleamed. "Let me know if you need assistance."

"Thanks, Mrs. P., I'll be fine."

"Tell me about your friend," Mrs. Parnell said.

"Not much to tell. I met her in university. We were in a special social issues reading course together and a couple of other classes, and we worked on a project."

"Yes," said Mrs. P. encouragingly.

"We worked well together. She was strategic and organized. I was young and passionate about justice. We aced the project with not too much effort, and the course finished. End of story."

"Did you become friends afterwards?"

"No."

"You didn't care for her?"

"She was a really pleasant person. She was about ten years older, I was just eighteen. We didn't really have much in common."

Mrs. Parnell snorted. "I'm forty-four years older than you. But who's counting."

"I guess you're right. Ten years can make a big difference in university, though. I had plenty of friends, and I was seeing Paul. We just never hung out together."

"You never saw her again?"

"Sure. This is Ottawa, after all, you run into people. Over the years, I'd see her at a concert or a movie. Lately, it's been in restaurants. We'd say hi, nice to see you, we must get in touch, that kind of thing. I never called her, and she never called me. I meant to. I guess she did too."

Mrs. P.'s eyebrows remained high. "When did you last see her?"

"Maybe early August. I saw her a few of times this summer at Maisie's Eatery. That's a new restaurant and spa in the market. Mostly female clientele. Before she left the restaurant, she stopped to talk to me. Both times."

"Was she alone?"

"No. She lunched with different women. I didn't really get a good look at them."

"What did you talk about?"

"Nothing much. Pleasant chit-chat about this and that. A

minute or two. She said she was doing well."

"Doing well at what?"

"She didn't say."

"And you didn't ask?"

"The conversations just didn't go that way. Funny, she had a great laugh. And she was smart as all hell. I think if she'd been in the next office, I would have had coffee with her, stuff like that. But it never happened."

"And you didn't recognize the women?"

"I didn't know them, and just because of the way we were positioned I suppose, she didn't introduce them. They seemed like friends. Could have been clients or co-workers. It didn't matter to me until today."

"You must have been important to her if she named you as next-of-kin."

"Not only that, but she named me as her heir. I found the will at her house. How weird is that?"

"Curiouser and curiouser. And you had no idea."

"None."

"In my experience, young women want to talk about their boyfriends or husbands. Did she mention anyone?"

"I wish she had. I would have followed up tonight."

"Was she attractive?"

"Yes, not beautiful but very nice looking, well put together, lovely skin and a lot of lovely auburn hair. She was on the curvy side of medium. She'd put on a few pounds over the years, and who hasn't. She had an absolutely luminous smile. She just lit up. My guess is she was single from choice."

"I thought if she had a gentleman friend, he might know something about the family."

"I never remember her having a boyfriend. Lots of guys were interested in her in university. She was quite beautiful back then. They used to hang around panting, but she just brushed them off. At the time, I thought they all seemed too young for her. Even her neighbours hadn't seen anyone coming or going."

"Oh, well. Did Laura ask about you?"

"A couple of years ago, she mentioned she hadn't heard about Paul. She was sorry to learn he'd died. Laura always knew how to say the right things. She asked about Justice for Victims. She said she'd read stuff in the papers. That's always a bit embarrassing for me."

"That's it?"

"Believe me, I've been trying to relive every encounter. All I have is a couple of pleasant chance meetings with a nice person. Nothing about next-of-kin, nothing about wills."

"Perhaps I am wrong, but is it not the custom for women today to exchange business cards?"

"Come to think of it, I gave her mine the last time I bumped into her. She dropped it in her purse. She said she'd call me for lunch."

"And did you get hers?"

"She said she'd just run out. Not that it mattered. She said she'd call me. Oh, wait a minute. That's it."

"What's what, Ms. MacPhee?"

"She dropped the business card into her purse."

"Hardly unusual."

"That's what was out of whack at Laura's home."

Mrs. P. raised one eyebrow.

"Her purse." I said it more to myself than to her.

"What about it?"

"There wasn't one."

"Perhaps it was with her at the time of the accident."

"I don't think so. I was given her personal effects at the

morgue, and there was a fanny pack, but no purse."

"Hmmm," said Mrs. P., drawing deeply on her cigarette.

"Of course, it could be in her car, wherever that is. She might have left it there for safekeeping when she went for her walk."

"You'll find that out when the officers return your call tomorrow. And as next-of-kin, you'll have access to that car."

"I'll probably have to pay the parking tickets for it, the way things are going. But even if she did leave a purse in the car, she must have had more than one. I'm not the girliest of girls, and I usually just carry my backpack, but I still have a couple of handbags."

"I don't, Ms. MacPhee. Never got used to being tied down like that. Basic supplies, that's all."

I let that one go. "I'm thinking back. One time when I ran into her in the restaurant this summer, she had one of those slouchy leather shoulder bags. I noticed, because at the time my sisters kept telling me they were hot items, and they were pressuring me to go to Holt Renfrew and get one. Like that was going to happen."

"Aha."

"But the last time I saw her, she dropped the business card into a small, structured bag, looked like alligator or something. My sisters are always chattering about handbags, so it stuck in my mind. So my point is, there should have been at least two purses in Laura's house."

"And I gather you didn't find them when you searched the house."

"Bingo."

"Certainly that is odd. But perhaps they got damaged, or she tired of them and gave them away. I have seen young women with leather carriers slung on their backs, looking quite rakish, might I add."

"Point taken, but these were stylish and expensive handbags. Plus she had nothing aside from the fanny pack they gave me at the morgue. And if she had given them away, she would have bought something nice to go with her wardrobe."

"I see."

"Glad to hear it, Mrs. P., because I don't see. If she has people in her life, where the hell are they? I'm betting if we find the purse, there'll be something to help us track her down."

Mrs. Parnell loves digging for details. She wouldn't mind the "us" part either. Right up her alley, in fact.

"Maybe the police can give me some answers in the morning," I said.

"Don't worry about it until then. Would you like your drink topped up? Help you relax."

I covered my glass fast, before she could slosh in any more Bristol Cream. I needed my wits about me.

Mrs. Parnell shrugged. "Suit yourself. Get a good sleep, Ms. MacPhee. Shall we reconnoitre at Young Ferguson's new place? He'll give us tea."

"So early?" I squeaked. I find Alvin's interior decor mind-bending at the best of times. Think nightmare theme park. I couldn't imagine walking through his door at dawn. "Can't we just meet him at the field?"

"Perhaps you are correct. I'll let him know. So we'll be at the launch site at 0530. Up, up and away."

*   *   *

Maybe that should have been up, up and awake.

I jerked back to consciousness at three in the morning, dislodging Mrs. Parnell's cat and giving Gussie a serious fright.

"Don't bark," I whispered.

Gussie hadn't yet fully grasped the concept of "don't."

Ten seconds later, I recognized the familiar thump on the wall.

"Shhh. Quiet, and I'll give you a treat," I whispered.

Gussie does understand the word "treat". I could tell by the tone of his next bark.

Again the thump on the wall. I thought about thumping back, but reason prevailed. I got up, found a couple of milkbones and returned to bed. I lay there, listening to Gussie crunch, then snore, and the cat purr. I would have preferred to be crunching, purring or even snoring myself but, in addition to the missing handbags, something else was bothering me. There must have been hundreds of students who'd come into contact with Laura Brown when we were at Carleton. Why couldn't I think of any names?

That's when the light went on.

Of course. The girl who knew everybody. Miss Congeniality. The one and only Elaine Ekstein.

Nine

I figured Elaine might be awake too. She was always puttering around all hours of the night, painting lampshades, stringing sequins, decoupaging cigar boxes. That's one of the nice things about obsessives: they don't relax even when they're not working.

Plus, even when she has the odd weekend off from her job as executive director of Women Against Violence Everywhere (WAVE), Elaine is unable to refuse help to anyone who asks. I didn't think twice about dialling her number.

Turned out I was wrong about the awake part. I let her phone ring four times, and when she didn't answer, I hung up. I remembered how hard it was to wake her up when she does go to sleep. That was dumb. Since I really needed to leave her a message, I dialled again. Elaine fumbled the phone on the third ring.

"It's me," I said. "Just need a bit of information."

"Holy moly, what time is it?"

"Latish."

"It's three-thirty in the morning. What's wrong? Are you in the hospital?"

"No."

"Jail?"

"Sorry, Elaine, were you sleeping?"

"Sheesh." It's not like Elaine to sound grumpy. Wacky yes. Grumpy, no. I guess I'd just caught her at a weak moment.

"Well, I didn't realize it was quite so late."

"Can you call me back in the morning?"

"Listen, you make your living rescuing people in distress, battered women, abused children, anyone with a problem. Are you telling me you only take calls during business hours?"

"Don't be ridiculous. But there's a big difference between outside of business hours and three-thirty in the morning. Whatever you want, it can wait. And I mean wait until after ten in the morning." She hung up. That was not at all like her. I figured that, in her sleepy state, she'd dropped the phone.

Since it really couldn't wait, I called back. How many times had I bailed her out when one of her clients needed a quick off-the-record legal opinion? I'd like to say Elaine's not quite so impulsive when she gets arrested herself, but in truth, she's always pretty much the same. If you're in a real pickle, she's there for you. She obviously didn't realize that this constituted a pickle.

Yet.

She answered on the fifth ring.

"Elaine. Quick question."

Long sigh.

"You remember Laura Brown from Carleton?"

"If I answer your inexplicable question, will you promise not to wake me up again?"

"Sure." Unless, of course, it was necessary.

"Yes, I remember Laura Brown. What about her?"

"She's dead."

"Did you say dead?"

"I did."

"Oh no, Camilla, that's awful."

"Yup."

"You're sure it's the same Laura Brown we knew at Carleton?"

"I'm sure."

"What happened to her? Car accident or something?"

"No. Do you remember how you met?"

"Gosh, I don't know. We were probably in a class together. Or maybe the pub. Is that important? Had she been ill?" Elaine isn't one simply to accept information.

"No, apparently she fell."

"Fell?"

"Off that escarpment behind the Supreme Court of Canada."

"Holy moly."

"The police are saying it was an accident."

Like me, Elaine is no fan of the police. "Mmm. The police. Listen, I didn't know you were friends with Laura. Mind telling me why it's so important to you at three-thirty in the morning?"

"Long story, but I'm the next-of-kin."

"Oh, you are not next-of-kin."

"Am."

"You've never even mentioned seeing Laura Brown since Carleton."

I decided not to mention the will at this point. "Trust me. And I'm just as surprised as you are. It's unsettling, and I would like to get the whole thing over with. I need to check out a couple of facts for my peace of mind. Then we can both go back to sleep."

"Well, I can't go back to sleep now. I'm wide awake."

"Okay, so who else might have known her?"

"You can't really expect me to remember that right off the bat."

"Why not? You never forget anything or anyone."

"Let me think. She must have known a lot of people, but she kept to herself. Remember?"

"Exactly. I also remember her walking around with one other woman, but I can't remember her name. I'm grasping at straws here, but I really need to find someone who might know how to reach Laura's relatives."

"Check the house."

"Done. I combed through the whole place thoroughly and didn't find a single thing."

"That's so weird."

"Tell me about it. Do you remember where she came from? I remember she said it was a small town some place here in Ontario. I thought it began with a C."

"Really? I always had the impression she was American."

"American? No, I'm sure she told me Ontario."

"My mistake. Calaboogie?"

"No."

"Clayton?"

"Uh-uh."

"Crow Lake?"

"Sorry."

"Okay, I'll try to figure out some names. But now, maybe I'll just go back to sleep."

"Thanks, Elaine. I'll talk to you in the morning. I know, not before ten."

"I'd say any time, but I'm afraid you'd take me up on it."

"Hey! What are friends for?" I said.

*   *   *

Maybe Elaine went back to sleep, but I couldn't. For some

reason, I was hungry. I couldn't really remember the last time I'd had anything aside from coffee and Harvey's Bristol Cream.

I headed for the fridge, although there's never all that much to eat in mine. Not like Laura's. I thought back to the orange juice, the milk, the chicken and vegetables.

I stood staring at a container of margarine and two open cans of pet food lit by my fridge light. There were still a couple of bottles of Moosehead left over from Ray Deveau's last visit. I picked up a small cappuccino yogurt with a best before date of June 1.

I could feel Gussie's hot breath on the back of my knees and the swish of Mrs. Parnell's cat's tail on my ankles.

"Go back to bed," I said. I found the box of Godiva chocolates and took them out to the balcony. It was nippy enough to need a blanket. I watched the crescent moon hang over the glittering river. I enjoyed the fact that no one was bugging me. Gussie and the cat snuggled up, but that didn't count as bugging.

"There's always something to be thankful for," my father used to say. I was thankful for pets and for chocolate. Laura probably hadn't been able to indulge much in that.

Wait a minute.

That was it. If Laura Brown had been diabetic, where was her insulin?

Ten

The trouble with having a brainwave is you need to confer about it. I don't know much about diabetics and their requirements. The only person who might know was Elaine Ekstein. Since she was already slightly pissed off at me, I figured I couldn't make things worse. I called.

"Elaine. Does your brother take insulin?"

I didn't hear anything like an answer. After a while I said, "Hello?"

"What?"

"Eddie, your brother, doesn't he take insulin?"

"Oh, that's why you woke me up again. I understand now why you couldn't wait until the morning. Yes, he does, thanks for asking. Goodnight. The phone will be off the hook from now on, Camilla. I hope you don't find that too terribly inconvenient."

"Come on. Where does he keep his insulin? Isn't it in little vials? Doesn't he need to take it everyday?"

"Are you crazy?"

"Apparently Laura Brown was diabetic."

"I didn't know that, and I don't see what it has to do with anything."

"She had a MedicAlert bracelet."

"Oh. Did the diabetes have anything to do with her fall? Did she lapse into a coma or something?"

"Maybe. The police suggested it. Anyway, so if you don't mind answering a question or two…"

"What choice do I have?"

"Where does Eddie keep his insulin?"

"In the fridge."

"Would he have a supply of it at any time?"

"Always. Naturally."

"What do you mean, naturally?"

"He's hardly going to take a chance with insulin, is he?"

"Right. But he must run out sometimes. Get too busy at the office and forget to pick up a new supply."

"I can't imagine a diabetic who'd let themselves run out of insulin. You'd have to have a death wish."

"Okay, Elaine. I'll let you go now."

"Sure, now that I'm up. Why are you asking these peculiar questions? Didn't Laura have any insulin?"

"I don't remember seeing any in her fridge. But maybe I'm wrong."

"I hope you are wrong, because if you're not, there's something fishy."

Of course, I already knew that. Okay, it was time to face facts. In the wee hours, I couldn't do much to find out what was going on. Particularly troubling, since I now had this insulin thing to fret over.

"Thanks, Elaine," I said. "Let's try to get some sleep now."

*   *   *

My own attempt to get back to sleep was less than successful. I tried my usual approach when I can't sleep because my head is whirling with a problem. I got up and read the newspapers. I had enough of them. Even the apartment building newsletter and the *West End News* were there to take my mind off things.

I skimmed the *Ottawa Citizen* and the *Globe and Mail*. When I really need to relax, I focus on the items that have nothing to do with social issues. I read stuff I don't care about. I read the fashion section, the homes section, even the cooking section. I read a detailed piece on installing your own insulation, and another one on dealing with mold in basements. Soon, I felt a pleasant grogginess stealing over me.

Unfortunately, just as my eyes started to get heavy, I noticed an item by my sometime friend, P. J. Lynch. Apparently, in one of the late summer tragedies, a number of cats in the nation's capital had been taking refuge in their neighbours' garages or basements. There was no harm done unless the neighbours headed off for holidays. Several beloved family pets had ended up dead of heat or starvation in empty houses. P.J. had done heartbreaking justice to the story.

I picked up Mrs. Parnell's calico cat and gave her a little stroke. "Now do you see why you have to stay in the apartment?"

The thump of Gussie's tail meant more strokes were called for. I gave Gussie a couple of reassuring pats.

"You too, Gussie."

Mrs. Parnell's cat, sensing that Gussie was getting ahead in the attention game, slid up my chest and rubbed her head under my chin.

"You're right," I said. "It is a good thing that P. J. Lynch, star police reporter and occasional political pundit, is looking after your interests and keeping an eye on issues of importance to the feline community. Smaller minds, however, might suggest P. J.'s star has fallen at the *Citizen*."

Gussie leapt onto the sofa and snuggled in. The cat wasn't going to get all the action.

"Too bad P. J.'s not talking to us," I said. "Otherwise we could find out how he feels about these assignments."

They both had drifted back to sleep. They weren't pleased when I woke them up to go back to bed.

Half an hour later, I was no closer to dreamland. The cat story hadn't helped.

I lay back and summed up what I knew.

Laura might have slipped into a diabetic coma. But if she was diabetic, why did I have no recollection of seeing insulin in her fridge or anywhere else, including the fanny pack?

Maybe I was being silly. Maybe she was now on some other form of treatment. A transplant or a patch or something.

I could ask her doctor about this, but there had been no indication of who her physician was and how to find out. Not a prescription, not a note. Not an agenda with appointments listed.

Her doctor would be on record at MedicAlert, but even if I got the name in the morning, what were the chances that the doctor would be around that weekend? By Tuesday, I'd be a wreck.

I was beginning to conclude that someone had scooped out every identifying feature of Laura's existence. Had that someone taken Laura's insulin too? Why? Or did I just not know enough to recognize it? The most important question was, if someone had taken the insulin, was it before or after Laura died?

I could see where the answer might make a big difference.

Gussie and the little calico cat didn't like it much when I tossed and turned. And I was definitely outnumbered.

Finally, I got out of bed and slipped into jeans and a light fleece jacket. There was only one way to find out.

It was just short of four-thirty on Saturday morning when I slid Mrs. Parnell's Volvo into the driveway on Third Avenue and let myself into Laura Brown's house again. I keyed in my code, 1986, and held my breath.

No alarm sounded. But the red light hadn't been flashing. I guessed that I hadn't quite got the hang of the instructions from the security company. I hate gadgets.

The house was deliciously cool. Laura Brown had liked her luxuries.

As so-called next-of-kin, should I have been turning off the air conditioner? I left the lights off. There was enough brightness from the street lamp to see. The kitchen end of the house was softly visible. Someone at the neighbours' house must have had trouble sleeping. Their lights were on.

I headed right for the fridge. It seemed just as I had left it. I moved the container of milk. Nothing. I moved the container of OJ and checked. More nothing.

Very peculiar. It gave me an idea. I decided to call another person who I knew for sure would be up and around, erstwhile reporter, P. J. Lynch. Just because someone's really mad at you doesn't mean you no longer remember their cellphone number.

"P. J.," I said cheerfully.

"Who is this?" he said.

"It's me."

"Goodbye, Camilla."

"Your choice. But I got a story for you."

"I've heard that before."

"And didn't you end up with stories?"

"Yeah. And getting arrested and you not being much help."

"Put the past behind you and move on."

P. J. sighed.

"Fine," I said. "If you're not interested. Bye."

"Okay, Tiger, what's the scoop?"

I was heartened by that. P. J. hadn't called me Tiger for a while. Maybe he was getting over my perceived betrayal.

"Well, it's about a woman who…hang on a second, will you? I heard something odd. I just want to check it out."

"Don't put me on hold. I'm in the middle of a story."

"Who are you kidding? Your deadline's long gone. We both know you're sitting there watching infomercials. Don't be so impatient. I'm not putting you on hold. I'm just walking to check something. I've got the phone in my hand." I figured it was just my imagination acting up in a strange house. The air conditioning was still humming, probably that. But what if someone's favourite feline was stuck there in the garage? With Laura gone, it would be dead before anyone found it. I didn't plan to come back soon.

"Call me when you're finished. I'm really busy," P. J. bleated from the cellphone.

"Don't you give a hoot about the welfare of animals?"

"What are you talking about?

"Cats trapped in vacant houses. Ring a bell?"

"That's cruel, even for you, Tiger."

"What do you mean, cruel? I'm serious. It's not why I called, but just keep your shirt on until I check out this noise. Then I'll give you the scoop on the woman without a history."

I knew he wouldn't hang up after that. I clutched the phone and moved toward the stairs to the basement. I opened the door and peered down into the darkness.

I didn't plan to go downstairs and check. I've seen way too many teen horror movies for that.

72

"Here, kitty kitty," I said.

"What?" P. J. squawked from the phone.

No kitties emerged.

The nice thing about an alarm system is that you know you are alone in a house. The not-so-nice thing is you might not be correct. I felt rather than saw the movement from the dining room. I had no time to turn around fully before the impact of the blow between my shoulder blades pushed me forward. The phone shot out of my hand and bounced down the stairs. I grabbed for the walls, trying for anything to stop my fall. I connected with the vacuum hose, which slid off the hook and rattled down the stairs. I howled as I tumbled through the dark after it.

The only image in my mind was the concrete floor below. The impact when I hit the bottom put an end to that.

Eleven

I opened my eyes to see a familiar paramedic. I didn't remember which of my many recent disasters he'd shown up for.

"Have we met before?" I said.

Apparently this wasn't all that intelligible.

"Try not to move until we check you out, ma'am." I closed my eyes again. I liked the sound of his voice, soothing yet uplifting, like ice cream. Mint chocolate chip.

That voice was an appealing contrast to the sounds of my three sisters fussing in the background. What were they doing here? Where was here?

I said, "Is it a cliché to ask, where am I?"

"You're at the bottom of a staircase in the basement of someone else's house in the middle of the night giving everyone you know heart attacks, Missy. That's where you are."

Ah, Edwina. Always one to stab a manicured nail into the real issue.

For some reason, there were two of her. And two of Alexa and Donalda. I didn't see any of my father. Two Mrs. Parnells stood close by, hunched near the wall and smoking a couple of Benson & Hedges. It was possible they stood next to some Alvins, but I couldn't be quite sure. It hurt to turn my head.

"Try not to move," the mint chocolate chip voice said.

Meanwhile, Edwina was warming up for a rant.

"Save me," I whispered to Mrs. Parnell. All I got was smoke rings. Quite a lot of them.

"Ladies," the paramedic said, "you'll have to move off. We need quiet and light. And we don't want the patient upset. That goes for you too, gentlemen."

I spotted two P. J.s lurking in the corner, next to the two gas furnaces. Four policemen were making notes in matching notebooks.

"I repeat, you'll have to clear the area." The paramedic sounded like he meant business.

Edwina grumbled. "Of course, let's not upset her. She can scare us out of our wits, so we can drive an hour into town in the middle of the night, and that's all right."

A slight scuffling ensued. Alexa said, "Come on. You can give her hell later."

"Sure, rough me up when there are no witnesses," I mumbled.

A cloud of sisters ascended the staircase, followed by a pair of P. J.s. The Alvins' ponytails flicked out of sight along with them.

The paramedic had less success with Mrs. Parnell.

"I am equal parts disabled and litigious," she muttered darkly. "And I had more than enough trouble getting down here."

"Let her stay," I said. "Believe it or not, she's a force for good." I did not add that she was only seriously disabled when it was in her interest.

The paramedic went back to tapping my toes and shining lights in my eyes.

"Will I make it?" I said, pleased to note my words were actually intelligible.

He stopped peering into my brain and smiled a chocolate sauce kind of smile. "We have to stop meeting this way."

"No argument here," I said.

*　　*　　*

Lucky me, the emergency room was quiet. My injuries were judged to be minor, but as we were dealing with a head trauma, I was X-rayed and examined without too much delay. "Let's see. Mild concussion, some bad bruising, cuts, possible sprained wrist. This isn't the first time I've seen you for a concussion, is it?" The emergency room physician also looked familiar. He stifled a yawn.

He was tall, dark and handsome and spoke with a Newfoundland accent.

I read his name tag. Dr. Abdullah Hasheem. I was glad he'd mentioned seeing me before. I had started to think all doctors looked alike.

"Mild concussion you said the last time. I haven't been here for ages." That was the best I could come up with.

"Then you know the drill. Watch out for dizziness, enlarged pupils, sudden headaches, changes in vision. Mood swings. That kind of thing. Have a quiet weekend. Give your head time to get back to normal. No sports, no vigorous activity."

"Not a problem."

Magic words, I guess. I was pronounced too fit for the hospital and released faster than you can say toss her down the stairs.

*　　*　　*

Back in my apartment, Gussie and Mrs. Parnell's cat welcomed me with nervous sympathy and kisses. My sisters bustled about, making tea. They don't do sympathy. No wonder the animals were on edge.

Having the girls on the premises was not good news. They'd interrupted their weekend, and I'd racked up yet another pile of psychological debts which I had no intention of repaying.

"Doesn't she ever clean this place?" That was Donalda from the kitchen. "Do you think there's any bleach, or is that too much to ask?" The swish of water followed, then the scent of citrus.

Edwina was whipping the sheets off my bed, although Alexa had already raced her to the washing machine with the contents of the hamper. Not one to admit defeat, Edwina snatched up the various piles of newspapers and made off with them down to the recycling room near the elevator. So what? With the shape my head was in, I couldn't read anyway. Plus, the only time my place ever got a really good cleaning was when I got injured. Maybe there was a better way to keep on top of the chores.

My head buzzed a bit as I turned to Mrs. Parnell. I was grateful her many interests did not include housework. "How did you find me, Mrs. P.?"

"You can thank our young Mr. Lynch."

"P. J. called you? But I didn't tell him where I was. Oh, I get it. Did the alarm go off?"

"Apparently, you made quite a racket falling down those stairs. Screamed your head off. An alarm was unnecessary."

"Did the neighbours hear? Their lights were on."

"No, our Mr. Lynch heard your terrified shrieks and hotfooted it to your apartment looking for you."

"Terrified shrieks?"

"A direct quote."

"Hmm. He came here? I guess I didn't tell him I wasn't calling from home."

"I could not help overhear him hammering on your door."

"Ah." If you don't sleep much and keep your door open on the off chance the neighbours will do something interesting, occasionally you'll hit the jackpot. Not a complaint. This wasn't the first time Mrs. Parnell's curiosity had worked in my favour.

P. J., who had been loitering palely, broke in. "Lucky for you, Mrs. Parnell was able to let me in."

"But I wasn't here. How did you find me?"

"Technology, Ms. MacPhee."

"We checked the callers on your phone to see if there was a clue there," P. J. said.

"There wasn't," I said.

"But there was. Perseverance. Cardinal rule," Mrs. Parnell said.

"Violet pressed 'Last Call Redial'," P. J. said.

Mrs. Parnell looked suitably modest. "We were fortunate enough to reach Ms. Ekstein."

I said, "You mean her phone wasn't off the hook?"

"No, but what a mouth on her," P. J. said, "worse than yours. That's one woman who shouldn't get behind on her sleep."

"But Elaine didn't know where I was going either."

Mrs. Parnell tapped the side of her head. "Using the old noggin, Ms. MacPhee. Once Ms. Ekstein stopped shouting, we were able to ask her why you had called."

"She kept going on about insulin. And refrigerators," P. J. said.

"All of which was in reference to your recently departed friend. Ms. Ekstein seems to have taken umbrage at your nocturnal calls," Mrs. Parnell said, happily lighting a Benson & Hedges.

"Violet put two and two together and remembered you had been concerned about something in this Laura Brown's house."

"But you didn't know where it was."

P. J. said, "You'd mentioned she lived on Third Avenue so we hopped into my car, since Violet's was not where she parked it, and we were off to the Glebe."

Oops. I'd borrowed the Volvo.

"We drove down Third until she spotted her car parked in a driveway. We deduced that was it."

"How did you manage to get into Laura's house, Mrs. P.?"

P. J. answered for her. "We hammered on the door. When you didn't open up, we called the cops. Then we just opened the door."

"Just opened it? But I left it locked."

P. J. seemed to be in an exceptionally good mood. I thought I knew why. "You'll get a great story out of this, won't you? Local lawyer attacked in vacant house. 'Ghosts in The Glebe'. A little something for the comeback trail to get you out of pet story hell."

"I think I can get a better hook than that."

"I can give you a hook. That's why I called you. The hook is Laura Brown."

Mrs. Parnell interrupted. "First things first, Ms. MacPhee. I'd like to know what happened to you."

"Well, I decided to head over to check out the fridge for insulin, because I didn't remember seeing any."

"I thought it was handbags you were concerned about."

"That too."

"At nearly four-thirty in the morning?" P. J. said. "What made you think either handbags or insulin were urgent?"

Mrs. Parnell looked hurt. "You could have called me to go with you. I was at loose ends."

"I assumed you were asleep, needing to rest up for the balloon festival. Anyway, I don't know what I was thinking."

She sniffed. "You might not have been injured if you'd had backup."

"Don't sulk, Mrs. Parnell. If it's any consolation, I regret investigating without you. And I shouldn't have taken your car without asking. I figured I'd be there for just a couple of minutes. What time is it now?"

"Eight."

Double oops. "Mrs. Parnell, you must have missed the balloon launch today because of me. Sorry."

"The best laid plans and all that. As it turned out, the balloons did not go up this morning. Too windy. Young Ferguson is quite crestfallen. Did you see him this morning? He was also quite concerned about your wellbeing."

"Never mind. Give him time. I'm sure he'll be mad at me again, soon. Will there be a launch this evening?"

"It looks most promising."

"I'll get your shots then. Honest."

"Back to the matter at hand, Ms. MacPhee. What happened in that house?"

"I was checking things out. I didn't turn the lights on, just in case the people next door called the police or something. They know Laura's dead."

"Excellent strategy."

"So I called P. J. on my cellphone, as you know."

"Indeed."

"I was talking to him when I thought I heard something. There was no reason for anyone to be in the house. I've been reading P. J.'s articles in the paper, and I got it into my head a cat might have been stuck in the basement. I went to look, and someone pushed me down the stairs."

"Lucky for you, the vacuum hose fell in front of you and broke your fall. You probably would have fractured your skull," P.J. said. "That's crossed my mind."

From the next room, I heard Edwina call out, "I bet that's the closest Camilla's ever come to a vacuum cleaner."

Mrs. Parnell didn't want to get sidetracked. "But Ms. MacPhee. I am puzzled. How could anyone get into the house without you knowing about it? Did you neglect to set the alarm when you entered?"

"That's the weird thing. The alarm was off when I got here, and I set it when I came in. No one could have gotten in without me knowing."

They exchanged glances, which is one of my least favourite things. "Don't do that," I said.

"What?" P.J. said.

"You know perfectly well what. You're looking at each other like I'm crazy."

"No one would suggest such a thing, Ms. MacPhee. But the alarm wasn't on when we entered."

I said. "I've been thinking about it. Logically, whoever did this knew the access code to the alarm. That means there's someone around who knew Laura well enough to have the code. I bet the security company didn't disable Laura's old code."

"Are you sure someone pushed you?" P.J said. "You'd been up half the night. Violet tells me you'd had to identify Laura Brown's body, which must have been rough, even for someone of your disposition. You were walking around an unfamiliar house in the dark. You were a prime candidate for catapulting down the basement stairs."

"There was plenty of glow from the street lamp and also light from the house next door."

"I am troubled, Ms. MacPhee. Why would you leave your cellphone in the kitchen and venture into a dark basement by yourself?"

"That's right, Tiger. Sounds like a bad horror movie. Were you wearing a bikini when you ran into the dark basement alone?"

"Funny, P. J. I didn't go into the basement, and I had my cellphone in my hand, just like any sensible person, so it was not being totally useless."

"You just thought you did."

"No, for sure, I had it. Hey. Where is it? I hope it didn't shatter on the concrete floor."

Again with the looks.

Mrs. Parnell held out my cellphone to me. "I picked it up."

"Thanks," I said.

P. J. said. "Violet picked it up from the kitchen counter."

"What?"

"On the counter by the fridge. You must have left it there. That's what we're saying."

"Don't give me that crap, P. J. I had it in my hand."

"As the doctor no doubt told you, sometimes the brain does strange things," Mrs. Parnell said.

I said, "I am not imagining this."

Of course, everyone denied everything. My sisters insisted they hadn't touched the phone. Who did I think they were? Come to think of it, who did I think I was? I gave up arguing, and the three of them resumed rearranging the molecules in my apartment.

Mrs. Parnell puffed huffily at the suggestion she might have picked up the phone and moved it to the kitchen.

"I am not absent-minded, Ms. MacPhee."

"I thought perhaps in the confusion of finding me and all that."

P. J. said, "I found you sprawled on the concrete floor. Violet stayed upstairs and called 911 from the kitchen. That's when she found the phone. She came down to the basement after. I don't even know how she managed the stairs."

"I am not an invalid," Mrs. Parnell snapped. "That mobility aid is just for balance. I'm fine on stairs if there's something to hold on to."

I said, "This proves my point. Someone pushed me and deliberately placed my cellphone upstairs so I couldn't call for help if I happened to survive the fall. They put it where it would appear I had forgotten it. Then they left me. By the time I'd be found, game over. It could have been weeks, since Laura didn't seem to have company. Now we know someone else had a key and the code. Means and opportunity for the perfect crime."

Mrs. Parnell blew smoke rings. "What about motive, Ms. MacPhee?"

"We're a little light on motive. I suppose I had one, since I'm the heir. I didn't have much to gain by attacking myself. But if you hand me my backpack, I'll get out the number of the security company and find out who else had an access code."

"Good thinking, Ms. MacPhee," she said, handing over the bag.

P.J. scratched his nose.

I called the 1-800 number and gave my name and mother's maiden name. I asked who else had an authorized access code to Laura's place.

"We cannot give out confidential information like that," the voice said.

"But it's my house now."

"When we get the proper legal papers to prove that, then we can release the information."

"Wait a minute. Can you tell me if anyone, without naming names, was officially authorized. Besides me."

The voice hesitated. "I suppose I can confirm that. You are the only one, ma'am, except for Ms. Brown herself."

I hung up and said, "Okay. I guess it's just me. This whole situation started less than eighteen hours ago, when the cops showed up. All this weird stuff is connected with Laura's death, but damned if I know how."

Mrs. Parnell lit a Benson & Hedges. "How curious, Ms. MacPhee."

"Yeah. It's an intriguing story, Tiger," P. J. said, "and, like you said, so far you're the only one with a motive."

Twelve

N o," I said firmly. The main thing with my sisters is to be wary of their body language and never let yourself feel outnumbered. They'd finished my apartment, my laundry and swept my balcony, considered some options for painting the place and made the usual remarks about my lack of matching china. Now they turned their attention to the last untidy detail.

Me.

"Look here, Missy," Edwina said. "We can't leave Daddy and the boys at the lake by themselves at lunch time. God knows what damage they'll do."

"That's right," Donalda said. "I've packed your suitcase."

"Listen carefully. Read my lips if you have to. I am not going to the cottage."

"You really need a new bathing suit," Alexa said. "I wouldn't be caught dead in yours."

I said. "I'm not planning to be caught dead. So it doesn't matter."

"Of course it matters. I don't think there's a scrap of spandex left unsprung in it."

"Here's a scrap for you: I won't need a bathing suit, because I won't be at the lake."

"Don't be silly," Edwina said.

Donalda would have picked up my suitcase at that point, except she was already holding it.

Alexa frowned, "I suppose you can always wear one of mine."

"Are you all hard of hearing? I'm not going. I have a concussion. My legs are all bruised. I'm cut, I'm grubby. I feel like crap."

"We can hardly leave you on your own with a concussion and other injuries," Donalda said with her peculiar MacPhee logic. I should have anticipated that.

"For the last time, I'm not going. I'll be fine here."

"I don't think so, Missy," Edwina said.

"Then think again. May I remind you, I am a functioning adult."

"There is absolutely no need to yell," Edwina sniffed.

I said, "I'll go Monday evening for the party. Which reminds me, shouldn't you start preparations? What about marinades? Do you have enough ice? Is there gas for the boats? Are there tiny tears in the personal flotation devices? Is someone on the lookout for salmonella at the BBQ? Who's getting the spare ribs?"

Edwina said. "Get a move on. The doctor said not to stay by yourself. And may I remind you, Alexa was a nurse."

"Not in the last twenty-five years, she wasn't. Anyway, I am not by myself. I have Mrs. Parnell. Plus P. J. And Gussie."

Mrs. Parnell raised her sherry glass in confirmation. P. J. blanched.

"Yes, well," said Edwina, implying a world of things.

"You'll be better off with the family," Donalda said.

I hardly thought so, especially since two out of my three brothers-in-law were not speaking to me and the third lived in his own fishing dream world. "I'll be careful."

Alexa said. "How do we know that you won't head right out and get injured again?"

I took a deep breath. "You can trust me."

"Me too." Mrs. Parnell blew a couple of spectacular smoke rings. Lucky me, she never mentioned balloons once.

*   *   *

As the morning wore on, I tried Yee and Zaccotto again. The switchboard put me through to their voice mail. The same thing happened when I tried to reach Major Crimes. Maybe the constables were on the four to eleven shift, but where the hell was everyone in Major Crimes? I didn't think the fact it was Saturday before noon should make much of a difference.

My brother-in-law didn't answer his cellphone at the cottage, where he was in charge of father-sitting, and I got a chilly reception from the only other person I could think of, Detective Sgt. Leonard Mombourquette. I tracked him down at home.

"Yes, well, I'm not in Major Crimes right now. I'm on extended sick leave, as you may remember."

"I know that, Leonard."

"I have an SIU investigation to get through. Do you have any idea what a frigging nightmare that is?"

"I can imagine."

"No, you can not imagine it. After that, I'll face a Professional Standards investigation. Then once those are over, I can look forward to testifying at the Coroner's Inquest. Try having that hanging over your head. My actions and my decisions will be under the microscope in both investigations and again at the inquest."

"But you did what you had to. You had no choice at all but to shoot."

"Well then, I feel better. I can relax while they turn every part of my life upside down."

"Look, Leonard, the point I want to make is…"

"If I hadn't been dealing with you, it wouldn't have happened. Okay? I wouldn't be spending every night questioning myself, what if I had planned better, if I'd been more alert, if I'd aimed lower. I am not going to get involved with any of your harebrained schemes. Clear?"

"I take your point, Leonard, and I understand how you must feel."

"You do not goddam well understand how I feel. I have to deal with it every time I look in the mirror. And when all the investigations are finished, I'll still have to live with it."

"Okay, here's what's happening: this friend of mine died, and the circumstances seem to be quite suspicious."

"People die around you all the time, Camilla. Have you asked yourself why that is?"

"I think she was murdered. I need to talk to someone in Major Crimes. Conn's fishing with my father, and I can't reach the constables who informed me about the death. Maybe they're not even on duty this weekend. They won't be in Major Crimes anyway. The more time that elapses, the harder it is to solve a crime. You know that."

"Yes, I do. When you do connect with Major Crimes, they'll be glad to have you explain how the police screwed up."

"I'm not saying the police are at fault. I'm asking for help, Leonard."

"You're on your own, Camilla."

* * *

One good thing about being next-of-kin: you're entitled to

information. Mrs. Parnell needed no urging to drive me back to the hospital to see what I could find out from the pathologist.

The results of the post-mortem were bad or good, depending on your perspective.

"Are you sure?" I said.

The pathologist was small and puckered looking, as though he'd been stored in formaldehyde. His face was dominated by thick dark glasses and even thicker eyebrows. The eyebrows were dramatic enough to take your mind off his other features.

"I think she was murdered."

He wiggled one of the dramatic eyebrows. "Not according to our findings."

"Well," I said, "there's a few things you should take into consideration."

"This woman died because she tumbled a hundred feet on to rocks. Her blood sugar was extremely low at the time. There were witnesses around. She climbed over the protective fencing in full view of other people. Then she must have passed out or become dizzy."

"I can't believe she would climb that fence. She was a sensible middle-aged woman."

"Not the first one to meet a nasty end defying the laws of physics."

"You were trying to find the cause of death, and you found one that made sense to you. But I'm saying there are factors at work you may not have been aware of."

"Thank you. And you are…Doctor?"

I drew myself up. "No need for sarcasm, Dr. Varty. I may not have a medical degree, but let me remind you, I am the next-of-kin. Here are the facts: some of Laura's belongings were stolen from her home; I was attacked there the night after she died; and someone definitely removed her insulin from the fridge."

"I am very sorry for your loss. I understand this is difficult for you. It's not the first time I've dealt with a death like this. And there's nothing to indicate Laura Brown's death was anything but a tragic accident. If you have evidence to the contrary, it's a matter for the police, not for pathology. If it's any consolation, because of the nature and location of the death, there will almost certainly be a Coroner's Inquest. In the meantime, we can release the body to you for burial. Do you have a funeral home in mind?"

*   *   *

"Are you certain you'll be all right without a vehicle, Ms. MacPhee? I really must be off," Mrs. Parnell said as she stopped the Volvo at the door to our building.

"I'm not going anywhere. Thanks for taking me to see the pathologist."

"A shame you couldn't get him to see reason. Would you like me to help you make the arrangements?"

"No, thanks. I'll just call the funeral home."

"You should rest. Save yourself to fight another day."

"I will."

"I hate to go, but I did promise Young Ferguson I'd head over to the festival site. He's volunteering for a few things, and he wants me to drop by." She picked up her digital camera. "I'll take both cameras. I am sure he will understand if you can't manage photos today."

I experienced a brief flash of what life would be like with Alvin if I didn't do photo duty this time. I reached for the camera.

"Happy to do it, Mrs. P. I'll be there for take-off. Don't you worry about a thing."

"Are you certain, Ms. MacPhee? I am concerned about

your physical state."

"Nothing wrong with me. I'll cab it over. It will keep me from being bored." I managed a martyred smile.

Back at my apartment, I patted Gussie and let the cat in from the balcony. I hunted for a paper and pen while the cat had a nap on the freshly vacuumed sofa. My sisters, of course, had cleaned up all those unesthetic writing supplies, and it took a while to find them.

I started a list. It turned into three lists, then four.

LAURA—SEEN—WHO ELSE?
FOUL PLAY – Indications
ONTARIO TOWN?
ACTION

LAURA SEEN was the easiest. I racked my brain for who else at Carleton University in 1986 would have remembered her. The eighties tended to be a blur for me. From the moment I met him, life had been about Paul.

I had few recollections of Laura outside of class. I did remember her in the library and occasionally in the pub. I did remember her walking with another woman near one of the beautiful spots by the Rideau, where you could enjoy sun on a rock in the spring and fall. But I couldn't remember the other woman's name. Sophie? Sally? How do you recall the names of the people who were in your classes nearly twenty years after the fact? Wait a minute. Sylvie! But Sylvie who?

I'm not the kind of person who would have bought a yearbook, even if Carleton had produced one at that time. Of course, the Registrar's Office was closed for the weekend. I'd tried to phone just in case they would release some information from their old files. After all, I was the next-of-kin. That reminded me of an unpleasant duty. I called the only funeral home I could think of to start the process of getting Laura's body. Apparently you need an appointment for that. "I'll get back to you soon."

I closed my eyes, ignored my pounding headache and went back to the lists. Think think think. Eventually the thinking paid off. There was Frances Foxall, of course. I didn't remember ever seeing them together, but they must have known each other. Frances had been tough and hard-nosed. The kind of person who thought everything that happened was her business. She'd been closer to Laura's age than mine. I figured she'd be a good bet to remember Laura's hometown and possibly even details about her family. I put Frances Foxall's name on the list. At the very least, she'd probably remember Sylvie's last name.

Like Frances, Sylvie had been about Laura's age. But that was the only similarity. I remembered Sylvie being quite beautiful in a delicate way, but for all her looks, she had been shy and easily embarrassed. Except for Laura, she'd kept to herself.

I wrote Sylvie? on my list. These memories weren't much to go on. I tried calling Elaine Ekstein, but she didn't answer. Next I made a note to contact Carleton and ask for Laura's home address. Tuesday would be the earliest. I had visions of administrators screeching about privacy and the rights of students. I shook myself. I wasn't sure if they'd still have that information. I intended to find Laura's family well before Tuesday. With luck, Major Crimes would be deep into the investigation by then. For sure, it would be faster if I could find just one person who remembered the name of the damn irritating little town that started with C.

I began with Frances Foxall.

Thirteen

Naturally, Frances Foxall wasn't in the phone book. A lot of people still changed their names when they got married back in the eighties. That didn't seem like a Frances Foxall thing to do. Come to think of it, getting married didn't seem like a Frances thing to do. If Mrs. Parnell had been home, I could have asked her to check Canada411. She would have found not only a phone number but a full address with Postal Code.

Sometimes the old-fashioned ways pay off.

I dialled 4-1-1.

The automated system didn't care for my vague request. A real operator turned up good old Frances in a small community south of Ottawa. Whole name, no initials.

Frances wasn't home. Naturally. I was the only person in Canada hanging around the house on the Labour Day weekend. A man who sounded like he had a bad cold said to leave a message after the beep. I left my name, my cellphone number and a vague yet compelling reason to call. I chewed my nails and thought hard. Who were the women Laura had been lunching with? Why hadn't she introduced them to me? Why hadn't I been interested enough to look at them?

I had an idea how to find out. It was getting close to noon.

I decided to head downtown for lunch and a side order of information.

Just to be safe, I called a cab.

* * *

Maisie's Eatery sits on the fringe of the Market and, lucky me, that meant it was open all weekend. Although I'm pretty down-to-earth as a rule, I enjoy the atmosphere at Maisie's: soothing white tablecloths, fresh flowers, pretty yet undemanding paintings on walls, plus the tempting aroma of fresh rolls. Except for the fact you had to climb a flight of stairs to get in, it was the perfect spot for lunch. I forced my bruised body up the steps, knowing what I'd find there would be worth it.

My first questions didn't get me far with the young woman at the desk in the front of the restaurant. "Sorry, but your friend sounds like a lot of women who come in here."

"She does? Oh. Can I have a look at your reservation list for July please? That could help me solve the problem."

"Gosh. I don't know. I'd have to check with Norine, the owner, and she's not here right now."

"I'd just take a quick peek. I wouldn't take it away. Cross my heart."

"Sorry. There might be privacy issues. I'd really have to get authorization."

I loved that. Privacy issues in a restaurant. That's the trouble with servers nowadays. Half the time they're MBA students or actors or perhaps even out-of-work lawyers, and they know way more than you want them to.

This girl seemed nervous. Probably because the place was nearly packed, and she was taking time from her tables.

I said, "This is an easy question. My friend lunched here quite often during the work week. She always sat at that table in the sun. I just need to know if you know the name of any of her companions."

She shook her head. "I just do weekends."

"Anyone here today who works lunch weekdays?"

She glanced around. "Let me see. I guess Chelsea." She pointed to a foxy-faced girl who had spiky hair with multi-coloured tips. Chelsea was balancing three full plates on her way from the kitchen to the opposite end of the restaurant. She served her tables and chatted with people. I liked her wicked grin.

"Okay, I'll talk to her."

"She's busy right now."

"No problem. I'll have a look at the menu while I'm waiting."

"Sure. You want a table?"

"No, thanks. I'll just stay here. I'll let you know if I decide to eat."

She smiled and skittered back to her customers. I kept an eye out for her as I leaned over the desk and flipped back through the reservation book. No point in alienating anyone, since I still hadn't found what I wanted.

I couldn't remember the dates when I'd seen Laura, except for one. I'd dropped in with a colleague after a hearing toward the end of July. I glanced at the reservations for the last week in July and didn't find Laura Brown's name. That was probably good. If her companion had made the reservation, that could be the break I needed. I noticed the reservations were usually first names and phone numbers. Good. I needed an opportunity to write down everyone who'd reserved for that time period. Without getting permission or getting caught. I was digging for my pen when Chelsea walked toward the desk. She nodded to me and said, "I'll be right with you." She led the newcomers to a table, handed out menus with a flourish and returned before I found my pen.

"Hi. I'm Chelsea. I understand you want to speak to me?" she said. Up close, she looked older and wiser than her foxy grin and spiky hair suggested.

I tried a new approach. "I'm looking for a friend. It's a matter of life and death." True enough, if somewhat misleading. "I saw her having lunch with another woman, sometime in late July. They sat there." I pointed. "My friend is medium-tall, a little bit plump, dark auburn hair, mid-forties, attractive but not stunning. She was wearing a linen suit, professional looking." I stopped. "She came here quite often."

"Hmmm," she said. "I remember meals, not faces or clothes."

"I don't know what she ate. She had an alligator handbag, if that helps."

She gave a short bark of laughter. "It doesn't. And to tell you the truth, I don't even remember meals that long after I've served them. Well, sometimes I remember faces, but I'd have to see her. You don't have a photo?"

"That's part of the problem. There's not a picture anywhere of her. She was diabetic, though. Maybe she needed special meals. Does that ring a bell?"

"Jasmine might know. She's got a knack for remembering people. She often works that corner. And people are always telling her about their diets and their problems. She's your best bet."

"Can I talk to Jasmine?"

"She's not on shift right now."

"When will she be here?"

"Not sure. She works a couple of jobs. She's putting herself through university. Hang on, I'll check the schedule. It might take a couple of minutes, we're really frantic, as you can see."

"I'll wait."

"You having lunch?"

"Yes, I'd like that table." I pointed to the window where I'd last seen Laura lunching.

"Sure. That's one of mine today."

I sat down at the table with relief, because I was feeling a bit woozy. It crossed my mind that I hadn't eaten for a long time, despite my sisters' best efforts. I loved the Maisie's Eatery menu.

"I'll order too," I said. "Something with chicken. Pick the best one. And a cappuccino for dessert."

"You want soup or salad?"

"Sure. Surprise me there, too."

I waited and watched Chelsea whirl from table to table. I used the time to try to remember what Laura's companions had looked like. Being in the same spot helped. One had dark hair, I knew that much, pulled back in a sleek ponytail. I wondered if she might have been Sylvie after eighteen years. I didn't think so. The eyes had been too dark, the cheekbones too prominent. But then I wasn't sure how accurate my impression had been.

Fifteen minutes later, I had my lunch, hot and sour soup, followed by chicken with coconut and fruit.

My cappuccino arrived with a bonus. Chelsea somewhat breathlessly, "You're in luck. Jasmine's in at five-thirty. That's not a bad time to talk. The restaurant doesn't get overwhelming until later. You won't have much luck if you come when we're full. The owner's here and, well, you'll see."

I could see my day going even further down the toilet.

"Could you give me Jasmine's address? That would save me a lot of time." I tried to smile harmlessly, but she wasn't buying it.

"No chance. I'm pushing our policy by giving you her name and schedule."

"Right."

"See you tonight," she said, with a sly wink.

At least I'd be getting regular meals.

*　　*　　*

Since I was on foot and well-fed, I had nothing better to do than push my way through the crowds of tourists and walk west. It made sense to take a stroll behind the Supreme Court and check out the unlikely place Laura had died. I made my way through the Market, turned on to Sussex and hiked along Wellington Street past the Parliament Buildings until I reached the parking lot that separates the Department of Justice from the West Block. Usually, I enjoy looking up at the historic stone buildings with their copper roofs. I think of them as Canadian Baronial in style, although my father once told me the correct term is Gothic Revival. No joke. You've got to be grateful for turrets and gargoyles in this day and age.

This time I had other things besides architecture on my mind. I zigzagged through the terraced levels of the exterior parking lots, clearly marked "No Public Parking Any Time", until I reached the last set of wooden stairs. They connected to the bike path that runs along the foot of the escarpment that the Parliament Buildings, Department of Justice and Supreme Court are built on. Everything ached as I lumbered down the steps. It was a relief to connect with the nice flat bike path.

The route is spectacular, no matter how many times you've been along it. To the East, the Interprovincial Bridge. Across the Ottawa River on the Quebec side, the magical dune-like structure of the Museum of Civilization and the more pragmatic E. B. Eddy Plant. On the Ottawa bank, the vast glass walls of the National Gallery glittered in the afternoon sun. Silver ripples on the river. A pair of matching balloons floated by, reflecting green and purple stripes in the river. The path was thick with people, probably a mix of locals and tourists, distinguishable by their cameras.

I turned west toward the Supreme Court of Canada Building. I rounded the corner, and the river spread out before me. As pretty as it was, the dramatic solid rock cliff that reached up to the Supreme Court overwhelmed it. I stood there staring up, over a hundred feet. I could see barbed wire and stone walls far above.

I retraced my steps and made my way back up to the small street parallel to Wellington. As far as I could tell, it existed for the convenience of the toylike green Parliamentary vehicles.

A few minutes later, I was behind the Supreme Court in the parking area I assumed was reserved for the Justices. This lot had a surprise feature: a lookout with benches. It was a nice place for lunching or clearing your head. To the left, a broad stone staircase swept down to another level with deciduous trees, well-kept grass, more benches. A 180° view of the river. A high iron gate blocked off one side, barbed wire on the right side, blocking the foolhardy from the drop. Straight ahead, a metal fence about four feet high. A torn piece of yellow tape that said "Police Line Do Not Cross" fluttered in the breeze. A fresh strip of "Caution Tape" had been added. I imagined the tape was intended to keep anyone from getting too close to the fence. Like that made a difference to anyone who was foolish enough to go over that fence. I slipped under the tape.

On the far side of the fence, there was a few feet of grass, then nothing. I spotted two dark parallel marks, where something had skidded. Was this the spot where Laura had gone over?

Laura had been fairly sporty and on the tall side of medium. She could have gotten over the fence with a bit of effort. But the risk was obvious. Was she trying to escape from someone? The pathologist had spoken of witnesses. Someone would have heard if she'd called for help.

None of it made sense.

For the first time, I began to feel angry. What the hell had Laura Brown been playing at? And why had she chosen to involve me?

Fourteen

Angry or not, I still had to deal with the problem. I damn well wanted to talk to those witnesses. I turned around, ducked back under the tape, sat on the nearest bench and tried Yee and Zaccotto again.

My messages suggested strongly that they return my calls at their first opportunity. I requested the contact information for the witnesses to Laura's death.

Five minutes later, I got up and started walking, passing by a clump of tourists with digital and video cameras. Maybe it was foggy thinking as a result of my head injury, but only after I'd spotted the twentieth video camera did I remember Elaine Ekstein.

Elaine had everyone she'd ever met on video.

I wasn't going to take a chance on her phone being off the hook. Although it was a bit of a hike, I walked straight to Elaine's, which is on Spruce Street, convenient to both Little Italy and Chinatown and their excellent restaurants. Elaine loves ethnic. She has the second and third floors of a crumbling wooden house with a history. She also has more security than the Pope. Not surprising, since she's had more than one death threat due to her work at Women Against Violence Everywhere. Elaine's home wasn't far behind the

WAVE office in the security department.

"Elaine!" I shouted as she unhooked two chains and unclicked a pair of deadbolts. I knew she had a motion sensitive light on her balcony and motion detectors on her living level.

"Why are you shouting, Camilla?"

"Because I just realized something."

"And why are you leaning at that odd angle?"

"Just a concussion. Someone tried to kill me by tossing me down a set of stairs. But, hey, I'm getting better." As I moved past her, she closed the door and reset the alarm.

"Holy moly. Is that why P. J. kept calling last night? I finally had to answer his stupid questions just to get some peace. I thought he was drunk. You were attacked? Does this have anything to do with Laura?"

"Yes."

I followed Elaine up the stairs to her second floor living room.

My bruised knees did not care for yet another set of stairs. Once I got my mitts on her videos, I planned to associate only with people with elevators. No exceptions.

Elaine sported tangerine capris and a lemon-coloured sleeveless blouse. Her red curls were held into an unstable ponytail by a pair of scrunchies, orange and yellow. She wore size ten flipflops with large daisies. Only Elaine could manage that look. I felt very, very beige.

She reached over to the radio, set as always on Radio Two. She turned down the volume of the opera just enough for us to talk.

She said, "I couldn't stop thinking about Laura after you called last night. What a tragic death. Even if I didn't like her much."

"What? You didn't like Laura?"

"Not really."

"I liked her, and I'm not nearly as accepting as you are."

"I never warmed to her. I found her dogmatic and inflexible."

That was a jawdropper, considering the source. On key subjects, Elaine elevated inflexibility to a religion. I kept that to myself.

Elaine said, "Actually, I'm surprised you liked her."

"Well, I'm surprised you didn't. Anyway, it's a creepy situation. I think the person who attacked me was involved in Laura's death."

Elaine said, "Oh, come on. This is Ottawa. We don't have killers running loose. Don't you think you're being a bit dramatic?"

After dogmatism and inflexibility, drama was Elaine's best thing.

"I don't believe Laura's death was an accident."

"Maybe you're imagining things because of your concussion. I've had clients with brain damage, and they're often fuzzy on facts."

"I'm not fuzzy on these facts, Elaine. And I'm not in the habit of imagining murders."

"Seriously, you don't look good, Camilla. You're pasty, like old dough or something. Better sit down," she said.

I let the pasty old dough thing slide and looked around for somewhere to sit. Easier said than done in Elaine's house. Every surface was covered with piles of paper, CDs, magazines, files, craft projects, you name it. For no reason I could imagine, the coffee table was covered entirely in hats. Plus there were hundreds of plants, green and luxurious and just a tad overwhelming.

I'm no Suzy Homemaker, but Elaine has every scrap of paper, book, magazine, record, article of clothing, receipt, pair of shoes and tacky gift she's ever received. I liked that about her. I enjoyed visiting. You could relax once you found a place to sit. And this time, I was betting on her packrat habit to pay off.

I scooped a teetering stack of Christmas cooking magazines off the sofa and crumpled onto it.

"Were you in the middle of your video phase our first year at Carleton?"

"I see what you're getting at."

"Were you?"

"In other words, do I have Laura on videotape? No. I'm sure I got into videography a couple of years later."

"That's too bad. I thought if we could see who she was with at a social event, I might find someone who could lead to her family. It's a long shot. Aside from talking to the servers at Maisie's Eatery, it's all I could think of."

"I was in my photography phase at that time."

"That's right. It wasn't videos, it was photos you were shooting. Even better. You still have your pictures, of course."

"Do I have pictures? Ha."

"Let's have a peek at them. I'm looking for a pretty girl named Sylvie. I don't remember her last name."

"Dumais?"

"Dumais. That's it. That's amazing, Elaine."

Elaine peered at me strangely.

"What?" I said after a while.

"Sylvie Dumais is dead."

"You're not serious."

"She drowned. Her kayak overturned on a lake in Algonquin Park."

"When?"

104

"Just this past June. Another accident. Like Laura's."

I said. "Let me recap: Laura's death was suspicious. And I don't think I fell down the stairs by accident."

"No need to snap. Let me get the photos. We'll see what turns up."

Be careful what you wish for, I believe the saying goes. I followed Elaine up another flight of stairs. Her third floor study was full of photos. They were organized in dozens of fabric-covered boxes. Feminine and homey. Of course, it would have been easier if some of the boxes had been labelled.

Nineteen containers later, I'd confirmed that chronological filing wasn't Elaine's strong point.

"Never mind," Elaine said. "It's been fun catching up, hasn't it?"

"Sure," I said.

"Get a load of you when you were called to the bar. What a party that was. I had a week-long hangover."

"That was eight years after I took that course with Laura. Let's focus on finding photos with her in them," I said. "Early years, remember?"

Elaine stood up and stretched. "Break time. Want some coffee?"

I always want coffee. "Yes, but I don't want to lose momentum."

I thought I saw her roll her eyes. She tucked a stack of photos on a chair and headed downstairs.

Elaine is passionate about so much, including coffee. Hers is always excellent. No decaf chez Elaine. I kept sifting through the boxes of photos while the aroma of the fresh brew rose up the stairs.

"Gotta be here somewhere," Elaine said, returning with two WAVE mugs, full to the brim and steaming hot. "One of these days I'll take a weekend and put them all in albums with nice commentaries. Oh, here's one of Sylvie. You can just see her in the corner. Candid shot. She didn't like to have her picture taken. Come to think of it, neither did Laura."

I remembered Elaine's flash going off that entire year, every time you put a fork in your mouth, raised a glass or yawned. No wonder people resisted having their pictures taken.

"It's hard to believe we've known each other for eighteen years, isn't it?" Elaine said, swishing through shots. "Hey, here's Laura, turning away from the camera. Nice shot of her back. And there's Frances Foxall. What an ego. But even she wouldn't face me."

"I'm trying to reach Frances," I said. "Where is everyone this weekend?"

"Oh, my God."

"What? You found one of Laura's face?"

"No. I found Joe Westerlund. Holy moly, remember him?"

"Remember him? He was my hero. I couldn't forget Joe Westerlund."

"All the women liked Joe. Like a Viking god with a Ph.D."

"He was awesome, in the old sense. I loved every course I took from him."

"Me, too. And it wasn't just a man/woman thing." Two bright spots appeared on Elaine's cheeks. "He made you think about social justice."

"You're right. Joe had more impact on my personal philosophy than all the rest of the undergrad faculty."

"And he was easy on the eyes."

"Come on, Elaine. Joe was way more than just a pretty face."

"And body. We're adults here. Allow me my vices. He was yummy. Lust lust lust."

"You know what? Joe Westerlund taught the class that

Laura and I did together."

Elaine was riffling through the photos, hunting for more shots of Joe Westerlund. "I always thought it was too bad he was married."

"A lot of girls wanted to have a shot at Joe."

"Except you, Camilla."

"He put his wife on a pedestal. Which was nice. Remember, he brought her to all the social events? Of course, it might have been to protect himself from the salivating females, no names mentioned. But looking back, she was so damned gorgeous and sophisticated."

"Speaking of pedestals. You were all wrapped up in Paul in those early days, I'm surprised you even noticed Joe."

I didn't want to go down the conversational path to Paul. "Do you think Joe Westerlund still lives in Ottawa?"

"Don't know. I haven't seen him since my undergrad years. You could call the school and find out."

"They're closed this weekend."

"Too bad." She grinned evilly. "Want another look at him?"

"Put a sock in it, Elaine. Joe was connected to his students. Laura was quite smart and capable. He'll probably remember her. He might even know where she came from."

"Can't hurt to ask."

"What was his wife's name?"

"I've blocked it out. Raging and deep-seated jealousy. When all else fails, try the phone book."

Elaine continued to scramble through photos, tossing some back into boxes, keeping some on her lap, sliding some into empty spots on chairs. "Boy, do I have some great blackmail material here. The hairdos alone should bring in a fortune. Look at your hairdo. Of course, at least you had a hairdo back then."

"Can you find a phone book in the middle of this stuff?"

Elaine said, "Can you try to be less high and mighty when I'm doing you a favour?"

"Me? I'm not making digs about *your* hair. And you're not really doing me a favour, Elaine. You're helping find Laura Brown's family, which is the decent thing to do. So never mind putting it on my tab."

"Don't be so fatuous." She slapped the phone book down in front of me. In that orange and yellow Elaine way.

Fatuous. Sheesh.

I found Joe Westerlund right away, a listing on a quiet street I thought ran off the Vanier Parkway. I didn't have to remember his wife's name. Their answering machine took care of that. A woman's voice said, "If you have a message for Joe or Kate, leave it after the beep, along with your name, telephone number and the time of your call."

There's something about leaving a message saying so-and-so's dead, it's four-thirty, that didn't seem appropriate. People have been after me to work on my sensitivity. When I remember, I give it a try.

"It could take days to get through these shots," Elaine said when I hung up. "I can't believe there's not a single picture of Laura's face in this pile."

"Keep hunting. We have to find out something about her. I have to arrange her funeral. People have to know."

"Maybe she didn't have family," Elaine said.

I was about to say "can't live with them, can't live without them." I bit my tongue in time. Elaine never mentioned her own mother and father, just her brother Eddy. I had no idea if her parents were dead or alive. But I was sure they weren't part of Elaine's life.

"I'm hot on the trail," Elaine said. "But I have someone

coming to the house for an appointment, so I can't do it now. I should try to clean up after you leave."

"I'm not going anywhere."

"Yes, you are, Camilla. Just until after I talk to this person." She stared at her oversized yellow watch. "It's too late now to do anything about the chaos."

The apartment didn't look any more chaotic than it had before the photo sorting, if she wanted the truth, which she probably didn't. "I have people to see, so I can't hang around here all day," I said.

"We'll get back to the photos after my session is over."

"Perfect. I appreciate what you're doing. Even if you spot someone who spent time with someone else who might have known Laura. If that makes sense, we'll track them down. We have to do something."

With her head stuck in a box, Elaine said, "I'll put everything that might be relevant aside, and you can go through it later. Except for the eighties hair and fashion blackmail material, of course. I'll keep those. Oh, there's another one. Where did you get those god-awful spangled sweaters, Camilla?"

I felt like saying, the same place you got your leopard print stockings and platform shoes. But I bit my tongue. "I'm pretty banged up, so I don't think I can manage the walk home. Not sure if I mentioned the Honda's in the shop again. I'd better call a cab."

Elaine swallowed. She is naturally generous and helpful, at least during her waking hours. Her instinct would be to lend me anything she owned. Except for her beloved vehicle. She clutched a batch of photos and bit her lip. She loves that Pathfinder.

I said, "It'll be hard to get a cab now. How about if I hang around in the bedroom and promise not to listen to your session?"

Judging from the expression on her face, she sure wanted me gone. The keys to the Pathfinder jingled in my hand as I limped out. Elaine clomped down the stairs after me and set up the security system.

I smiled as the deadbolt clicked.

Fifteen

Elaine's Pathfinder was piled with empty Tim Hortons cups, Timbit cartons, plastic bags, half-finished notes, overdue library books, dry-cleaning and much, much more. Sort of like an archaeological find but without the time lag. I was glad I wasn't a passenger, because only the driver's seat was clear. Still, I was grateful. I was on a mission. Mission Phase One was a quick buzz of Laura's place on Third to confirm something. This time the security system was flashing properly. I keyed in 1986 and headed straight for the fridge. I kept my ears open and my back to the wall as much as possible. I opened the stainless steel door and peered in. Sure enough, insulin containers and syringes. Okay, was my mind playing tricks on me? I didn't think so. But someone sure was. And that someone would be banking on the idea that people would blame my recollection of the missing insulin on my head injury. My family and friends already thought I was nuts on the subject. This would just convince them.

But it told me a couple of things. Whoever had pushed me had access to Laura's house, a key and stranger still, the security code. So that would have to be someone close to her, someone trusted. I formed a hypothesis: this person had tampered with Laura's insulin, maybe all of the vials, just to be sure. Then afterwards, they'd slipped back into the house under cover of darkness to replace the insulin, perhaps in case there was an issue from the autopsy. If anyone checked after the fact, the insulin would be back in its place. Laura Lynette Brown would appear to have died a natural if foolhardy death. Exactly as the pathologist had said. Good work on the part of the murderer. I was betting that I'd interrupted the return of the insulin, and that's why I'd got shoved down the stairs.

My hypothesis still had a few holes in it. Such as how you could count on no one seeing you enter the house, twice. I had my crazy theory, but I was no closer to having a clue about who would want to kill Laura or why. And I wasn't anxious to spend a minute longer than necessary in that house.

*　　*　　*

In front of Laura's place, I blinked in the bright sunlight. A small, round, white-haired woman walking a pair of tan dachshunds smiled at me. I smiled back. I've learned from having a purely temporary dog that you walk dogs, and then you walk them again and then you walk them again. And you're still not done. You become a neighbourhood fixture.

"Hello," I said. "Nice dogs. Do you live around here?"

She pointed across the street. "Yes. I'm Mary Buttons. The boys and I live across the street and down three in the blue house."

I said. "I don't know if you heard that Laura Brown, who lived here, was killed in a tragic fall behind the Supreme Court yesterday."

Her hand shot to her mouth. "Oh, no. That terrible accident. You never think of these things happening to one of your neighbours."

"You never do," I agreed. I tried to ignore the two hungry-looking wiener dogs sniffing my ankles.

"Very sad. Are you…?"

"Next-of-kin," I said. "I'm trying to locate her friends and co-workers before her name is released to the media."

"Naturally," she said.

"Did you see her coming and going?"

"Sure, I did. I'm around with the boys three times a day."

"Do you know where she worked?"

"I thought you were next-of-kin."

"There is an issue about where she was working."

She frowned. "I see. That's a bit strange, but no, I don't know where she worked. Or if she did. She was around a lot during the day. Maybe she worked at home."

"That would explain it. Did you see clients coming and going?"

"No. Hardly ever saw her with anyone. Just exchanging a word with the neighbours over there, that's all." She pointed toward the house next door, which now had the mums neatly planted.

"Oh," I said, disappointed.

"I saw her early yesterday afternoon with someone, though."

"Really?"

"Yes. She went into the house with another woman. And a while later they went out again."

"Did they walk off together? Did you see where they went?"

"They drove off. Then later, she came back alone. Then she went out again. Heavens, that must have been just before she died. How sad."

I interrupted the sadness. "What did the other woman look like?"

"I didn't really get a good look. Just an ordinary person."

"What about hair colour? Height?"

"Everyone seems tall to me. I couldn't see her hair or eyes. Not that the old sight's that good any more, but even if it were, they were wearing straw hats and sunglasses. They were having a good time, laughing, putting stuff in the car, like they were heading out to a picnic or something. They looked cute. I had some scooping to do, thanks to the boys, and when I glanced up, they were gone."

"And then Laura came back later?"

"Yes. And then she went out again."

"A long time later?"

"Maybe half an hour. Mid-afternoon, I guess. We had forgotten to mail some letters, hadn't we, boys? So we had to go out again before we missed the afternoon pickup. We're always forgetting something. Must go up and down this street twenty times a day. You'd think we'd be skinny."

"And where did she go?"

"She came out with a box, then she went back in again and got another box and put them both in her car. I was about to offer to help, but she got in and drove away. I waved, but I guess she didn't see me."

I handed her my card and scrawled my cellphone number on it. "If you think of anything else, can you call me?"

"We will. Sorry for your loss."

The boys barked in agreement.

*   *   *

That gave me something to think about. And just enough time to get something accomplished before I had to be at the balloon festival. First, I tried Joe Westerlund's number twice

114

from my cellphone. No luck. Both times I hung up without leaving a message. What if Joe and Kate were out of town for the weekend? Everyone else seemed to be. Worse, what if Joe Westerlund were on sabbatical? I figured he was in his mid-fifties, at least. He could even be retired from the university and on a six-month hike in the Himalayas.

I checked my watch. I had plenty of time to swing by the Westerlunds' house. And I had nothing better to do. Someone in the neighbourhood might know if Joe was in town.

Next, I called Alvin's home number. Lucky me, he picked up.

"Alvin, can you do a search for me?"

"Violet says maybe I jumped the gun yesterday. I'm sorry I got angry when you missed the flight last night and this morning. I realize you didn't have any choice."

"I thought it didn't take off this morning because of wind."

"It didn't, but if it had, you would have missed it. Anyway, I hope you're feeling better. I understand you're in this sad situation."

"Tell you what, all is forgiven and, as a bonus, I won't get upset in the future when you continue to remind me I missed the launch."

"That sounds reasonable. What's the catch?"

"I need you to get a list of towns in Ontario that start with C."

"Lord thundering Jesus. We're in the middle of the balloon festival."

"Save it, Alvin. You and Mrs. P. can find this on the net in seconds."

"So could you."

"But I don't have a computer at home. You have your laptop. Use that. Didn't you just tell me you were sorry for being upset?"

"You're the one who wants the information. You could go into the office."

"I'm in the middle of something. It won't take you long, and you can give me the list when I meet you at the launch grounds this afternoon. That way I don't have to dock your pay for being AWOL yesterday."

I clicked off. That's often the best policy with Alvin. Show a little kindness and you're toast.

Time to try Joe Westerlund's number again. A woman answered. "Wrong number," I said and hung up.

Fifteen minutes later, I pulled up in front of a slate-coloured bungalow on River Road near the Vanier Parkway. I checked the number, but it was the right one. The house had a row of new-looking skylights and a huge conservatory. I was surprised to see the property looked neglected, even rundown. It was a far cry from the elegant brick house Joe and Kate Westerlund had owned in Centretown back in the eighties.

Alongside the flagstone staircase, with its weed-filled cracks, a long wheelchair ramp provided another access to the front door. The paint on the ramp was cracked and peeling. Three birdfeeders stood on long poles near the front. Each one had a different variety of seed. I spotted sunflower, niger seed and a mix. Each feeder had a different and more complicated squirrel baffle. I recognized the baffles as types that the bird lovers in my family had tried. Unsuccessfully. As I walked toward the door, a grey squirrel with a dramatic and luxurious tail turned from regarding the birdfeeders and chattered at me. Such confidence. We both knew who'd win the battle of the baffles.

The birdfeeders stood at the edge of a large garden bed that must have been splendid at some point. Now it was choked with creeping Charlie and nettles. People are starting to cultivate natural gardens, to my sisters' horror, but this went way beyond that.

I hobbled down the flagstone path to the entrance and

knocked confidently. Kate Westerlund opened the front door. The last time I'd seen her, she'd been in her mid-thirties, radiating sensuality. At parties, she'd be barefoot, sporting woven clothing from Third World countries. The styles always accentuated her long arms and legs. On her, the no-makeup look had seemed naked and frankly sexual. My last memory was of a party where she sat by herself, smoking a joint on the back porch, while a trio of sophomores drooled in the background. Now, the dark hair that had once cascaded to her waist was pulled back in a short no-nonsense salt and pepper ponytail. She wore black linen Bermudas and a sleeveless black tank. Her deeply tanned skin spoke of many hours not worrying about the sun. She wore no jewellery, except for a plain gold wedding band. She looked a lot more sophisticated now. And substantially more intimidating.

"Yes?" she said.

"You probably don't remember me," I said. "I was one of Joe Westerlund's students back in the eighties. Could I speak to him, please?"

She said. "I didn't catch your name."

"Camilla MacPhee," I said, leaning against the door frame.

Her brow furrowed. "Joe had so many students over the years. Are you all right?"

"No problem. I didn't expect you to remember me."

"MacPhee," she said, uncertainly.

"Don't worry about it. Is he around? I don't want to interrupt your weekend. This will just take a couple of minutes."

"You'd better come in," she said, standing aside and holding the door open for me. The foyer was wide, with only a spectacular woollen wall hanging and a stylized metal table with a portable phone. I followed her through the foyer to the living room.

The inside of the house was furnished mostly with books

and artwork, much of it woven. That had been Kate's medium. Every wall held at least one huge woven piece of art. Some were handspun wool in rich vegetable dyes, others free-form quilts with raised images. Trapunto, I think Kate had called that technique. At one time, a Kate Westerlund wall hanging had been quite a status symbol. Her huge commissions dominated many public buildings. I wondered if my art-loving burglar client, Bunny Mayhew, had ever made off with any. I hoped not. Kate's works still had warmth and power, although a filmy layer of dust indicated they'd been hanging for years in the same spots.

The living room was roomy, with bare, dark oak floors.

"Have a seat," Kate said, pointing to a ochre-coloured leather sofa with a minimalist design. I was happy to sit. Kate said nothing. I looked around, wondering if Joe was about to stick his head in through the doorway. The living room was large, but aside from the sofa and a coffee table with a huge vase of sunflowers, there was little to detract from the art on the walls. In the far corner, French doors opened on to the out-of-control garden. A reading lamp and a leather arm chair with a small area rug to the side of the door were the only signs that someone did any living in the room.

Kate had never been a woman who made small talk. She probably wouldn't expect it from others, I decided. "Is Joe here?"

"I guess you could say he is."

Where I come from, people are either there or not there, or occasionally not all there. "I don't understand."

She hesitated and after a while seemed to reach a decision.

"Come with me," she said.

I got up from the sofa and followed her down a long hallway into a room at the back of the house. It had a wall of windows with a Western exposure like my apartment and the same late afternoon sun. This view looked across the park. A dozen birdfeeders were set up outside the window. There was more action here than at the front feeders. I spotted the usual clusters of industrial sparrows and a few blue-black starlings. A pair of goldfinches alighted as I watched. Blue jays hovered and screamed, and a couple of pigeons pecked at the grass underneath the largest feeder. From a nearby tree, a black squirrel kept an eye on things. I stood, wondering if Kate were going to call Joe from some remote part of the house. It was only when I turned away from the window that I saw the man in the hospital bed. A few seconds passed before I recognized him. I could only hope he didn't hear my gasp. The majestic Joe Westerlund had shrivelled to a shadow man. I remembered him being well over six feet. This man was skeletal, bent and twisted.

He made an effort to speak. I tried to understand. I thought perhaps Kate might translate the sounds.

She said, "Here's a nice surprise, Joe. One of your students to see you."

The man in the bed made a questioning gurgle.

Tears stung my eyes, something that doesn't happen often. "It's Camilla MacPhee." I moved closer. "You may remember me from Carleton back in the eighties."

More garbled sounds. I decided they meant yes.

"You were my favourite prof in eight years of university. I just wanted to thank you for the principles you instilled in us."

What could do this to a person? A stroke? His handsome face was now shrunken and gaunt, mouth distorted. The powerful hands were clawed. I couldn't tell if he was glad to see me, or even if he understood what I'd said. Was that intelligence behind the faded blue eyes or just wishful thinking?

"I hoped you would remember my friend, Laura Brown."

He understood that, all right. His head lashed from side to

side, limbs jerked with agitation, the unintelligible grunts grew louder. One clawed hand knocked over the glass of water on the table by the side of the bed.

Was he saying, no no no?

Kate moved forward and put her hands on his shoulders. "It's okay, Joe. Nothing to worry about. I'll get you some more water," she said, picking up the glass. With her other hand, she took my arm and propelled me from the room. She had the kind of grip that leaves bruises. Joe continued to make horrible, agitated noises as Kate closed the door behind us and pushed me toward the front of the house. "You've upset him. I shouldn't have let you in. I thought it would be good for him to see a student."

"What happened to him?" I said.

"ALS happened. It's killing him."

"What is that?"

"He has lost the use of his muscles. He can't eat by himself, he can't turn a page, he can't really communicate."

"My god."

"Such a waste," she said. "Such a waste of his wonderful mind. It's trapped in a ruined body."

I seemed to spend all my time bringing nice people to tears. I touched her shoulder. "I am so sorry."

"Everyone is."

"But he's young." My father was still walking three miles a day at eighty-one. I figured everyone had that ahead of them. Especially someone like Joe Westerlund.

"Fifty-nine. Up until a few months ago, he could get himself into the wheelchair. Now he has to be lifted in and out of bed."

What do you say after you've said sorry? And what the hell good is sorry anyway? I said, "I remember you used to have these great parties in your other house. Huge rooms full of kids."

She attempted a smile. "We had to sell that house once the

disease started to make headway. We needed a single storey. But even this is too much to manage now."

I tried not to dwell on what Kate Westerlund's life had become.

"I had wanted to ask him about my friend, Laura Brown. She died recently, and I need to locate her family and close friends. I didn't realize her name would upset him."

This time, Kate dropped the water glass. "Laura Brown is dead? What happened?"

This wasn't the moment to mention my suspicions about Laura's murder. Just her name could cause distress in this house. "She died in a fall yesterday. I should have realized that you would have known her too. I could have asked you about her and spared Joe that upset."

"Of course, I know her. I kept in touch with a lot of Joe's students."

"Why do you think Joe got agitated hearing her name?"

"I doubt it had to do with Laura herself. The medication has an effect on him. The disease has an impact on his emotions. He's unpredictable. He has bad days and good. This is a bad day. I'm glad you didn't tell him she was dead."

"Me too. Did you know anything about her family?"

She shook her head.

"Sorry to have bothered you. I remember Joe as such a compassionate teacher. He influenced my notions of social justice," I said.

"That's Joe. Passionate."

"I ended up being a lawyer because of him."

"A lawyer? Really? Law is not always on the same team as justice. Joe used to say that."

"Well, I tried to be one of the white hats. That's why I'm searching for information about Laura." Not that I was feeling defensive or anything.

"He'd like to hear that he was an influence for good." Her manner toward me seemed to have warmed.

"Thanks. I'd better head out."

She didn't argue. "Will there be a memorial service for her? I'd like to go."

"That's part of why I need to find the family. I'll make sure you know what's planned as soon as things are settled."

She stopped at the door. "What if you don't find them?"

"Then I'll arrange something. A memorial. I'll put a notice in the paper, I guess. Wait a minute. You said you knew her. Had you seen her lately?"

"Not for ages."

"That's too bad."

Kate said, "She should have had lots of friends. She was pleasant. Not really outgoing, but charming and warm. I remember her smile."

"Yes. Do you know what she did for a living?"

"No, but she will have succeeded at whatever it was. She should have gone to grad school. She was Ph.D. material. Joe used to say she had the capacity to carve out a major place for herself in the academic world."

"She was bright, hard-working and serious."

"Impressive. Once, years ago, we had her to the house for dinner when we still lived in Centretown. He tried to convince her not to throw it all away. They got into a shouting match. Well, Joe did. It was a one-man shouting match. She said the academic world was not for her."

"And she didn't lose her cool. That must have been hard with Joe."

Kate Westerlund laughed suddenly. "She held her own with him. He could be overwhelming."

"I remember."

"She stuck to her guns, and we didn't really see her after that. I wish I'd kept in touch."

"Can you think of anyone she could have stayed in touch with? Someone who might know her family?"

"I don't think she had any family. If she'd had family, I'm sure she would have mentioned Christmas or a birthday. Something."

"What about her home town?"

Kate hesitated then shook her head.

I said, "Can you let me know if you think of something else? Here's my card. Home number and cell. Especially if you remember someone who might have known her."

I hurried down the walkway. I was anxious to get away from the house and the stranger that Joe had become. At the same time, I felt unkind, unfeeling and inadequate. Something about Kate bothered me too, but I was in too much turmoil to think clearly about her.

Sixteen

My hands shook when I tried the ignition. Was it the reaction to seeing Joe? Or lack of sleep and the presence of painkillers? I closed my eyes, but that just made things worse.

I hoped I wasn't going to have to arrange a funeral when I didn't even seem to be able to turn a key.

The Pathfinder seemed hot and stuffy, even though the air was cool. I opened the windows. On the lawn, the birds were gone, and the grey squirrel had repositioned himself to take a run at the nearest birdfeeder. At the sound of the window opening, he turned to chatter at me. Do whatever it takes, he seemed to be saying.

Is it a sign of a worsening concussion when you start taking advice from squirrels? "You're just a rodent with a fabulous tail," I said. "Even if you do have exceptional analytical skills."

The squirrel went back to its business.

That reminded me of someone who might be able to help. Sgt. Leonard Mombourquette. No bushy tail, but otherwise quite rodent-like himself. Even better, he was just a short drive away. I figured Leonard could find some useful information, even if he'd already said he didn't want to. He'd have access to all the police files and connections. I'd never been inside his home, but I'd dropped Conn McCracken off once, so I knew where he lived. Like the MacPhees, Leonard Mombourquette is from Cape Breton, and as an added bonus, he was Ray Deveau's first cousin. Maybe he'd... No, I wasn't going down that route.

I strolled toward Mombourquette's red front door a short time later. Unlike the Westerlunds', this one was in good order. If you don't want visitors, you shouldn't have a tiny, perfect house with a tiny, perfect garden and a tiny, perfect flagstone walk with some tiny, perfect herb growing in the cracks.

My sisters could have identified the herb with their eyes closed. It smelled wonderful when you walked on it. I tried not to walk on it, because the entire garden and walkway looked like a labour of love for someone, a dream location in the middle of an old neighbourhood. It was all soft shades of sage interspersed with pink and white.

Most of the gardens I'd passed had an end-of-summer parched look to them. Not this one. It was small-scale and subtle. Fragrant. Every plant seemed to be at exactly the right stage and in precisely the right place. I can scarcely tell the difference between real and artificial flowers, but I know a work of art when I see one.

The house and garden reminded me of the illustrations in a Beatrix Potter story. Small rodents in flowered dresses and mop caps might greet me, while others scrambled to prepare for a welcome guest. Instead, Mombourquette answered the door wearing grey cotton knit running shorts and a well-washed grey T-shirt. He wore charcoal and white flip-flops with a little swoosh on them. He hadn't shaved, giving him a growth of soft grey bristles.

"What do you want?" he said, wrinkling his pointy nose.

Everything about him drooped. Where was the ill-tempered little ratlike figure I had come to appreciate slightly?

"I'd like a bit of advice."

"Forget it." His voice sounded suffused with self-pity. I gathered I wouldn't be getting camomile tea and poppy seed cakes.

"Come on, Leonard. Don't be like that."

"Oh, pardon me. Why don't I just await the results of the SIU investigation with a song in my heart?"

"Those sound like words to live by." I meant to sound supportive. Perhaps the tone wasn't quite right.

"Goodbye, Camilla."

I stuck my foot in the door. "I need help."

"Not my problem. I've already told you."

"What kind of attitude is that?"

"The attitude of someone who gets to live with the shit generated by you the last time you needed help."

"That was unavoidable. You can hardly hold me responsible." His whiskers twitched. "I'm sorry you have to go through this. Believe me." He still didn't meet my eye. "Fine. I get the message."

Mombourquette had the door half-shut, when I said, "One question. What do you call those little plants growing between the stones? They smell nice." I didn't say that they smell particularly nice if you walk on them, because I knew that wasn't the way to Mombourquette's small grey heart.

"Thyme," Mombourquette said. The door opened a bit more.

"Makes me sorry I live in an apartment." His noncommittal grunt gave me hope. "Who created this wonderful garden?" I burbled.

Bingo.

Five minutes later, I was sipping ginger peach tea in the

living room. The house was what my sisters would call a loving reconstruction of a unique heritage property. I figured the black metal fireplace was over a hundred years old. Leonard favoured antiques. A carved maple sideboard, a camelback settee upholstered in faded blue brocade. A hutch with some chintz platters. We took our tea in blue and white china cups. We sat on chairs with needlepoint cushions. Leonard slid a plate of old-fashioned molasses cookies onto the polished maple table.

Tea and garden talk or not, Mombourquette was not my biggest fan. In fact, outside of arguments, emergencies and shooting incidents, we'd never really had a conversation. I realized it would be up to me.

"For what it's worth," I said, "you did the only thing you could. You saved lives. That's the conclusion they are going to draw."

"The SIU puts you through the grinder. It's one way to find out who your friends are." Mombourquette sipped his tea morosely.

"Yeah, well. With a union like you cops have, who needs friends? Lot of legal muscle behind the police association."

The sun glinted off his incisors. "It's bad enough we officers put our lives on the line to keep society safe, you don't think our union should stand behind us?"

Depends on what the officer has done, I thought, as a couple of high profile recent incidents came to mind. "Not saying that, Leonard. I'm glad you've got support. And, speaking of support, everyone in my family seems to hold me responsible for your situation."

He nodded. Pleased, I suppose.

"So listen, here's the problem." I sketched out the background from Laura's death, my newfound next-of-kin role, the on-again, off-again insulin, the will, my tumble on the stairs, the fruitless search for Laura's home town, her relatives and the women she had lunch with. "You can see how important this is. I can't arrange the funeral yet. That's pretty awful. But you have access to all the police systems, you could get someone's SIN number and their place of birth, and last ten addresses and so on. Since you're on leave, I figured you could help." I smiled brightly at him.

He did not return the smile. If he'd had a tail, it would have flicked dangerously. "You know something, Camilla?"

"What?"

"You frigging astound me."

"That's a yes?"

*   *   *

Turned out it was a flaming and dramatic no. Close to nuclear no. It seems that if you are a police officer on extended medical leave, it's a really bad idea to go over to Central and ask for information. If the brass spot you out of bed, you'll get slapped with a desk job.

Well, who knew that?

Sometimes you have to walk away from a situation. This was definitely one of those times. I hightailed down the street and around the corner to the Pathfinder and huddled with the Tim Hortons cups. I could have used a coffee to wash the taste of herbal tea out of my mouth. I pulled away from the curb and around the corner and angled the Pathfinder in again, thinking I'd figure out where the closest Second Cup was. Anyway, you shouldn't drive when you're really mad. I tried breathing deeply to regain my composure. My head felt like the inside of a jet engine. Talk about the mouse that roared.

Alexa's always suggesting meditation to calm down. I tried a few of her suggestions. I closed my eyes and thought of a distant beach. Blue soothing water, the sparkle of sun on the waves, the warm touch of sand on bare feet.

I woke up with a start. The sky seemed darker than it should have, but I checked my watch, and it was only four-thirty. Fall certainly comes early, I thought. I had to get hustling to make it to Hull for the launch. I picked up my cellphone to give Elaine a call and tell her I'd bring the Pathfinder back after the launching.

I held the phone away when I heard her voice. What a pair of lungs. What was her problem?

Spinning head and shaky hands notwithstanding, I got the Pathfinder on the road, heading down the Vanier Parkway to the Queensway, the fastest way back to face the raging redhead. I asked myself why everyone I knew was always so bellicose.

* * *

Elaine was still in outrage mode when she unlocked, unbolted and unchained her door. She said, "That was inconsiderate. For all I knew, you'd been killed in an accident."

"Hate to disappoint you. I didn't have an accident. Not even a near miss."

Elaine is not one to let go of an issue. "You never mentioned you needed the Pathfinder for hours."

"Okay, I'm sorry. But may I remind you, you practically booted me out before your appointment. If I'd had half a chance, I would have filled you in on my plans. Gladly."

"Fine, forget about it."

I could tell she didn't mean it. "I was shaken up after I saw Joe Westerlund."

"What do you mean?"

She went white as I described the ravages of Joe's illness. "ALS. I can't believe it."

"It's totally unfair. Can we go upstairs?"

She turned and led the way. "So sad. A wonderful person like that."

"Wouldn't matter who it was, it's still awful," I said.

"But if it was some miserable rat, that wouldn't be so tragic."

"Even then. That reminds me, I dropped in on Leonard Mombourquette. I was hoping he'd cooperate, but he's obsessed with the SIU investigation."

Elaine stopped at the top of the stairs. "You're calling someone else obsessed?" she said. "I feel sorry for Leonard. He's cute. I hope things work out in his favour."

The world is full of surprises.

"What's the matter now, Camilla?"

"Leonard Mombourquette? Cute? Have you forgotten that time you were arrested?"

"That wasn't personal. Just part of his job. Don't stand there gawking. Do you want to see the photos I found?"

That Elaine can always reel you in.

I said as I was being reeled, "Did you find some of Laura?"

"Plunk yourself down and have a look." She positioned herself on the sofa and picked up a batch of photos.

I sat beside her. She passed the pictures to me, one by one, sorting as she went. A few were doubles, I guess. She slipped those onto a nearby chair, next to the other pile.

"These pictures were taken during an end-of-term party, and then I shot these here during the winter term of first year."

I said. "You did well."

"Not as many as I wanted. It's a start, though."

I frowned as I worked my way through them. "You still can't see Laura's face in any of them."

"I know. Terrific shots of the back of her head, though. She always had great hair."

"What were you so excited about showing me?"

"Even though Laura doesn't show up, I found lots of other people."

"This is great. Look, I hope you don't mind if I take the Pathfinder again, because I have a real short time to get over to the balloon festival. I'll be back by ten at the latest."

"Sorry, Camilla, I have an appointment."

"Again? Is this because I was late?"

"No, really. I do."

"What's with all the appointments on the long weekend?"

"Holy moly. When did you sign on as my mother?"

"Fine, how about you give me this pile of photos, and I'll try to figure out who people are?" Before she could object, I dropped the photos into one of the small cloth-covered boxes stacked nearby. "Don't worry, I'll return them. Your pretty box too. And can you drop me off at home, so I can take the dog out? I'll get a cab over to the launch site. I have to be there by five to be sure to get some good shots. Why are you looking at me like that?"

"Did you say by five?"

"I suppose five-thirty would be okay. Why?"

"Among other reasons, because that was hours ago."

"Don't be crazy," I said.

"Check your watch."

I checked my watch. "Four-twenty. Told you. Oh, shit. My watch must have been damaged last night. That's about the time I fell."

"Even so, didn't you notice that it's practically dark?"

"That was a good watch, too. What time is it?"

"How does 7:28 sound?"

It wouldn't take a neurologist to tell me I wasn't thinking too clearly if I could make that kind of mistake.

*   *   *

I stayed around home just long enough to do my urgent park duty with Gussie and to provide Mrs. Parnell's cat with an evening meal suited to her high station in life. I wasn't prepared to admit it, but I liked looking after the animals. There's something soothing and relaxing about dogs and cats.

As a rule, Mrs. Parnell is happy to make a visit to my apartment, no key apparently required, and feed the animals when I'm tied up at the office. Throughout the summer, when I couldn't get home, she'd teetered around the park using her walker to give Gussie an outing. So in a moment of warm camaraderie, I had agreed to pop some fresh seeds into the cage for Lester and Pierre any evening when Mrs. Parnell wasn't home.

But before I fed the always ungrateful lovebirds, I wanted to check my phone messages. But perhaps I should refer to that activity as "Return to Voice Mail Hell."

*   *   *

BEEP

Alvin here. Got a list of towns in Ontario that begin with C. I printed it out and we'll have it for you at the launch site this afternoon. I think you could have got pretty much the same thing from a road atlas, but what the hell. Anything for our friend, Camilla.

BEEP

This is a message for Camilla MacPhee from Constable Jason Yee. Can you call me as soon as possible. I believe you have my cellphone number. Thank you.

BEEP

Camilla, this is your sister Edwina. Why aren't you answering? I'd better not hear you're wandering around town with a concussion, causing trouble for your family. I will assume you're in the bathroom, which you will notice is now spotless. Keep it that way. You have five minutes to return this call.

BEEP

Hello? I hope I've reached Camilla MacPhee. My name is Robert Watson. I'm Frances Foxall's husband. I'm afraid I have some bad news for you. Would you be kind enough to call me back? Thank you.

BEEP

This is Conn. I hear you're hounding Leonard Mombourquette. You know damn well he's going through a rough patch now. He's on sick leave, he can't even sleep. It is unconscionable for you to be badgering him. Just stay away from him. What is the matter with you?

BEEP
Camilla? This is Alvin...

Seventeen

There was nothing mysterious about the second message from Alvin. He was unequivocal. I'm surprised I didn't have blisters on my earlobes after listening. Still, I had a couple of things to attend to before I called back and explained why I'd missed the Saturday evening launch. I saw no point in encouraging either my sister or Conn McCracken. But some of the calls were worth following up on.

First, I tried to reach Constable Yee on his cellphone. It immediately went to his voice mail. Either he was on the phone or out of range. I left a message suggesting that he leave the specific answers I wanted on my voice mail and, further, if he had new information or questions for me, that he leave a detailed message. I reminded him I wanted the names of the witnesses who saw Laura fall.

Next, I located the piece of paper on which I'd written Frances Foxall's number. I didn't like the feeling in the pit of my stomach as I dialled. A man answered on the fourth ring. I asked for Robert Watson.

His hesitant tone went well with the soft voice. "This is he."

"Camilla MacPhee here. You returned my earlier call."

"Yes. You were calling Frances. I guess you didn't know."

"Know what?"

"Were you friends?"

I felt my head spin a bit. "We knew each other at university."

"Oh. That was a long time ago. So had you not heard?"

"We haven't really been in touch. I was calling because a mutual acquaintance was killed yesterday, and I wanted to let Frances know personally." Not a complete fabrication.

"I see. How dreadful. Well, unfortunately, there's no easy way to say this. Frances died this summer."

"Died? Oh my god. I'm so sorry."

He had a definite catch in his voice. "Thank you. It was unexpected. An accident."

"A fall?" I blurted.

"In a way. You may know we've had a hobby farm, south of Ottawa, for the past ten years. Frances did a lot of riding. She was thrown from her favourite mount."

The pause that followed was so protracted I thought for a moment he'd hung up.

"Mr. Watson?" I said.

"She broke her neck," he said, his voice cracking.

"That is tragic. When did it happen?"

"Six weeks ago. July 13th. That's the worst part. It was her birthday."

I scrambled for the right words. I had not liked Frances Foxall, but this sad-voiced man didn't need to know that. "Frances was a remarkable woman. This must be extremely difficult for you."

"Yes," he said. "Frances would have been pleased to speak to you. And I appreciate your call."

*   *   *

135

I sat on my sofa and stared at nothing. Another person from the same Carleton cohort was dead. With Laura Brown and Sylvie Dumais, that made three. Three women who'd known each other and died accidentally within a few months. No goddam way was that a coincidence.

Frances had died on July 13th. I tried to keep my buzzing head steady enough to think. July 13th. I had been caught up in the frantic search for Jimmy Ferguson. That would explain why I hadn't heard about Frances's death. A woman being killed in a fall from a horse would probably have made the local news.

The paraded on the back of the sofa and rubbed her silky head against my neck. Gussie put his chin on my knees and sighed.

"Thank you for your support. If only the rest of the world were like you two."

I had a couple of things left to do that evening. It was time to face the music. Lucky me, Alvin didn't answer his phone or his cellphone. Mrs. Parnell picked up her cellphone on the first ring.

"Mrs. P., I'm…"

"Tremendously exhilarating, Ms. MacPhee. I wish you could have experienced it."

"Well, I can't believe I missed it again."

"I'm sure you had your reasons. The flight was simply grand."

"You're not upset?"

"Spectacular views. Perfect clear sky. Like nothing else in the world."

"That's great. Alvin's message led me to believe you'd been becalmed, and you'd landed in the middle of a major roadway and everything was a disaster and that it was mostly my fault."

"We mustn't let small setbacks get us down, Ms. MacPhee. Esprit de corps and all that."

"You mean you *were* becalmed?"

"Nothing we couldn't get ourselves out of."

"Good attitude. I just wanted to mention the reason I missed out on taking the photos tonight was because of my watch. It must have been damaged when I fell down the stairs at Laura's place. I'm a bit confused because of the concussion, and, anyway, I screwed up, and I don't know what I was thinking. I'll be there tomorrow. For sure."

"These things happen. You have a lot on your plate right now. You'll be back to your old self in due time."

"Count on it."

"Hold on, Ms. MacPhee, Young Ferguson wants a word."

"That's okay. I don't want to tie up your cellphone. I can talk to him later."

"Camilla?"

"Oh, hello, Alvin."

"Yeah, right," Alvin said. "Did you tell Violet your watch was wrong? What kind of lame excuse is that? Did the dog eat your watch?"

Even on the phone I could imagine him, beaky nose ruby with outrage, cat's-eye glasses more pointed than usual.

"I wanted to be there. Things went wrong."

"These flights are important to Violet, you know. I don't think a few photos would be too much trouble for a friend."

Apparently, Alvin had been reading the same kind of motivational handbook as my sisters.

"See you tomorrow," I said. "What? What's that? Alvin. Can't hear you. I'm losing the connection."

I snapped the cellphone closed.

Call it self-defence.

*　　*　　*

The staff were bustling about Maisie's Eatery, resetting tables, when I puffed through the door.

"I'm looking for Jasmine," I said.

The woman at the front desk raised her sculpted eyebrow in a way that told me she'd be trouble. Her three-hundred-dollar highlighted hairdo, sexy navy suit and the shiny red four-inch heels said something, but it sure wasn't "welcome". I knew she was the owner-manager, but I guess she didn't recognize me as an occasional customer. I'd be in a bad mood too if I had a facelift pulled that tight.

"Ms. Thurlow is not available. We're busy."

"Right." Since the restaurant was less than half full, I doubted the rush would be beyond their control. But hey.

"Why don't you think of me as part of that rush? I'd like to be seated in Jasmine's section."

She pursed her glossy red lips. "I'm not sure I can do that."

I'd met her counterpart before. They make their presence felt in corporate headquarters, airlines, complaint sections and law offices. Not that they worry me.

"I'm a frequent customer, but I can always take my business elsewhere."

"Surely you understand we have policies."

"I have policies too. One of them is to get treated properly in the service industry. Oh well, it will make interesting reading," I flipped out my little notebook from my pocket and flicked the top of my pen.

Seconds later, I found myself seated at a corner table with a fine view of the kitchen. The owner was whispering intently to a tall, willowy young woman with a dark pixie haircut, a wide, expressive mouth and trendy angular glasses.

138

The young woman made her graceful way toward me. Years of dance training, I decided. My sister Alexa walks the same way.

"Sorry, if I caused you trouble," I said. "I didn't intend to."

She shrugged. "Don't worry. If not you, then it would be somebody else. That's just Norine."

"Is her bark worse than her bite?"

"Let's just say she barks, she bites and they can both be bad."

"I noticed. And you're Jasmine?"

"That's me."

"I was in here earlier, and one of the other servers suggested you might be able to help me."

"You spoke to Chelsea. Yeah, she left me a message."

"Chelsea, right. She mentioned me?"

"She's a bud. She thought I'd want to help you."

"Did she tell you what I need?"

"You were asking about a couple of women who came to the restaurant a few months ago." Her wide mouth twitched. "That was a lot of detail for Chelsea. But her heart's in the right place."

Finally, something was going my way. Jasmine was smart and pleasant and appeared to have a functioning sense of humour. Just the kind of person I'd been missing.

"Crazy, I know. Two among thousands of customers. But it's important and, at least, I got a good lunch out of it today." I glanced over and noticed Norine assessing us. "I think I'd better order dinner."

"Being watched? Let me take your drink order, first."

"Excellent diversionary tactic," I said, sounding a bit like Mrs. Parnell.

I ordered mineral water, San Pellegrino. It goes against the grain for me to pay several dollars for something that comes free from the tap. Still, it wouldn't fight with my painkillers.

Jasmine brought my drink and listened while I described Laura Brown and the woman she was dining with. I explained about Laura's death and my trouble finding her friends and family.

She said. "I heard about that accident. They didn't say her name on the radio. It gave me the shivers. I mean, right downtown in daylight should be the safest place, right?"

"Good point."

"Do you have a photo of your friend? That would help."

"There don't seem to be any photos of her, except for a batch from our college days. That's why I'm all over town with these strange requests. Your friend said you might recognize her from a description."

"It's possible. I am fascinated by faces."

I described Laura in detail. I even went so far as to talk about her purse on the table. "Small, structured bag, crocodile or something. Tan. Double handles."

Jasmine said, "We get lots of women in here with that general description. Plus I also work at a café in the west end, on my days off here. So I have a lot of faces in my head. I'll try to narrow it down for you. But it's not her you want, it's the friends and the friends' names. Right?"

"Exactly." Norine fixed her gimlet gaze on us.

"Is this going to bring you grief?" I asked.

"Well, it might be a good time to choose from the menu," Jasmine said. "Diversionary tactic, as you said."

I picked the filet of beef, with garlic mashed potatoes and beet salad. What the hell. We're only on this earth for a short time.

"Good choice," she said, taking my order with a flourish.

Norine drifted towards us. "The place is filling up, Jasmine."

"Your filet will be right out," Jasmine said with a wide smile.

Short minutes later, the steak showed up. Maisie's does an amazing filet, which would be worth going to a restaurant by yourself on a not-so-wonderful holiday weekend for, even if you weren't tracking people. But Maisie's is really famous for its desserts. And Jasmine was back with the two-page dessert menu seconds after I finished my meal. Norine had her eye on us, so I did my best imitation of a person fascinated by a selection of desserts. I pointed here and there and raised my eyebrows to indicate dessert-related questions.

"My friend probably didn't eat dessert. She was diabetic."

"Diabetic. That helps. And auburn hair, you said."

"She had an amazing smile. She always sat here in the window. She loved the sun."

Jasmine's own smile was pretty amazing when it flashed. "I think I know your friend," she said. "She came in often, if it's the right person. She was usually with one other woman, but there were others."

"How many other people do you remember her having lunch with?" I said, pointing to the specialty coffees to throw Norine off the scent. "Was it always lunch? Did you ever see her at dinner?"

"Hard to say." Jasmine pointed at the Chocolate Triple Threat.

"And you don't have any names?" I said, nodding my head.

"We don't usually know our customers' names, so I didn't know your friend was called Laura. If we do take a reservation, it's usually just the first name."

"Every bit helps." I didn't say what I was thinking.

Everything in our world except maybe the personals, revolves around last names. Phone numbers, addresses. The kind of things I needed. Why would restaurants have to be different?

"Don't people leave their numbers when they make a reservation?"

"They do. So if I can remember a first name or you can give me one, I could try to match it up with the reservation list."

"And you could give it to me."

"Afraid not," Jasmine said. "Serious legal implications there."

"Don't tell me, let me guess. You're studying..."

She laughed "Not yet. I start first year law at University of Ottawa this term. I don't want to start by violating people's privacy."

"U of O is my alma mater."

"You're a lawyer?"

"I run an advocacy agency for victims of violent crime."

Behind the trendy glasses, Jasmine's large grey eyes shone. "You do? What is it?"

"Justice for Victims." I felt a stab of guilt. JFV had been getting short shrift of late. Still, I enjoyed the flash of admiration from Jasmine.

"Justice is what it's all about."

There's a time and a place for idealism. I didn't want to disillusion Jasmine, so I just nodded.

"I can't wait to get to work in the field. That's why I've been working the two jobs all summer, so I can go straight through without having to take a year off. I know I can make a difference."

"You will. If we come up with a name, you can call the person and tell her I want to talk to her and why. Then it's her choice."

"Good plan," she said. "All we need is the name."

I snapped the dessert menu shut. "I'll have a double cappuccino. Chocolate sprinkles on top."

We smiled at each other under the watchful eye of Norine. Jasmine had earned my respect. Plus a healthy tip.

Eighteen

I was too woozy to walk home. Once again I caught a cab. You can't take it with you, as they say.

The cab ride was not without usefulness. Spotless, well-cared for leather seats. Holly Cole playing on the stereo. The driver was dark-skinned, with crisp short black hair. I sat in the backseat and stared at the chiselled features in his photo as my head throbbed and spun. His name was Youssef, with a surname I was unable to pronounce in my medical condition. He was a lot like my regular emergency room doctor, minus the little moustache and the Newfoundland accent.

"I don't suppose by any stretch of luck you were a doctor before you drove a cab?" I knew better than to say before you came to Canada.

He stared at me in the rear-view mirror. "Sorry. Engineer," he said.

"That's too bad. I was hoping for a doctor. I have this concussion. It seems to be getting worse."

"Civil," he added. "I can take you to the hospital if you want. I hear they have doctors there."

Everyone's a comedian.

I glanced again at his photo as we pulled into the driveway in front of my apartment building. That's when it occurred to me. Why hadn't I taken the box of photos with me when I went to Maisie's? What a dope. Just because I didn't know anyone, didn't mean Jasmine wouldn't recognize one of the people. I wasn't at my sharpest this weekend.

I thanked Youssef.

He handed me a card with his unpronounceable last name and a cellphone number.

"Let me know if you need any bridges built," he said. "Or if you just need a cab to Emergency."

"I'll settle for a ride downtown again in five minutes."

* * *

If cats have eyebrows, then Mrs. Parnell's cat raised hers when I limped through the door, as if to say, "It's you again, how boring." Gussie on the other hand, spun in a frenzy. I think he believes that seconds after I turn the key in the lock, there will be a walk.

"Not this time, Gussie," I said, checking my phone messages. Nothing. Not even "Unknown Name", "Unknown Number" or "Number Blocked". Not a single click. Talk about no social life.

Gussie continued to spin, on his third twirl knocking the cat off the chair with his tail.

"Sorry, no walk now."

My first mistake: entering the apartment. My second mistake: uttering the W word. Even with a negative. Gussie yelped with joy.

"Be quiet." This must have sounded like "walk", because it earned me a few more barks. In turn that led to Mr. Crab Head banging on the wall. Which set Gussie off again.

The banging turned to pounding. Gussie barked louder. More pounding.

I hated that man.

"Good dog," I said. "You'll have a nice ramble when I get back the next time."

My head was spinning more. My knees throbbed, and every scrape and bruise had its own little brand of pain. I decided the various aches and ouchies were probably making my head feel worse.

I picked up the flowered box of photos, slipped into my new jean jacket with the butterfly embroidery on the back, grabbed my backpack, swilled a painkiller and slipped out the door.

Gussie howled.

Even though it was a busy weekend, Youssef seemed pleased to get the extra fare.

*   *   *

"Tried to, but I just can't live without that dessert after all," I said to Norine when I waltzed through the door at Maisie's. "Chocolate, chocolate, chocolate."

Before she could seat me at some other server's table, I hustled across the restaurant to the table I'd been at before. Someone else was already sitting there, so I took the next one, hoping it was still in Jasmine's section.

Norine followed me, glossy lips compressed, body language screaming "Ready for battle".

I whipped the napkin out of my glass with a flourish and fiddled with the fork. I turned to the people dining to my right.

"Wonderful atmosphere here, isn't it? And the desserts! Don't leave without one. You'll only end up coming back. I did."

They stared, their forks suspended in mid-air. But this was Ottawa, so in the end they had to nod politely.

Norine knew when she was beaten. I could tell by the look on her face that she didn't intend to lose to me again. We'll see about that, I thought. Jasmine, on the other hand, produced her wide smile. Some tips have that effect on people.

I ordered the white and dark chocolate cheesecake with raspberry cognac coulis and caramelized pecans, because after all, it was Labour Day weekend, and I had a head injury, and no one I didn't care that much about had called me.

The dessert certainly felt like it had health benefits. Well worth the inflated price. I'd blown a wad of cash on a guy named Youssef that day, and I still needed to hang on to more cab fare, so I had to accompany Jasmine to the desk to use my cash card. Everything had started to hurt again, and my slight dizziness had been replaced by intermittent flashing.

"When you get a chance," I said, as I keyed in my PIN, "I need you to look at some old photos. You might recognize some of the people."

"I'd be glad to." She glanced in Norine's direction. "But I don't think I can do it here. She looks like she could put a stake through your heart."

"Does she?" I said, happily. Jasmine did not succeed in stifling a smile. "What time do you get off?" I asked.

"Usually by ten-thirty, it's pretty well empty here. I'm out around eleven, as a rule. Look out, she's on her way over."

"I can wait for you."

"I wouldn't do it here, if I were you," she said. "Norine will just keep me late doing set-up for tomorrow. She's made spite into an art form."

"We're ahead of her. I'll meet you somewhere else." She hesitated. "I'll be fast, honest."

"With two jobs, I need my rest. Could we meet tomorrow instead?"

"I know this sounds strange, but it's a serious matter, and I am desperate." I fished around in my full backpack and finally pulled out a business card, only slightly crumpled. I scribbled my cell number on the back. "I only need about fifteen minutes. You pick the spot. I'll be happy to pay you for your time."

"All fifteen minutes of it?" she smiled. The girl obviously knew her way around a toothbrush. "Double time and a half."

"You got it."

"How about I meet you at Legal Beagle? You know it?"

"I've seen it. Catch you there between ten-thirty and eleven." I could tell by the look on her face that a stormy encounter with Norine was on the horizon. I took the offensive and strode from the desk to head off Norine.

"Wonderful desserts. Well worth the return trip. I'll tell my friends."

She managed a smile that could chill soup. "Thank you."

I marched off with a jaunty step that belied the whirly stuff going on in my head.

Legal Beagle.

Cute.

*   *   *

I found myself at loose ends. Unfortunately, there wasn't much I could do. Couldn't annoy or be annoyed by my family, since they were at the cottage. Most of my friends had departed for the weekend. I'd already pissed off Elaine Ekstein, and anyway, she didn't answer her phone. I could hardly go back to Mombourquette's.

I certainly wasn't hungry.

I'd hit a wall with Laura Brown. And I had time to kill. I

wandered around the Byward Market, enjoying the evening scene. Restaurants were emptying, people were starting to trickle into bars. Foot traffic was heavy. Couples strolled by, holding hands, peering in the windows of shops and restaurants. I thought Elgin Street had a lot of restaurants, but new ones were springing up all over the place in the market. I wondered how long it would take to eat at every restaurant in the area, especially including all the fast food places. I love shawarmas. How many different types could I find there? It didn't take long to get tired of the food game. I strolled up and down the narrow streets, William and Byward, peering at the shrouded market garden stalls, dodging laughing pedestrians. The last weekend of summer, and everyone was having fun jaywalking.

Two girls roller-bladed by at breakneck speed, their matching blonde ponytails lit by the moon. Panhandlers stuck their hands out. I counted three buskers making music at different corners. The Roy Orbison lookalike was good, and the country guitar even better, but I was most impressed by a guy playing "Für Elise" on the accordion. I tossed a loonie into his cap on the sidewalk.

You feel safe in the Byward Market at night, whether you should or not. That's because there are always people everywhere. That set me thinking again. Having lots of people around hadn't helped keep Laura alive. Was I wrong? Had Laura's death really been just an accident? Tragic, but no more than being at the wrong place at the wrong time? Had my fall down her stairs been a bit of clumsiness on my part? Had I imagined the missing insulin?

Was I wasting my time and everyone else's trying to find out about her, when all I had to do was give the all clear for the burial, put the notice in the paper and see who showed up? Should I just stay home and rest until this head thing fixed itself?

Self-doubt is not my best thing.

I kept it at bay until it was time to meet Jasmine.

*   *   *

Legal Beagle was dark and swirling, black painted wood, matte finishes punctuated with the flash of stainless and the throb of neon. Pink, blue and purple neon accented signs, mirrors, doors. The bar was just starting to get moving. I felt like having a beer, but I ordered a San Pellegrino out of grudging respect for the drugs in my system.

"Quiet tonight," I said to the bartender.

He glanced at the clock with its pink neon frame. "Still early."

It was 10:30 on Saturday night on the weekend. I sat and sipped my designer water and tried not to feel peevish as the minutes ticked by. At 11:10, as my second bottle of San Pellegrino neared the end, I figured it was time to call it quits. Jasmine wasn't coming.

At 11:11, I got up to leave, just as the other server, Chelsea, flounced through the door. Her hair was gelled into spikes, all green tonight, and her colour was high, even flushed. She wore a leather bomber jacket over an orange bustier teamed with a black spandex mini-skirt. First time I'd ever seen hand-tooled cowboy boots paired up with fishnet stockings. And to think I'd felt self-conscious because there were butterflies embroidered on my jean jacket.

She ordered a Absolut Mandarin shooter before she said hello. Obviously an emergency.

"I'm sorry." She hopped up on the bar stool, showing quite a lot of fishnet. "I thought you might have left."

"Where's Jasmine?"

"You can't believe what that bitch Norine put her through," Chelsea said breathlessly.

"I bet I can."

"She's a real piece of work at her best. At her worst, which I think I've just seen, she's unbelievable."

"She gives that impression even to the casual observer," I said.

Chelsea's shooter arrived, along with a dose of sympathy from our waiter. "The hag still giving you a hard time?" he said.

"She's spreading it around."

"What do you mean?" I asked.

"She's got Jasmine doing stocktaking plus cash out and shut down. And she gave her setup for tomorrow."

"That explains why she's not here. But I thought you weren't working tonight."

"Jasmine sent me a message through one of the other girls. I said I'd catch you here. She'll call you tomorrow after work."

I figured we needed to vent a bit, so I ordered my third San Pellegrino, or maybe it was my fourth. I'd be running to the bathroom all night, but so what. I didn't have anything better to do.

"When you have time," I added, figuring the bartender was prepared to hear Chelsea's story and offer constructive advice.

Chelsea snarled, "Jasmine has to refill the fucking salt shakers."

The bartender gasped. "You have *so* got to get a new job."

"I am out of there," Chelsea said.

"Well, you could do a lot better," he said. "Talk to management here."

"I might," Chelsea said.

"I'll have that San Pellegrino in the meantime," I said.

Chelsea said, "I think it was deliberate. She figured out

151

Jasmine was planning to meet with you, and she wanted to mess that up."

"Why?"

"She doesn't need a reason. She's a fifth dan black belt in bitchery."

"Hmmm," I said, wondering if I could use that line some time. "Too bad I caused Jasmine trouble."

"Not your fault. But next time I meet someone, it's gotta be in Hull. I really need a smoke."

"We could grab a cab and head over if you want," I said. "I'm in no rush."

"It's okay. I just dropped in to give you the message. I got people to see."

"Right."

"Jasmine told me to give you her phone number and said she'd be happy to meet you. But please don't contact her at work."

"Sure," I said.

Chelsea handed me a folded piece of paper. "That's it, really."

I glanced at the slip of paper. I hated to drop it into the chaotic backpack.

"Wait a minute." I put the photo box on the table. "Since you're here, maybe you can do something for me."

"Hope it won't take long."

I fished out my best shot. "Have a quick look. Here's a side view of Laura. Does she look familiar?" I slipped my last thirty dollars on the bar. It would mean a trip to an ATM for cab fare, but so what.

Chelsea flicked a glance at the cash. It seemed to help her decision.

"Not a great photo. What was she doing, hiding from the

camera? When was this taken?"

"A long time ago. And yes, I think she didn't want the camera to catch her."

"No wonder. Yuck. Where did people get those ugly sweaters?"

Fine words, considering the bustier and fishnets.

"You get a sense of her overall look, although she'd gained a bit of weight recently."

"I think I've seen her."

"Can you look through the rest of these photos?"

Chelsea gave a whoosh of exasperation. My bribe had worn off pretty fast.

I said. "Maybe I should get a refund on that thirty."

She narrowed her eyes.

"Come on, Chelsea. Just glance at these pictures and tell me if you recognize anyone from Maisie's."

At that point, the bartender arrived back with Chelsea's second vodka shooter. Plus a beer on the house for her and a San Pellegrino for me. Not on the house.

I signalled for the bill. I wanted to indicate a sense of urgency to the bartender. I didn't need to sit in on Chelsea's career planning. "Is there anyone you recognize?"

"Hard to say, with everyone looking so weird. The glasses are hysterical. Hadn't people heard of contacts?"

"Let's just go through one by one," I said. "I know you're in a hurry."

"You got that right."

"So if we can just clip along."

"I'm late for a date now because of meeting you for Jasmine."

"Can you call your date? Let him know you'll be delayed a couple of minutes?" I assumed it was a he.

"I guess I could leave a message."

"Excellent. So, no one in this batch?"

She shook her head. She didn't try to call anyone.

The second photo got a negative shake too. And so did the third. She wasn't sure about the next one. There was something familiar about two of the people, but that was all.

I squinted at the figures. The combination of the dark bar and the flashing neon and the post-concussion activity in my head made it hard to see clearly. I scrawled a note on the back of the photo. Elaine would have their life histories.

"But I see a lot of people, you know?" Chelsea said.

"I'm sure you do."

"And it's not like work is my entire existence."

"You obviously have a lively social life," I said.

"And intellectual life," she added.

"Of course. It goes without saying." It had never crossed my mind that Chelsea might have an intellectual life.

I decided to finish the photo project before the vodka shooters and beer chaser hit her like a typhoon.

I watched Chelsea flip through the shots in a desultory fashion. I was about to abandon hope when she gave a little start. Her foxy face lit up. "What's this worth to you?"

"Come again?"

"Information is a commodity. You need it fast?"

"Perhaps you have forgotten I've just given you thirty dollars."

"Well, I definitely recognize two people here from Maisie's. They were fairly regular customers. They used to have lunch with another woman. Auburn hair, tall, a bit overweight, big smile."

Laura. Chelsea must have known who she was all along.

"I know someone else she used to have lunch with. But she's not in these pictures. And like I said, it's going to cost you."

"Be serious."

"You need it. I have it. What's it worth?"

"We are talking about people finding out that a close friend has died."

"So in that case, say a hundred each."

"I'm astounded."

"Okay. No problem, got to go. I told you I was late."

"I don't believe Jasmine would take this approach."

"Why don't you wait for her then? You can get together by Monday or Tuesday."

"I don't have that kind of money."

"There's an ATM up the road."

I stared at her. This little minx thought information about Laura and her friends was a commodity. I had to admit she had me in a corner. But my chequing account didn't have a spare three hundred just waiting for an extortion attempt.

"End of season sale," I said. "Two hundred for the three names. Take it or leave it." I was about to hop down off the bar stool and head for the cash machine when I remembered the bills I'd found in the file at Laura's. According to Laura's will, it was all mine anyway. And this was for Laura.

"All right." I dug around the backpack and fished one of the hundreds from the envelope. "Let's get a face first before we get the other hundred."

Chelsea shrugged. She stretched out a sharp green fingernail to point at Frances Foxall.

I swallowed. "When did you see her?"

"Back in the summer. Late June. July maybe."

"Frances Foxall."

"Want the other one?"

I nodded and extracted another hundred.

This time Chelsea pointed at Sylvie Dumais. "This one's name is Sylvie. I haven't seen her for a while."

"There's a reason for that. She's dead."

Chelsea shrugged. The second hundred vanished into some hidden pocket.

"You want that third name? It will cost you another hundred."

"We had a deal."

She licked her lips. "I don't recall agreeing to it."

I hated to give in, but on the other hand, Laura's money was there, and no matter how much I felt like giving Chelsea a swift kick instead of a large bill, she had provided me the identity of two people who had been at Carleton with Laura, who had had lunch with her, and who were now dead. I needed that third name. I slapped the last hundred dollar bill on the bar. I kept my hand on it. "After this, do you have more information?"

"This is it." She reached forward to pick up the bill.

"The name," I said, keeping it firmly under my palm.

She shrugged. "Bianca."

Not enough to let go of the cash. "I don't know a Bianca."

"Your friend Laura did. She had lunch with her all the time. Including last week."

"How do you know her name?"

"Bianca used to make the reservations when they had lunch together. You get to know the regulars at Maisie's."

So sly little Chelsea had known who Laura was all along.

"Do you have a last name?"

"Just Bianca."

"What about a phone number?"

"That will cost you another two hundred."

"Be serious. I've given you more than enough for a single name."

"Your problem. Another two hundred or forget it."

"I don't have another two hundred." If I'd feigned a lack of interest earlier, it might have put me in a better bargaining position. "Maybe I could pay you tomorrow."

"Call me at Maisie's when you have the cash. I'm out of here." Chelsea snatched the hundred. I sat with my mouth hanging open as she skittered out to the sidewalk.

Nineteen

I slipped Jasmine's number into my pants pocket and hopped off the bar stool, jarring my knees and creating a few new stars in my brain.

"Going somewhere?" The bartender plunked the check in front of me.

"Hang on until I speak to Chelsea."

"I don't think so."

"Right." I reached into my backpack for my cash card and came up empty.

He raised an eyebrow.

I patted my pockets.

He curled his upper lip.

I said, "It's in here somewhere."

He crossed his arms.

Pockets, no luck. It didn't help that my head was spinning.

"I can't imagine what happened to my card," I said. That must have been a familiar tune, because the bartender had slipped around the bar and neatly blocked my exit. I patted my pockets again. Thinking back to the last time I'd had the card.

Maisie's.

I closed my eyes and tried to remember if I'd picked it up after I'd paid for my dessert. No. The card must still be back on the cash at Maisie's. And Maisie's was probably closed.

I could still see Chelsea through the window of Legal Beagle. She was engaged in an animated conversation on her cellphone. She gestured toward Legal Beagle. Most likely making her excuses to the boyfriend and placing the blame on me. If I'd had any money left, I'd have bet she didn't mention her recent windfall.

If I could get to Chelsea fast enough, maybe I could "borrow" a bit of Laura's cash back, write her an IOU and repay her the next day, considering most of the tab was for her vodka shooters. Dealing with Chelsea would be easier than making an arrangement with this particular bartender. My luck held. Someone called to him, and he turned his head long enough for me to sidle away from the bar.

By the time I reached the sidewalk, Chelsea was gone. I peered up and down the street. No green tips anywhere.

Maisie's was my only choice. I hightailed it up the road, turning to see if the bartender was in pursuit. I hoped to find someone still at Maisie's, collect the card, get to an ATM, return and pay my tab, before the bartender called the cops.

The telephone poles were doubling and threatening to triple. The street lights shimmered. They were all kind of pretty in an unnerving way.

I made my way with caution, occasionally putting my hand on a wall to steady myself. I suppose passers-by thought I was just another drunk, but that was the least of my problems.

I clutched the box of photos under my arm. I sat on the curb for a while, watching out of the corner of my eye for unsavoury late-night types who might see me as prey. People left me alone. Looking drunk probably helped. I struggled up the stairs to Maisie's without falling over. I banged on the locked door. No answer. I pressed my nose to the glass.

I shouted. "Please open up. I forgot my cash card."

No one came. Something told me those shadows in the back of the restaurant were people who could damn well hear me but wouldn't come to the door. But that could have been the concussion talking.

I raised my voice. "I know goddam well you are in there."

Nothing.

"As long as you have my card, I'll keep hammering."

Ten minutes later, I added sore knuckles to my list of ailments. This no longer seemed to be the best use of my time.

"I'll be back," I yelled. "You can't steal cards and get away with it." Fine words from someone who'd skipped out on a bar bill.

I slunk down the stairs and onto the sidewalk. At least in the crisp late night air, I could think better. I was way too dizzy for a forty-five minute walk. But I did have people to rely on.

Mrs. Parnell is reliable, willing and never sleeps. But she didn't answer her phone or her cell. Ditto Alvin. Probably off kicking up their heels to celebrate their flight. My sisters would send their husbands in a heartbeat, but I didn't want to wait an hour for them to get into town. Or get dragged back to the cottage.

P. J. must have been prowling the city looking for doomed cats or something. I left him a message with my whereabouts in the hope he'd get the call soon. But I could hear sirens wailing towards Hull, so that was bad news. P. J. would probably be checking out whatever had stimulated the sirens.

I could have called the cops, since the Maisie's people had my card illegally, but I knew damn well they wouldn't take it seriously.

Elaine didn't answer her phone. I left a message saying

160

where I was and what had happened.

I even thought about calling Youssef, but cabs require cash. So I was stuck.

In the end, I called Leonard Mombourquette. I had nothing to lose.

Maybe Mombourquette was tending to his tiny, perfect garden in the moonlight. He didn't pick up.

It was getting harder to stand up straight, so I plunked myself on the curb again. I left a detailed message for Mombourquette. I may have exaggerated the seriousness of my predicament. But only slightly.

I was sure he wouldn't want my death on his conscience, in addition to his other troubles.

There are worse things than sitting on a curb for twenty minutes while everyone parties around you on what is supposed to be the best weekend of the year. But at that moment, I couldn't actually think of any of them.

I stared at the shimmering people and buildings, fiddled with my cellphone and tried to figure out a better course of action. I found myself mesmerized by the minarets on the sign of the Turkish restaurant across from me. They reminded me of something.

What?

The minarets did a subtle yet elegant belly dance. Interesting culture, I thought.

But what was I trying to remember?

Something.

Oh, yes.

A name.

A place name. Turkish.

Istanbul?

That was the name of the restaurant? Something like it.

What did that remind me of?

Stop the swirling, I'm dizzy.

I know I know I know what it is.

Constantinople!

In the excitement of remembering, I let down my guard. I felt myself propelled forward into the late-night traffic. I lay on the road, stunned. Hands grabbed my shoulders and pulled. Or were they pushing? I did my best to fight them off. The last thing I remembered was yelling out Constantinople again. A lovely light show played in my head, rivalling the Canada Day fireworks, but much, much closer to home.

I heard the faraway blare of horns and the screech of brakes.

Twenty

A few words of advice: try not to pass out cold, sprawled half on the street, half on the sidewalk, in the Byward Market on a Saturday around midnight. Especially if you have been sitting on a curb immediately prior to this. In addition, do not yell at passing cars. Such behaviour brings out the police officers, but not the big friendly ones you learned about in elementary school.

"Constantinople," I said confidently as I raised my head to greet the constables who were approaching. "I need to go to Constantinople immediately."

The female officer snorted. "Constantinople? Ma'am, you must mean detox."

"Detox?" I batted away her helping hand. "I'm not drunk."

"Do you want to try standing up, ma'am?"

"Hey, where's my box of photos, they're important. And my backpack. What happened to that?"

"No idea, ma'am."

I squinted at a lump halfway down the block. "That looks like it. What's it doing way down there?"

The officers exchanged glances, but one of them trotted the half-block and picked up my backpack.

"Now just try and stand up, ma'am."

"I don't feel like standing up. Somebody rolled me into the traffic. That's not legal."

I twisted around to see who that somebody might have been. The sidewalk swam, the cops divided into doubles, then triples. No problem. I was used to that. But quadruples were new. I didn't like them at all. I closed my eyes. "My head is out of control."

"We can see that, ma'am."

"Did I mention I hate being called ma'am?"

"No, ma'am."

A wave of nausea washed over me. I opened my eyes and tried not to upchuck Maisie's Chocolate Triple Threat onto the eight pairs of regulation style police footwear in front of me.

"Come along into the car, ma'am," the not-so-nice officer said. "We'll make sure you're all right at the station."

"Hold on. I may have a concussion, but I haven't lost my law degree, and last I heard, there was nothing in the criminal code or in the civic ordinances about sitting on the goddam curb." Fine words, although even I could tell they were coming out a bit slurred. I sank back to the same curb while speaking.

"True enough," the officer said, with a too-wide grin. "But we have complaints about you disturbing the peace."

"What?"

"Dis–tur–bing the peace," she said with entirely unnecessary emphasis.

"What are you talking about, disturbing the peace? Look around. You have me mixed up with hundreds of drunken louts."

I had drawn quite a crowd. There's nothing more entertaining than someone else getting arrested.

"Attempted break-in, too. That has some teeth," she continued merrily.

"What?"

"And don't forget uttering threats. That was still illegal when I signed on tonight."

This would have been a good time to demonstrate grace and dignity. But I felt a surge of panic at the thought of being arrested and probably strip-searched and tossed into a cold damp cell. I never understood how anyone could get through that. I used to imagine jail cells and holding tanks when I had legal aid clients. The images helped me to work up a good head of steam for court. I didn't want to be in one of those cells, ever. I tried to stand up. On the third try, I managed, but without dignity, let alone grace.

"Let's see if I understand. You are saying I uttered threats? Me?"

"You got it."

"Who accused me?"

"How about getting into the car, ma'am?"

"Don't call me, ma'am. I have the right to know who accused me, and that hasn't changed since you signed on tonight." Slur slur.

"We got a call from Maisie's Eatery."

"Ah. Probably from the person who kept my cash card tonight."

"Then someone of your exact description took off from Legal Beagle without paying."

"That's because of the cash card."

"Explain it at the station, ma'am."

"Do you know officers Yee or Zaccotto? They can tell you I have a concussion, and I am a lawyer, not a drunk, and definitely not a criminal."

"I think those guys are on days this week."

"Okay. Maybe you should call my brother-in-law. He's a Detective Sergeant on the Ottawa Force. Really. Major Crimes."

"Is he on duty tonight?"

"No, he's at the family cottage."

"How about you use your one phone call to reach him from the station?"

"Wait a minute. I'll call him now. Hey, where's my phone? Shit, it's not in my backpack. Who stole my phone?"

I just hate it when people roll their eyes. She said, "Check for a phone, guys."

"And my jacket's gone. Do you see a jean jacket? New. With butterflies."

"We'll look around, but it's time for you to get into the car, ma'am."

Lucky me, I was saved from a trip to the cells by a furtive scurrying through the crowd. Never thought I'd be so glad to see Mombourquette. Every mean thought I'd ever had about him evaporated.

"Oh, hey, Sarge," the female officer said.

The other officer gave Mombourquette a respectful nod. A gesture appropriate from a junior colleague. A subtle expression of support.

Mombourquette took a minute to huddle with the constables. They relayed a quite animated version of what I was supposed to have said and done. The female officer waved her arms a lot.

"I'll look after this, if it's all right with you guys," Mombourquette said.

"Who are you calling 'this'?" I said.

"She did have a head injury last night. And she is Conn McCracken's sister-in-law. I'll take her to the hospital to see if the concussion is causing her bizarre behaviour."

The female officer wasn't so quick to let go. "We got a fistful of complaints."

I said, "What do you mean, bizarre behaviour?"

Mombourquette's dear little whiskers twitched. "If anyone lays charges, I'll see she shows up at the right time and place."

"No problem," the male officer said.

I said, "Charges? I'm the one should lay charges."

The female winked. "Careful, Sarge. She's a handful."

"I hear ya," Mombourquette said, leading me toward his car, conveniently parked on the sidewalk. I guess old habits die hard.

"Hey, Lennie," I said as I fumbled my way into the passenger side. "You sure took your time."

"Something tells me I should have left you there."

"But they would have tossed me into the ladies drunk tank."

"You got it."

"I already had a concussion, who knows what I have now. I could have died in a cell."

"Don't put thoughts in my head," Mombourquette said.

*   *   *

"We need to get to the bottom of this situation," I said as we cooled our jets in Emerg.

"One more time," Mombourquette said. "There is no 'we'. There is only you and I. You were acting like a lunatic, and I helped you out for the sake of your family. You're damn lucky you're not being arraigned as we speak. And just so there's no mistake, as soon as you get cleared by a doctor, we will both go to our respective homes. Stop making things worse."

"Whatever. Can I use your cellphone?"

Mombourquette's jaw clenched. "Use your own cellphone and…"

167

"I told you it was stolen. So were my photos, and my new jean jacket is gone too. I love that jacket. Those cops were no help."

Mombourquette said nothing. I fished in the backpack for Jasmine's number, but I didn't have any luck. "There's someone I need to talk to, and I'm having trouble seeing. Can you find a slip of paper with a phone number on it? It should say Jasmine, and it's in here somewhere."

"Even if you find the number, you're not allowed to use a cellphone in the hospital. You, of all people, should know that."

That was one of a million ordinary life details I was having trouble remembering.

"What harm can it do? We're nowhere near the operating rooms, and as you keep pointing out, it's the middle of the night. This person could be the key to the case."

"That's another thing I'd like to make clear. There is no case."

"Is."

"Isn't."

"Is."

"Look, Camilla, if you think there's a case, then you get on it. I am on administrative leave, and if I get tangled up in anything like a case, the shit will hit the entire cooling system. So, for me, there is no case."

"Okay then." I felt my head clear briefly. "It doesn't matter if you get involved, because there is no case, since according to everyone in the police, there was no murder. See? It depends on how you look at it."

Mombourquette said. "The answer's still no."

"Once we get out of here, all you have to do is help me in one of these ways, which are not illegal, not dangerous, and

168

not out of line for a private citizen such as yourself."

"No again."

"Let me tell you what they are, first."

"Nope."

"One, retrieve my cash card from Maisie's. That way I can get some money, pay off Legal Beagle—maybe I didn't tell you about that."

"I don't want to know."

"Two, help me get my photos back. I've been trying to explain to you that this girl, Chelsea, is one of the servers at Maisie's. I met with her a few hours ago, before the incident at the curb. She recognized three people in the photos of the old Carleton crowd. Elaine dug out the shots for me."

Mombourquette massaged his temples.

"The thing is that two of these people are dead. Dead. So-called accidents."

"Accidents happen."

"We're talking three women in their forties, friends from university. One drowned in June. One was thrown from her horse in July. And now, in August, we have the third, Laura, falling to her death in downtown Ottawa."

"Coincidence."

"I need to show the photos to Jasmine. She's a lot more intelligent than Chelsea." I didn't say less grasping. "I'm hoping she'll recognize other people. Maybe one of them can help us."

"Let it go."

"The photos are in a flowered box. The cops didn't care, because they thought I was drunk. But if *you* ask them to look around. It's so important."

"I believe the term is 'belligerent drunk'."

"Fine, then if you could just find Jasmine's number, then

169

you can be on your way. Can you see a small sheet of paper in my pack?"

"No."

"Two seconds of your time. Please."

"For the last time, I am not taking any part in your investigation."

"It's just a piece of paper. And what are you doing here? If not taking part in an investigation?"

"I am spending way too long," he made a big deal out of glancing at his watch, "in an Emergency waiting room because of your fondness for getting concussed."

"We're already in one of the examination rooms. And what do you mean my fondness for..."

Before I could finish, we were interrupted by a doctor, holding a file. Wouldn't you know, it was my regular guy.

Dr. Hasheem shone a lot of lights in my eyes. "This is getting to be a bad habit," he said.

Mombourquette said. "She's in and out all the time."

"It's not necessary for you to stay during the examination, Leonard." I injected just enough firm warning into my voice.

"We need to know what the doctor says about you sitting on curbs in the Market in the night and then rolling into the street. I want to hear if he thinks that's a good idea."

"I don't, actually," the doctor said.

"Well, you're not aware of the circumstances," I said. "Let me explain."

The doctor was checking the record. "Weren't you here this past June?"

"July," I said.

"And I remember something about the winter. Hypothermia?"

"Yes."

"And a broken leg, if I am not mistaken."

"Not such a big deal, really."

"And then twenty-four hours ago. Fall down a flight of stairs. Possible concussion." He gave Mombourquette a speculative glance. "I'd like to speak to your wife alone. Would you mind waiting outside, sir?"

Mombourquette squeaked, "What do mean, wife?"

The doctor shrugged. "Fine. Significant other. Partner. Girlfriend. Doesn't matter. Please wait outside."

"We're not together," Mombourquette said, bristling.

"Whatever you do, don't corner him, Doctor," I said.

Dr. Hasheem meant business. "Outside."

I managed not to laugh, but only because it would have hurt. "He's not responsible for any of my injuries."

"He'll wait outside anyway."

I said, "I'll let you know when the cat's away, Lennie."

There was no humour in Dr. Hasheem's face as he held the door open. Mombourquette slithered through and vanished.

It took a while to convince Dr. Hasheem that Mombourquette was just an innocent bystander. Five minutes later, the doctor let him back in the room.

I continued to check out symptoms. "So, forgetting things. Even important things? That's a sign?"

"Sure is."

"Nothing to worry about then?"

"Depends."

Dr. Hasheem wrapped up the exam and sat on the little stool. "You have a Grade Three concussion. We're going to have to keep an eye on you for a while. Did you say you live alone?"

"Happily."

"I think we're going to admit you. We're waiting for a bed."

"No, no. I can't be admitted. I have animals to look after."

"Animals to take care of. Well, that's not actually our

guiding principle for treatment." If I'd closed my eyes, I would have imagined Rick Mercer talking. I kept them open. Life was weird enough already.

"I feel much better already. Probably just being reassured."

"We are talking about a brain injury, and we don't want to take any chances. Someone needs to monitor you."

"Not a problem. Leonard will be glad to do it. Won't you?"

Dr. Hasheem managed to overlook Mombourquette's squeak. He said, "You may find she seems restless, agitated or irritable."

Mombourquette said, "What else is new?"

Dr. Hasheem blinked. "Watch out for vomiting, one pupil larger than the other."

"I don't think…" Mombourquette interrupted.

But Dr. Hasheem was in charge. "And slurred speech," he added.

Uh-oh.

"Right," Mombourquette said.

"Convulsions and seizures, it should go without saying."

"It should," I said, clearly and crisply.

"No booze," he added.

"No problem," I said.

"And make sure she's not alone for the next day or so."

"What?" Leonard said.

"Make sure she's not alone. Is that hard to understand?"

"Well, there's a big difference between monitoring someone and not leaving them alone."

"How else are you going to watch for deterioration in her condition? You don't want her slipping into a coma, do you?"

Mombourquette showed his incisors.

Dr. Hasheem snapped the file shut. "Get her back in here right away if you see any of the those signs I mentioned. You'll need to wake her up every couple of hours to check."

Mombourquette said, "But we don't even like each other."

"Don't be petty, Leonard."

"She'd be better off in the hospital. Camilla, did you ask the doctor if your concussion would cause you to shout out nonsense at the top of your lungs?"

"What are you talking about?"

"You. According to reports you were in the market, rolling in the street and shouting 'Constantinople. That's the answer.'"

"Did not. Oh, wait a minute. That rings a bell."

"You have to admit that's more than a little bit strange, Doctor," Mombourquette said.

"Right. I'd forgotten about Constantinople. I was walking through the Market earlier in the evening, and I saw this restaurant called Instambouli, or something like it, with a little graphic of minarets. It's coming back now. Is that typical of a head injury, Dr. Hasheem?"

Dr. Hasheem was already halfway out the door. "Shouting out the names of historic cities? First I've ever heard about it." He closed the door behind him.

I said, "Don't worry, Leonard. I have plenty of friends. You just need to get me home. Let's make tracks. Health resources are stretched to the limit, as you know."

"You mean take you home and hang around all night. You heard the doctor, someone's got to wake you up every couple of hours."

"No problem. I'm sure my sisters will understand if I die. Alone. And in terror. I'll leave a note."

Mombourquette turned pale. "Don't bring your sisters into this. You're not going to die, for God's sake."

"I might."

"Fine. I'll take you to your sisters now."

I called his bluff. "Excellent. They're at the cottage, an hour north of here, maybe a bit longer, because it's slow going on the back roads at night."

A nurse stuck her head in the door and said, "Can you move along? We need this examination room."

Mombourquette narrowed his beady eyes at me.

I said, "What'll it be, Leonard? Your place or mine?"

Twenty-One

The first light of dawn was turning the sky pink when we settled into my apartment on Sunday morning. Mombourquette seemed skittish sitting on my sofa. Perhaps because Mrs. Parnell's cat was watching him intently. Gussie ogled the cat with much the same expression.

Mombourquette was having a rough time lately. I felt kind of sorry for him. He was bravely camping out where the cat might get him, just so I didn't lapse into a coma. It wasn't like we were friends or anything. He didn't even like me. But when no one else was available, he'd gone the distance. Even bailing me out in the Market could have meant big trouble for him. But Mombourquette was an old-fashioned cop who believed in doing the right thing. I admire that. I remembered how relieved I'd felt when he'd shown up. I felt a surge of gratitude.

"Thanks, Leonard," I said.

He stared at me warily. "What?"

"I appreciate what you're doing. Keeping me out of jail and taking me to the hospital and all." His mouth hung open. "I'm grateful. Did I already say that? Why do you have that expression on your face, Leonard?"

"I was just wondering if this uncharacteristic civility meant your condition was worsening."

"I don't feel like fighting any more."

"You're scaring me."

"I'm restless. I need to take action. Oh, I know what I can do."

"Please don't do anything."

"I was just going to hunt for Jasmine's telephone number in my backpack." I dumped the contents of my backpack on the coffee table. My vial of painkillers rolled off and landed on the floor. I picked them up. "Glad I didn't lose those. I don't know where that phone number could have gone. It was right in here. Hey, wait a minute. Where's the will?"

Mombourquette said, "I'm going to hate myself for asking, but what will?"

"Didn't I tell you about the will? Maybe I didn't. Okay. Laura Brown named me as the sole beneficiary in her will."

"Huh."

"I found the will in her house when I was searching for the names of her contacts, and I had it in my backpack. Now it's gone. So someone took my phone and the photos and the will and my favourite jacket. But they left my keys and my ID and my new book. You know what's weird? I can understand someone taking the phone and even the jean jacket, but why would anyone steal a will? And the box of old photos?"

"Tell you what," Mombourquette said after a deep sigh. "If you're doing okay in a bit, I'll drive to the Market and see if your things turned up. According to the uniforms, you fell right into the road, maybe the will rolled into the gutter. Could be the photos blew away."

"Crap. I wonder if the phone number blew away too. I'll have to catch Jasmine at the restaurant when I get my cash card."

"Listen, Camilla. Not a good idea to go back to that restaurant. I'll get your card for you."

"That's decent of you. Can you ask about Jasmine? Please don't keep sighing like that. It's important. There's something else about Maisie's, but I can't think what it is. My brain is so fuzzy."

"Just try and recuperate. You'll remember soon enough," Mombourquette said through a giant yawn.

I yawned too. More than once. But I really needed to tell Mombourquette something. What? Oh, yes. "That reminds me, Leonard. I remember why Constantinople is important. Before I forget again..."

But he was already snoring. Or maybe I was.

*　　*　　*

Someone shook my shoulders.

I gasped and opened my eyes. "Are both my pupils the same size?" Mombourquette nodded. "Good. What time is it?" I said.

Mombourquette checked his watch. "Seven."

"Oh, no."

I hobbled over to the window. Sure enough, the sky was full of bright balloons, floating dreamily along the Ottawa River and off toward the Gatineau hills. Poster perfect.

I'd missed another goddam launch. So much for being a person you could count on.

I couldn't even take it out on Mombourquette, since we were going through this nicey nicey phase.

I reached Mrs. P.'s voice mail and apologized at length. I knew she'd give me the benefit of the doubt, but I didn't want to contemplate Alvin's reaction. "Long story, Mrs. P. I'll explain later. I'll make up for it tonight. Should get some great shots."

Mombourquette had dozed off again. He looked kind of cute in a soft, rodential way.

As long as things were going badly, I decided to let Elaine know about the missing photos. The sun was up, so she might be too. Apparently not. I held the phone away from my ear. Across the room, Mombourquette's eyes popped open at the sound of Elaine's voice. He scurried into the kitchen.

I said, "Not such a big deal, Elaine. We had great results. We just need to find some more photos from the same grouping. If…aw, don't be like that. Anyway, it's only if they don't turn up when Leonard checks out the Market later."

"She'll get over it," I said to Mombourquette in the kitchen after I'd hung up.

He said, "That is one scary female."

"Oh, she's not so bad, once you get used to her," I said.

"If you say so. Do you know there's nothing to eat in your house? That's not good for you. Your brain needs proper food."

"I have coffee," I said.

"There's no cream for it. Not even milk."

I considered that. My nausea had subsided. Mombourquette had a point. "Food. Great idea. I don't usually eat at home. Let's go out for breakfast."

"You should stay here. It's safer. You can't get into trouble."

"I guess we could call for take-out. What do you want? Chinese? Italian? Greek? I've got all the menus."

"I was thinking more like breakfast. Bran buds? Porridge? Muesli?"

"Muesli? What is muesli anyway?"

"You stay here and be good. I'll go find us some decent food."

*   *   *

Be good. Not as easy as it sounds. Gussie had an idea involving the park. However, if you've been rolling in the gutter, scuffling with the police and then sleeping fully clothed sitting up on the sofa, next to a person you don't know all that well, you're just not ready to run into the neighbours. I was definitely well enough to take a shower.

"Soon, Gussie," I said.

When Mombourquette left, I hopped out of my clothes. I wasn't sure whether to toss them in the empty hamper or drop them into the incinerator. The hamper won. My wardrobe's not that extensive. As I emptied my pockets, I found a crumpled piece of paper with Jasmine's telephone number.

I hustled to the phone and dialled. Oddly enough, considering it was early morning, the line was busy.

I tried again after I'd showered and dressed. "Hang on, Gussie," I said. "This is important. And it won't take long."

This time Jasmine answered on the first ring.

"Jasmine? It's Camilla MacPhee. I know it's early, and I apologize for that. I realize you are working a couple of jobs, and I was afraid I'd miss you. I need to talk about Laura's luncheon companions. Can we meet somewhere? Anywhere but Maisie's. It's really urgent."

Jasmine let out a long, eerie wail. "She's dead."

I kept my cool and spoke slowly. "Of course, she's dead. That's why I have to talk to you. I need to find out about a woman called Bianca. I must get in touch with her. Can I meet you before you go into work today?"

There was such a quaver in her voice, I couldn't make out what she was saying.

"Sorry, Jasmine, could you repeat that?"

179

"Chelsea. My friend."

"What about her?"

"She's dead."

"Chelsea's dead?" I sank back onto the sofa, my throat constricted. "I can't believe it. I was just talking to her last night. What happened?"

It took Jasmine a couple of tries to explain. "The police said she was walking over the bridge to Hull, and she jumped or fell into the river. They asked if she might have been on drugs or been drunk or something. Can you believe that?"

"I had a fall myself, and the police took that exact attitude."

"Anything close to the market, and they act like everyone's a criminal or a druggie."

"But Chelsea had more than a few drinks. I know because we were together at Legal Beagle."

Jasmine stopped sobbing. A steely note entered her voice. I thought I detected the lawyer she was going to become. "Chelsea could hold her liquor better than anyone I ever met."

"I'm sorry. I'm not saying she was drunk, but she might have been vulnerable to someone. Let down her guard. Maybe someone tried to rob her." All I heard were sobs at the other end.

I waited for Jasmine to calm herself. "I'm sorry about your friend."

My heart was thumping. Chelsea had been alive and lively, laughing and looking after number one just a few hours earlier. I'd hardly known her, and she'd done her best to take advantage of me in her own high-spirited way. She'd known something about the women who lunched with Laura. Now she was dead. There just had to be some connection.

"I know this is tough for you, but where can we meet?" I said.

"I don't want to see anyone. Leave me alone."

"Be careful who you talk to, Jasmine," I shouted.

I hate dial tones.

Was it my imagination, or was it getting harder to stay alive in safe little old Ottawa?

*   *   *

"Of course, I'm all right, Leonard. You've only been gone forty-five minutes. Hey, what's in the box?"

The cat, who had been snoozing languidly on the sofa, woke up and licked her lips.

Mombourquette's nose twitched. All four of them did, in fact. He had developed a distinct silvery shimmer. It was quite appealing, in a disturbing way. Perhaps the appeal was heightened by the fact he'd brought two large double doubles from Tim Hortons. The box also held an intriguing selection of doughnuts. Even if you divided by four, it was a feast. My symptoms seemed to be coming back, but I figured those puppies would fix them. This new thing about being polite to each other certainly had side benefits.

"Sorry, I couldn't find anything more nutritious."

"Are you kidding? This is great. Thanks."

He frowned. "You look quite pale."

"I'm okay, but I have something to tell you," I said, peering into the jumbo box of doughnuts. "I've got some bad news and some good news. What do you want first?"

"You'd better have breakfast first."

"Excellent point, Leonard. I could use a doughnut to steady myself. This beats muesli any day. Speaking of news, any luck in the market?"

"I checked around for your stuff. Sorry, there was no sign of anything. And Maisie's is still closed. I got in touch with the guys on patrol. They were just going off shift."

"And they hadn't seen anything?"

"They said there was no box or anything else near you when they arrived. They looked, because apparently you were making quite the fuss."

"I didn't think they took me seriously."

"Probably didn't, but they told me they checked anyway. I believe them."

"Someone must have stolen it."

"Doesn't make sense. I can understand why someone took your new jacket. If they'd also taken a watch, I could understand. A piece of jewellery, sure. ID or credit cards, no question. Drugs. Car keys. Even your shoes. Fair game with someone passed out. Even your rings."

I stared at my wedding band and engagement ring. "God, someone would take those?"

"Happens."

"Well, that proves my point, Leonard. Why the photos and the will? Doesn't that tell us something?"

"No street person or druggie or casual thief is going to leave your ID and prescription painkillers and take a bunch of photos."

"Exactly. But someone did. Don't you wonder why?"

Not one of the shimmering Mombourquettes made eye contact with me.

I said, "It's a setback, but the will's on file, and Elaine has tons of pictures. I'll call her back."

Mombourquette sighed. "I wish that was all you had to worry about, Camilla."

Twenty-Two

I refuse to worry about anything," I said, "until I finish my coffee and doughnut. I'm thinking about the double chocolate glaze and the honey almond next. Unless you have your eye on them."

"Good thinking," he said. "The problems aren't going anywhere. I'll have the maple glaze and the Boston cream."

"You got Boston cream? Boston cream is my favourite."

Mrs. Parnell's cat had been positioned on the table next to Mombourquette, regarding him speculatively. Despite the presence of doughnuts, Gussie had dozed through everything, farting with contentment.

After we'd eaten, I said, "Let's take Gussie for his walk. I promised him. It's a matter of some urgency."

Gussie woke up and barked as if to prove the point. For added effect, the neighbour next door banged on the wall. The little calico cat licked her chops. Mombourquette headed for the door.

When Gussie and I caught up to him at the elevator, I said, "Not that I'm not ready for whatever it is, but everything in its own time. My rule is, bad news first, good news second."

"No argument here."

"When we get to the park, I'll give you my good news," I panted.

That worked too. There was no holding Gussie back, and we were in the park in what seemed like seconds.

"Here's the best thing, Leonard. I remembered what Constantinople meant."

"Okay, and what does it mean?"

"Contrary to interpretation, I wasn't shouting out nonsense because of my head injury."

"So what was it?"

"Laura's home town. I've been trying to remember the name ever since this whole thing started. No, not in the flower bed, Gussie."

Mombourquette seemed underwhelmed by the news.

I said, "Now that I know where she was from, I should be able to find someone who knew her."

"Huh."

"It could be the break we need. You got an Ontario road atlas in your car?"

"I better tell you what I found out."

"Sure, it's your turn, Leonard."

"Don't interrupt until I've finished talking. Okay, Camilla?"

"Won't say a word." This newly polite relationship with Mombourquette had something going for it. "Bring it on."

For some reason, Mombourquette kept staring at his flip-flops. "Here goes."

"I'm ready," I said.

"Maybe not. That girl you met with last night? Chelsea? I'm afraid she's dead."

"I know. That's the bad news I had to tell you. I found out from Jasmine while you were out."

"You promised you wouldn't interrupt."

"It wasn't exactly a promise."

"Better let me finish. I heard from a solid source that foul play might be involved."

"Jasmine said they told her Chelsea probably fell or jumped. But people don't fall off the bridge, and Chelsea sure didn't seem suicidal. I think it's connected with Laura. That makes four deaths in four months. I better talk to Jasmine fast. Hey, I have an idea. You could talk to someone in Major Crimes and fill them in on the connected deaths, and that wouldn't be investigating, but it could stop whoever is doing these things before there's another murder. Like maybe Jasmine or this Bianca. I need to find her too and warn her."

"Listen to me. This is off the record. A guy in Major Crimes told me when I was picking up the stuff at Tims."

"My apologies. Go ahead."

"They got a tip about Chelsea last night."

"That's great. Does it give them a suspect to focus on?"

"Oh, yeah."

"They're not thinking robbery or sexual assault, are they?"

"She had several hundred dollars on her when they pulled her out of the river. So I'd say no to robbery. No one mentioned sexual assault, so I'm guessing there were no indications."

"I told you it had to do with Laura. Did anyone see her walking with the suspect? Or getting into a car?"

Mombourquette cleared his throat.

Gussie tugged at his leash.

"Yeah, they got a detailed description."

"Well, that's good."

"Not really. A waiter from Legal Beagle got in touch. Apparently, you were seen having a big argument with her in the bar. Then you raced out and chased her down the street, yelling."

"Oh."

"Yeah. Not all that long before you collapsed, but it was enough time for Chelsea to get killed."

"But that's crazy. I didn't have anything to do with it. She was meeting someone. She was talking on the phone with the person. We just need to find out who she was talking to. They can get the cellphone record. Can you set them straight?"

"Try to understand, it was coffee shop talk. People know we have a connection, some of them blame you for what happened last summer. They thought I'd be pleased to hear it, I guess."

"You told them I didn't do it, right?"

"I said I didn't believe it, but they've got witnesses, and they want to talk to you. I'm surprised they're not here already."

"What do you mean, witnesses?"

"Apparently there was more than one tip. You were seen near the Interprovincial Bridge with this girl."

"But I never went near the bridge."

"One of them described your jean jacket with butterflies on the back."

"That's my missing jacket. Oh my God. Do they know you took me home?"

"They do. And we're both in deep shit."

I said, "Okay, Leonard. So what's your good news?"

"I'm afraid there is none."

*   *   *

A few minutes later, a grim-faced Mombourquette headed off to see if he could pry more information out of some friendly soul on the force. Mrs. Parnell's cat looked disappointed.

He paused at the door. "You going to be all right?"

"Of course, Leonard."

"You won't go anywhere?"

"I have no car, no money, no cash card, and no desire to connect with my relatives. Mrs. Parnell and Alvin are off in a balloon. Where could I go?"

"I'll check in as soon as I have news."

I wasn't exactly lying. I didn't say I wouldn't go anywhere. I did have the VISA card I keep for travel, and I didn't mention that either. Elaine's name never came up. I didn't plan to sit on my bum and wait for the police to bang on the door. Better Mombourquette didn't know that. For his own mental health.

As soon as the door closed behind him, I tried Jasmine's number. Busy. I fed the animals and tried again. The third time I called the operator. According to her, the phone was off the hook. Neither Mrs. Parnell nor Alvin answered at home or on their cells. Must have been out of range. I got P. J.'s voice mail three times too.

Luckily, Youssef answered the phone in his cab.

"Of course, I take VISA. See you in five minutes," he said.

*   *   *

A couple more brownie points for Youssef: one, he had an Ontario road atlas; two, he didn't mind finding Constantinople for me, since my vision was still wonky; three, once we arrived on Spruce Street, he had no problem idling his cab until a bleary-eyed Elaine staggered down the stairs and undid the zillion locks on her front door. He waved goodbye as I dodged past her and lumbered up the stairs to the living room.

"Sorry to wake you again, Elaine, but you're my only hope."

Elaine tilted her head. "Why are you standing at that weird angle?"

"What are you talking about?"

"You. You're standing at a 45° angle."

"Nothing to worry about. The big thing is the police are probably after me."

Elaine's mouth hung open. Most gratifying. "Why?"

"That's not all," I said. "It's goddamed inconvenient, because now they'll never give me the names of the witnesses who saw Laura fall."

"Sit down, Camilla. You're making me dizzy."

I sat. "It's all connected with Laura. Did you know Frances Foxall died this summer?"

"Holy moly."

"She was killed in a riding accident, and she had also been seen with Laura at Maisie's. Bear with me. I'm having trouble remembering things, and I want to get it all out. Sylvie Dumais, who is also dead as you told me, was seen lunching with Laura. Then Chelsea, the girl who told me this, went off the Interprovincial Bridge last night. She's dead too. Probably killed by the same person who stole your photos, my cellphone, and Laura's will and pushed me into the traffic in the market. They stole my jacket too and probably used it to make it look like I killed Chelsea. I guess you didn't get the message I left you last night."

Elaine merely stared.

"The police tried to arrest me for being drunk in public. That was before they knew Chelsea had been murdered. Luckily, Leonard Mombourquette got me out of the situation."

"I don't believe it."

"Too true. But apparently now we're friends. So now I have to go to Constantinople, which seems to be north of Kingston, and find Laura's family. I need to replace the photos with similar ones and show them to Jasmine, the other server from

188

Maisie's. I think I told you about her. She needs to be warned, too. Plus I need to locate a woman named Bianca, because she's involved somehow and may be in danger also. Did I mention I can't get my cash card back from the restaurant?"

"It's too much to take in this early," Elaine said.

"Right. So if you can just lend me the Pathfinder and your phone and maybe a couple of bucks, I'll take care of this stuff before the police track me down."

"If you can't stand up straight, how can you drive the Pathfinder on the highway without killing yourself or innocent parties?"

"No choice, Elaine."

"The police won't come after you for being drunk in the Market on a Friday night."

"Which I wasn't. The head injuries made it look that way."

"They've got better things to do. It's small potatoes. You don't need to worry."

"Mombourquette warned me that Major Crimes is investigating Chelsea's death. And they've got witnesses who identify me fighting with her and chasing her down the street, yelling."

"They *will* want to talk to you."

"Since I don't officially know that, I want to take care of these things first."

"Hear me: you can't drive."

"Sure I can. Where are your keys?"

Elaine said. "I'll take you."

"That's kind of you."

"Holy moly, like I've got a choice."

Twenty-Three

Constantinople turned out to be tucked in the tangle of dirt roads that run off Highway 38, north of Kingston, in a mix of farming and cottage country.

"Wouldn't want to try to farm here," I said, as we passed another fine example of pre-Cambrian shield.

The late summer weather had been hot and dry. We raised a lot of dust as we crested another blind hill. Elaine kept her eyes straight ahead. "You know what? If we haven't found it in three hours, I'd say that's a bad sign."

"We've been relying on the map. And we know about the problem with maps. I say we ask someone."

"We're in the middle of hell. Just who do you suggest we ask?"

"Someone in one of the general stores we passed."

"But they're back on the highway."

"So what?"

"We'd have to backtrack."

"Big deal."

"I hate backtracking."

"Let's keep going in circles, then. There's that 1950s Pontiac up on blocks. Third time we've passed this place."

Elaine took a bit more gentle coaxing. "We can't just go in

190

and ask about some people named Brown. There must be only a couple of million Browns in this country."

"What is your problem, Elaine? We're women. We can ask directions to Constantinople or anywhere else. If it helps, sit in the car and keep your face hidden."

"Very funny. I'll come with you."

Elaine's worst fears seemed to be realized. People stared at us like we'd just landed from Venus and asked for a short cut to the Vatican.

Everyone shook their heads. I thought they showed unnecessary emphasis. They spoke slowly and made dramatic gestures, indicating they had no idea where Constantinople was, or even if it existed. The name Brown drew more blanks. I imagine they collapsed into laughter as soon as the door slammed behind me.

I hit the second store by myself. Elaine opted to stay in the car. Okay, no success. Still, I held out for one last store.

Smith's General Store had the smell of an establishment with a long history. A dust-covered red pick-up was parked in front. A rusted Corvair was up on blocks at the side of the store. A load of wood sat stacked near the front.

Inside the store, a quarter-inch of dust decorated the tinned soups. Smith's sold soap without packaging, loose candles, fly paper and big boxes of safety matches. Bait appeared to be their specialty. I noted two new coolers full of nightcrawlers.

A pair of ancient fellows in red baseball caps were the proprietors. I figured they were brothers and that they had about six teeth between them. I asked if they knew how to find Constantinople.

"Constantinople?" the first one said.

"Yes."

"Constantinople?" the second one said about thirty seconds later.

Of course, it may have been the first one again.

"Does that ring a bell?"

"Yep," the first one said.

I looked at the second one. He said yep too.

"Good," I said. "Can you tell me how to find it?"

"Not that easy," the first one said.

Somehow I had already figured that out. I smiled at the second brother. After a longish minute, he said, "Not that easy."

"Okay. What would be the nearest community to it? Maybe we could ask someone there to direct us."

"We'll direct you," the second brother said.

"Need a map, is the best thing," the first brother said.

"Do you by any chance sell detailed maps of this area?"

Turned out they did. Five minutes later, they had the route traced out for me.

"I guess I'll be able to find the Browns now," I said.

"Who?" they said in unison.

"The Browns. I'm looking for the parents of Laura Brown, an old friend."

They exchanged glances. The meaningful kind.

"Thank you for your help," I said.

"You want Ralph and Sadie then. Why didn't you say so, ma'am?"

"You know them? I asked at a couple of other places, and no one knew anything about the Browns."

Brother One spat. "Newcomers. Can't tell their arses from their elbows."

Brother Two spat a bit further. "Come in from somewheres else. Change everything. Give people crazy ideas."

"Useless conceited parasites," I said, getting into the spirit. Brothers One and Two grinned in approval.

"Won't do you no good to go to Constantinople."

"Why not?"

"Won't find Ralph and Sadie there," Brother One said.

Brother Two shook his head sagely. "They moved when Laura was just a tyke."

"Where would I find them?" I said.

A hush fell over the store. My head throbbed. I sat down on a wooden bench and decided to wait them out. I hoped they wouldn't direct me to the nearest graveyard.

Twenty-Four

"Well, I'm sorry," I said to Elaine. "Apparently, the Browns moved to a place called Daken, years ago. It's supposed to be really hard to find, but they said they'd show us the way."

"Let's hope we're alive when we get there."

"What can go wrong?"

I found out what could wrong soon enough as we shot down the twisting dirt roads in full pursuit of Brother Two in his dirt-covered Ford pick-up. Every bend in the road seemed to produce another choice of directions.

"Holy moly. Does he have a rocket engine in that thing?" Elaine muttered. "If we lose sight of him, we're sunk."

She had a point. I figured Brother Two might have had a career in Formula One before he went into the nightcrawler business. Whatever engine he had in that old truck, the Pathfinder couldn't match it. I thought my head was going to splinter into a thousand painful fragments.

"Speed up! You're losing him," I said.

"Well, I don't want to be in the line of fire if some of that wood comes flying out of the back."

"But if we can't see him…"

Elaine said, "I guess we get lost out here in this godforsaken bit of wilderness. We'll be lucky if they find our bleached bones."

"Do you think maybe his directional signal isn't working?" Not that I'm such a geographer, but we'd turned north, south, east and west and had now started north again.

"Nobody lives here," Elaine said.

"Come on. You can see houses every now and then through the trees."

"I'll take your word for it."

"People don't live near the road, I guess. I wonder how they manage in the winter?"

Elaine was bathed in sweat, and I was pretty damp myself when Brother Two whipped his truck into a ninety degree turn and shot down a half-hidden single track road. He must have used the OFA sign, which I guessed meant Ontario Farm Association, as the marker. Or it could have been the weather-beaten "Property For Sale" sign.

We slid precariously across the road and just missed a fine example of Canadian shield on the far side. Brother Two was completely out of sight by the time we got on the road. Lucky for us there were no more splits, turns or choice of directions. Just a couple of dips that caused my stomach to fly up to my throat, and there was the truck, stopped in front of a small conventional yellow brick bungalow. The house sat on a large lot. A cluster of outbuildings loomed in the back. A well-tended vegetable garden occupied a substantial space near to the side.

I got out of the car, knees weak and head buzzing. On the upside, I only saw one of everything, if you don't count cedars and spruce.

Elaine stayed put. She seemed jittery.

Brother Two nodded briefly as I passed the truck. Apparently, he was staying put too.

I walked back to Elaine, who was clutching the steering wheel like a life preserver. "Let's go."

"I'll stay here."

"You're the one who counsels people. Come with me."

"Can't."

"This is not about us, Elaine. We've got to tell the Browns their daughter has been killed. It's the right thing to do."

"You'll do the right thing," she said.

I marched up to Brother Two.

"Thanks for showing us the way. Please don't leave without us."

He grinned, giving a nice view of his chewing tobacco.

"I imagine they'll be pleased," he said.

"Pleased? I don't think so," I said. I stiffened my spine and set out toward the front door. Elaine stayed in the Pathfinder. Probably trying to get her heartbeat back into normal range.

Brother Two stuck his head out the window and called to me. "Best try around back."

I edged my wobbly way around the side of the house. A German shepherd cross bounded toward me, snarling.

Thanks to Gussie, I had a few Liver Snaps in my pocket, and that earned me a new friend. Even watchdogs can be bought. Beyond the dog, a grey-haired man in a black and red checked shirt took a break from chopping wood.

I raised my hand in greeting. The dog sniffed at my pockets.

"Mr. Brown?" I said.

He nodded.

"My name is Camilla MacPhee. Can we talk inside?"

*   *   *

From the look of it, no one sat in the immaculate living room much. Mrs. Brown called it the front room, and it was plainly reserved for company. I would have preferred the warmth of the kitchen we'd walked through, where the smell of fresh bread hovered. The shepherd cross hovered in the doorway, whining, not daring to put a paw on the beige wall-to-wall carpeting.

Dust-free photos of a young smiling girl with dark braids occupied every available surface. I didn't see a single picture of Laura. Was this Laura's younger sister? She'd never mentioned a sister. No wonder, with such obvious favouritism. At the least, I would have expected Laura's high school and university grad photos.

Sadie Brown was small, slim and just short of seventy. Her steel-grey hair was trimmed almost to the roots. She shook my hand with a powerful grip. She'd done her share of wood-chopping.

They settled me with coffee and fresh cookies, neither of which held much appeal. I still had to tell them their daughter was dead. That'll curb your appetite.

She sat on the sofa. He remained standing. They looked at me expectantly. Whatever they were expecting, it wasn't bad news.

"Before I go on, I want to make sure you are the parents of Laura Lynette Brown."

"Laura Lynette?" Mrs. Brown said in surprise.

Ralph Brown said nothing.

My mouth was dry. "I am sorry to be the one to tell you this," I began. I had already decided to leave the business of foul play to the police.

Their foreheads creased in puzzlement.

I felt my stomach turn over. "I'm afraid your daughter, Laura, has been killed. In an accident."

Mrs. Brown's hand shot to her mouth. Her husband sank into a chair.

I plowed on, gibbering. "It happened on Friday. A fall from an escarpment not far from the Parliament Buildings. I believe it was instantaneous."

They stared at me.

I felt tears rising. "I'm sorry."

"I don't understand," Laura's mother said.

Denial. I knew it only too well.

"Because of her diabetes, apparently she passed out and slipped."

"Diabetes?" he said.

Sadie Brown said, "What kind of terrible joke is this?"

Laura's father got to his feet. So did I, unsteadily.

He said, "You'd better go now."

Laura's mother remained seated. She said to no one in particular, "What's all this crazy talk about our Laura Lynette? I thought she wanted to see the house."

"I'm sorry," I said again.

She picked up the nearest photo and began to weep soundlessly. Her husband, white-faced, jaw clenched, held the door for me.

I didn't remember Laura ever mentioning her family's religion, but the University of Ottawa had been overwhelmingly Catholic, so I made an assumption. "Is there someone we can send for? Maybe your priest?"

She cried out, "Just leave. Leave."

I stood my ground. "I can't just leave you here on your own to deal with the shock of Laura's death."

"Why the hell not?" Laura's father said. "We've been dealing with it for the last thirty years."

Twenty-Five

I whipped open the car door and gave Elaine a bit of a scare. "You'd better get in there now," I said. "You've got to hear this."

It took quite a bit of soothing from Elaine to get the Browns to talk.

"We thought you were coming to look at the house," Mrs. Brown repeated. "We get lookers every year or two."

I bit my tongue before I said I was sorry again. Too much of that can backfire. "It's a beautiful place. Just a matter of time until you sell it."

"It's been on the market thirty years, since Laura Lynette died."

I blinked. Whatever I'd been expecting here, it sure wasn't that.

Elaine said, "It appears that my colleague has made a terrible mistake."

"Mistakes happen." Mrs. Brown glanced quickly toward her husband.

"That's right," I said.

"Some mistakes are worse than others," Mr. Brown said.

"I really am sorry," I said.

But he didn't really seem to be talking to me.

"Camilla didn't mean to upset you. I apologize for her unseemly intrusion," Elaine said, stressing unseemly.

Normally I would snap at such a remark. I said, "I am…"

Sadie Brown said, "It's a terrible mix-up. Now another mother will have to go through this." She picked up a photo of the girl and traced the smile. "She never made it past ten years old, our Laura Lynette. She'd be older than you if she'd lived. Wearing city clothes, I imagine. Maybe with children of her own."

Laura's father stood, his gnarled hands balled into fists, staring straight at the wall ahead, perhaps seeing the little girl who never made it past ten.

On the way back to the car, I stopped to speak to Brother Two.

"What happened to Laura Brown?"

"Godawful thing, that. Poor Ralph there. He never saw her behind the tractor. Never got over it, neither of them poor folks."

"You wouldn't," I said.

"If they sell this place," he said, "maybe they can get away from those memories."

"Not likely," I said, heading back to the Pathfinder.

* * *

"Well, that was horribly upsetting for me, and unnecessarily distressing to those poor people. And a complete waste of time." Elaine was doing well over the posted limit of 90 kph on Highway 7.

"Upsetting, yes, waste of time, no," I said.

"But she wasn't the same girl."

"Of course, she wasn't the same girl."

"We've spent three hours driving around the backwoods,

and it will take at least another hour and a half to get home. For nothing, except to resurrect all that grief."

"The point, Elaine, is if the woman we knew wasn't Laura Lynette Brown, from Constantinople, Ontario, then who the hell was she?"

"We'll never know."

"I'm damn well going to find out. When we get back to town, I'll duck in to my place to check on the animals, then we can go to your home and get to work on those photos."

"Count me out. I have an appointment, and it will be a miracle if I get there in time, so I can't look through the snapshots for you."

"Fine, we'll do it later. I have to drop on over to the Balloon Festival anyway. I promised Mrs. P. I'd take pictures, and I haven't been there for a single launch. I'll take a cab. Hey, wait a minute, what's with all the appointments on the holiday weekend?"

"What I do with my weekends is my business and, what's more, I think if no one found out who Laura was after all these years, a few photos won't do the trick."

"Maybe. But it's the best bet we've got. I think someone in those photos got Chelsea killed."

*   *   *

It was mid-afternoon when Elaine dropped me off and headed out for the appointment that was none of my business.

I said, "I'll call you later. And I'll pay you for the gas when we pick up my cash card at Maisie's." She pursed her lips in a way that could lead to serious wrinkles. "See you soon, Elaine. Thanks again."

Elaine gunned the Pathfinder, leaving me covered with

dust from the driveway. Sometimes I don't know what gets into that woman.

Gussie had his legs crossed by the time I arrived.

Needless to say, the phone was flashing. I started to peek at call display, on the off chance it was anybody interesting, but Gussie howled. And Gussie's situation seemed more immediate. The empty and half-chewed doughnut box explained why.

"Okay, Gussie, I get the point."

Maybe the brain injury was causing me to talk to animals. As I grabbed my keys and a couple of plastic bags for dooty duty, I caught sight of myself in the mirror. Some friend Elaine was. She might have mentioned that I had two black eyes. Well, black, dark olive with navy tinges. No wonder people had been giving me odd glances all day. Maybe that was why Gussie was howling. There wasn't much I could do except slip on my Ray-Bans. I tucked my hair under a Blue Jays cap and pulled the brim low. The up and down weather was down again. I was feeling a bit chilly, and since my beloved jean jacket was gone, I dug around in the back of the closet and found a Carleton sweatshirt. It was a measure of the state of my head that I put the sweatshirt on after the hat and sunglasses.

Gussie likes to take his time and frolic, and because he is a big dog who needs some exercise, and because he had been stuck in an apartment with quite a few doughnuts, and because I wasn't in frolicking condition, I decided to take something to read.

I spotted the Berger book from Laura's place, sitting on the dining room table where I'd dumped my backpack while hunting for Jasmine's phone number.

I stuffed the book back in, slung the pack on my back and departed, ready for anything.

*   *   *

Gussie and I were returning from our walk, during which Gussie had taken an inordinately long time to accomplish a straightforward matter, when we stopped in our tracks. A flurry of police cruisers idled at odd angles in front of the building. Nobody would be driving past them, in or out, as far as I could tell.

The roof lights were flashing, but there were no sirens.

We followed a pair of unfamiliar constables into the building. Gussie and I got into the elevator with them. One of the constables pressed sixteen. My floor. I was hoping they were all heading for my pesky neighbour's place but, deep down, I knew they weren't.

The constables stayed well on their own side of the elevator. That might have been because of the plastic bag I was swinging.

When the door opened, sure enough, the officers marched briskly down the hallway and joined a couple of others clustered outside my door. This didn't help the bad stuff going on in my head.

I hesitated by the elevator. Even if they wanted to talk to me about that business with Chelsea in front of the bar, it seemed like a lot of cops for a force that claims to be under-resourced.

Whatever their reason, they were taking it way too seriously, and I didn't want to be part of it. It was time for another painkiller, and I had just a short while to let the medication take effect before heading to Hull.

The baseball cap combined with my Ray-Bans to work in my favour. The sweatshirt added fifteen pounds and ten years to my appearance. For once, that was a good thing.

With two of the cops looking my way, ducking back into the elevator seemed like a red flag. I fished out my keys, and Gussie and I stopped in front of Mrs. Parnell's apartment, since I had a key to that. But which key was hers? I tried a few, hoping not to be noticed. One of the officers approached me.

He flashed a badge.

I tried for just the right amount of interest, not guilt, not anxiety, just normal nosiness. Gussie barked, protectively. Luckily, this guy wasn't any of the many constables I had come in contact with.

"What can I do for you, officer?"

"We'd like to talk to your neighbour." He pointed toward my door.

"How come?"

"Have you seen anyone enter that apartment lately?"

"No." This was true, if not the whole truth. You can't really see yourself without a mirror. I said, "A lot of people are away for the weekend."

"You know where she might go?"

"No idea." Aside from Mrs. Parnell's, I had no place to go at that moment.

"Nothing comes to mind?" I guess this guy had aspirations to become a detective.

"I wish I did." Very very true.

I hoped he wouldn't notice I wasn't familiar with the key to apartment 1608. Now with Laura's keys added to my clutch of home, mailroom, car and office keys, I had a fistful of metal. I felt a surge of joy as one key slipped into the lock. The lock turned.

Mrs. Parnell's lovebirds, Lester and Pierre, shrieked in dismay as the door swung open. What a pair of turncoats.

"Good luck, officer," I said.

He flipped open his notebook. "Can I have your name, ma'am?"

That might have been a pivotal moment, but his radio went off. We said "excuse me" simultaneously, and I slipped into Mrs. Parnell's apartment without committing an actual indictable offence. The door closed behind me, and I exhaled softly.

My hands shook as I dialled P. J.'s number. This time, he picked up.

"I have a story for you, P. J. Come to my place and find out why half the police force is banging on the door of my apartment."

"No shit?"

"No shit."

"I'm on it. This is great. Thanks, Camilla."

I read Mrs. P.'s telephone number to him. "After you find out, call me at this number and let me know what's happening."

"Where are you?"

"Just call the number."

For some reason, Mrs. Parnell prefers to keep her telephone number unlisted. I wasn't sure how long that would slow down a former crime reporter like P. J.

There's a lot to do in Mrs. P.'s apartment. You could read a hundred books on World War II history, strategy or military memoirs. You could listen to a thousand classical or jazz CDs on her high-end stereo system. You could sit at one of her computers and search the net, or you could park yourself in the black leather chair and turn on the big screen television and watch anything that VIP cable has to offer. Of course, for any of these activities, you'd need single vision, a clear head and an untroubled mind. Every minute felt like a year as I slumped on Mrs. Parnell's leather sofa and fretted. My instincts told me to lie low. What if the next cop recognized me?

P. J. would take a while to get to the bottom of things. Once he did, I could head to Elaine's. My key strategies were: avoid long, time-wasting interviews with the police, avoid getting dragged off to the cottage by overbearing relatives, avoid missing yet another take-off at the Balloon Festival and avoid more blows to the head.

Lester and Pierre continued to shriek throughout my attempts to think. "All right," I said, "I'll feed you."

In retrospect, this was a bad idea.

In the time it took to replace their VitaVittles Gold and special honey nut treats, Lester and Pierre managed to elude me and head for the chandelier over the dining room table. Gussie was thrilled. I'd never seen him jump on a table before. In fact, I'd never seen him jump anywhere. But deep in his fuzzy body were the genes of a hunting ancestor.

Lester and Pierre shrieked shrilly. Gussie barked joyously. The doorknocker sounded ominously. I said "shit," meaningfully. The phone rang. Naturally. No point in pretending there was no one home.

"Yes," I said, peering through the peephole.

"Police, ma'am."

"Hold on a second, please. The phone is ringing. Hello?"

"Camilla? It's P. J. You're not going to believe this."

"Can I call you back?"

"Are you crazy? You need to hear this!"

"I want to hear it, but the police are at the door."

"What's all that racket?"

"Hold on a second."

The doorknocker sounded. This cop had no attention span. "Can you open the door, ma'am?

"My pet birds are out of the cage, and the dog is threatening to eat them. You can probably hear him barking.

206

Can I get back to you, officer?"

"It won't take long, ma'am."

"It will if my birds escape. Can we talk through the door?"

I opened it a crack, hoping the space was too small for a lovebird to shoot through.

"Just a few questions about your neighbour."

"I don't have much to say," I started, when the miserable so-and-so next door shouldered his way past the officer. "But that's her next-door neighbour. He might know something. That will give me time to get the birds back in the cage. Or I could go to the police station later. Who should I talk to?"

He said something that was drowned out by the shrieking of Lester and Pierre. I swung around to see Gussie make an optimistic leap toward the chandelier. Lester and Pierre swooped across the room, touching down on a cluster of framed photos of Mrs. Parnell's World War II comrades. Gussie followed them, barking. The birds, the dog and the tinkle of breaking glass drowned out my words. "Thank you, officer. You'll hear from me."

"What is going on there?" P.J. said.

"You wouldn't believe it."

"And you won't believe this," P. J. said.

"Right. Did you find out why the cops are looking for me?"

"They have a warrant for your arrest."

"What?"

"Promise me I get the exclusive interviews."

"Don't be a jerk."

"Well, Tiger, looks like murder."

"Murder? That's not possible."

"To be more precise, two murders."

Twenty-Six

"Two murders?"

"So I'm told."

"Who the hell do they think I murdered?" I held on to the table as the room whirled.

"First, Laura Brown, and second, someone called Chelsea O'Keefe."

"That's just nuts."

"No yelling. I'm not the one with the warrant for your arrest."

"Sorry. I'm a bit shaken up."

"Can I get an interview from you about how it feels to be accused of murdering two women?"

"Come off it, P.J."

"You said if I found out what was going on, you'd give me a story."

"This wasn't the story I had in mind."

"Yeah, but fugitives from the law can't be choosers. Oh, wow, look at that."

"What now?"

"Two of your sisters just pulled up. Man, do they look dangerous."

"How did they find out? Is this on the news or something?"

"Someone on the force must have let your brother-in-law know."

"Is Conn with them?"

"Yeah. Ow. He doesn't look happy."

"I can understand that. Are all the cops still there?"

"Of course."

"Damn."

"So are you going to tell me where you are?"

"Not likely, P. J."

*　　*　　*

Elaine was bubbling when she picked up. Her appointment must have gone well.

"Elaine? Don't talk, and don't get mad. This is an emergency, and I need your help."

"May I at least know how and why?"

"How, yes. Why, no. You're better off not knowing."

"But..."

"The police are involved."

Elaine hates the police. Sometimes that's a bad thing. Sometimes it's a good thing. This time, it worked in my favour.

"Sure," she said.

"I need you to check out my apartment building to see if the police are still staking out the building. Check my floor too. Pretend to be visiting me, maybe. And if the coast is clear, I need you to call me back and tell me."

"The police have your apartment staked out?

"Yes. We might need a slight diversion."

"Consider them diverted."

"And bring those snapshots. I'll find you in the parking lot."

I counted on Elaine taking fifteen minutes, not including diversion. That gave me time to find something to wear in Mrs. Parnell's closet. Mrs. Parnell is about twenty pounds thinner than I am, six inches taller, and forty-five years older. Her feet are size ten, mine are a six. She puts her money into music and hi-tech gadgets instead of duds. Aside from that, no problem.

Eventually, I found the Tilley hat I'd given her for Christmas and a London Fog short trench coat possibly from the sixties. I kept the Ray-Bans. It was kind of fun. I always loved dressing up as a kid. Unfortunately, there wasn't much I could do to hide Gussie, but I figured we could still slip away in whatever confusion Elaine would generate. Just in case, I hit the kitchen, found some flour and sprinkled it on Gussie's coat. I wasn't sure what was more surprising: that Gussie looked like a different dog or that Mrs. Parnell actually had flour.

I was pretty well ready to go when the fire alarm went off.

* * *

Elaine was splendid in a lime-green tailored shirt, with matching capri pants. She had long, green, pointed slingbacks on her feet. Her hair was in some kind of updated French twist. She seemed quite elated, which gave her complexion a nice boost. Alvin would say she rocked.

I held on tightly as she took the corner at 80 kph. Gussie let out a yelp. A couple of tourists jumped for cover.

"Thanks, Elaine. Although you can get charged for pulling a false alarm. There are a lot of seniors in that building. Someone could have panicked and had a heart attack."

"You wanted a diversion, you got a diversion. Stop bitching and tell me what's going on."

"I can't. If I did you'd be aiding and abetting a fugitive."

"Are you a fugitive?"

"If I said yes, then you'd be aiding and abetting a…"

"That can't be good, if you're a lawyer. Can they charge you with avoiding arrest?"

"Yes, if they can prove I knew I was going to be charged."

"So now you're officially on the lam. Not that I'm aware of that." This is the kind of stuff that makes Elaine truly happy. More than, say, a long drive in the country.

"Being on the lam is not the official name of anything in the Criminal Code of Canada."

"You know what I mean."

"I have a pretty good defence for the avoiding part. What with the head injuries and all. Brain damage. My Emerg doctor will back me up."

"Right. A judge should be sympathetic."

"Depends on the judge, considering the seriousness of the allegations."

"Holy moly. What are they?"

"I still have to find out what's going on. Maybe you can follow the news and see what information they've released. In the meantime, I need to get my cash card back. And I have another little task for you. Feel like providing another diversion for me, no fire alarms this time?"

"Diversion is my middle name."

"I'm glad you have that nice outfit on. Head for the City parking garage, the indoor one in the market. We have to leave Gussie in the car for about twenty minutes. It will be cool enough in the underground parking for him."

"Will this be fun?"

"Count on it."

*   *   *

Inside Maisie's, the mood was typical, right down to the miserably elegant Norine, yattering into a small silver cellphone. We'd picked the late afternoon dead zone, too late for lunch and too early for dinner, so I didn't spot any servers buzzing about. Of course, Chelsea was dead and Jasmine was grieving.

"I left my cash card here last night," I said without any preamble.

"You didn't," Norine said.

"I did."

"We haven't found any cash cards."

"Wouldn't you have to look to know that?"

"My staff are all trained to return them." She curled her collagen-enhanced lip.

"And yet, I left here without my card last night. How odd."

"Perhaps you left it elsewhere." The lip curl mutated to a smirk.

"I definitely left it here." I resisted the urge to smack the smirk, since that would be assault and battery.

"You probably left it in an ATM." Her eyes slid away from me.

I knew from my time as a defence lawyer that eyes sliding away means someone's lying her arse off.

I smiled. "I used my card here, and I didn't have it when I left, and you deliberately ignored me when I tried to get it back last night."

"We get so many people here. Some are more memorable than others."

"I'm guessing not that many pound on your door after hours."

"Doesn't ring a bell."

"Rang enough of a bell for you to call the police."

"You'll have to excuse me. I have people to seat." She

nodded in the direction of Elaine, the only person in the restaurant. Elaine was lounging near the door, examining the specials menu intently.

"Dinner for one, madame? Or would you like to see the luncheon menu?" she said.

Elaine rose to her full splendid green height. "I'm just checking the facility for a special occasion."

"Oh?"

Elaine strode over and shook the manager's hand very, very firmly. "I represent a number of influential women's groups in town, and we are looking for the perfect venue for a big ticket fundraising occasion."

"Hang on," I said. "I was here first, and I don't think we have attended to this matter of my card."

"As you know, large groups of women can be pretty hard to please," Elaine said. "It's important to pick the right ambiance."

"Your group will not be disappointed in Maisie's. I guarantee it."

"That's what I've heard. But I need to be sure."

"Excuse me, ladies. But I wasn't finished. And I don't have all day," I said.

"I'd like a look at the regular menu," Elaine said. "This might not be the right place for us after all. You can't be too careful." She managed to convey the impression that she was about to bolt.

Norine flashed me an evil look. "I'm going to ask you to leave."

"And if I don't?"

"I'll call the police."

"Go ahead, since I plan to call them myself. Card theft."

Elaine glanced at her watch. "I'm almost out of time. Would it be possible to talk privately about this?"

"Please leave the premises," Norine managed to hiss in my direction.

"Fine," I said, turning toward the door. "I'll take legal steps."

Elaine was enjoying her role. "May I see the rest of the dining areas? We are seeking an intimate yet effective atmosphere, and it will be important to have good sound. How are your acoustics?"

"They're excellent."

"I understand you have a courtyard as well? Could we have an outdoor event if the weather holds?"

"Yes, we'll head over there now, shall we?" Norine glanced in my direction, and I flipped her the bird as I passed through the door.

Seconds after Elaine and Norine turned the corner, I ducked back in, slipped behind the desk and grabbed the reservation book. I wouldn't have more than a couple of minutes to find Bianca.

Luck was with me.

There was at least one Bianca who came to Maisie's often. For lunch and dinner. I found a phone number with the familiar Federal Government 9. I copied down the number quickly and rustled through the pile of papers, business cards, credit card slips etc.

I lifted the VISA machine.

Bingo. My cash card.

Finding the card was the good news. The bad news was the flash of roof lights I spotted through the window. There was no way to make eye contact with Elaine. The front door opened just as I slipped into the cloakroom and pressed myself against the wall. If the cops stopped to check, I would have been toast, since there weren't any coats.

I spotted the uniforms heading by and heard an unfamiliar female voice say, "Police." Looked like Norine had managed to call the cops after all. Elaine must have been losing her touch, if she'd let that happen.

I peered around the corner in time to see two female officers heading toward the far end of the restaurant. I moved as fast as my head would let me, out of the cloakroom and through the door. I'm surprised they didn't hear my heart pounding.

Another cruiser was edging traffic out of the way and heading up Dalhousie with two wheels on the sidewalk and two wheels on the road. And I saw what look like the red flash of more roof lights speeding along Clarence.

Sheesh. Bonnie and Clyde probably didn't get that much attention.

Twenty-Seven

In retrospect, I should have taken my chance with the cops. However, my first stop was an ATM, where I scored two hundred dollars. I didn't know how long I'd be away from home. Second stop, a souvenir store in the Market, where I bought a white baseball cap with a vaguely neon maple leaf. I selected a red T-shirt with the purple outline of a large tulip. Inside the tulip, it read OTTAWA. I couldn't believe my good fortune when I found a large backpack decorated with a Mountie on horseback. I added a small Canada flag and a disposable camera. I finished off my new look with a pair of cheap sunglasses with red lenses. A quick trip to the nearby McDonald's to change in a bathroom cubicle and, poof, the old Camilla was gone. I put my own backpack inside the new one along with Mrs. Parnell's hat and coat and my Ray-Bans. I headed back into the Market crowds, proud of myself for not losing consciousness. In addition to a disguise, I now had enough change to make phone calls.

It took everything I had not to wobble as I passed a constable leaning against a parked Ottawa police cruiser outside. My father always used to say, the best defence is a good offence. I grinned and waved my flag at him. "Hey, you one of them Mounties?"

"Sure am, ma'am," he lied.

I said, "Cool," and moseyed off, like any dumbass tourist without a double-decker warrant out for her arrest.

Five minutes later, I was in the parking lot, looking for Gussie.

I staggered around, confused by my fuzzy head but also by the large number of black Pathfinders parked in the garage. I had no idea what Elaine's license number was. The only thing I knew about the Pathfinder was that it was dusty and had a large dog in it.

Faced with a couple of Pathfinders in close proximity, I yelled "Gussie." A shaggy head popped up two Pathfinders down. Good. Now to get into the vehicle.

Elaine misplaced her keys an average of once a week, and she's always in a hurry. There had to be an emergency magnetic keyholder somewhere on the vehicle. They'd be in a place she could reach without getting her clothes dirty before whatever meeting she was late for.

I didn't have to test this theory, because Elaine hadn't locked the door. I hopped in and scrawled a note for her using an eyeliner I found on the floor by the accelerator and the back of a napkin which had been wedged between the seats. Elaine had lots of useful stuff in her vehicle.

Gussie was happy to see me and happier to get out of the Pathfinder. I figured the inside would air out in time. I hoped large lopsided smelly dog wasn't part of my police description.

Fortunately, you can find a pay phone without walking too far in the market. Youssef picked up first ring. Unfortunately, he wasn't on duty, but his cousin Akbar could take me, unless I had some objection. Did Akbar have an objection to dogs in the cab, I inquired.

"Is your dog smelly?" Youssef said.

217

"Not in the least." Of course, as the famous line went, he was not my dog.

My head and various body parts had begun to throb, ache and otherwise misbehave. My painkillers were inconveniently located in my apartment, surrounded by police. I used the waiting time to think. I needed a place with a phone, a radio and a vial of Tylenol 3. The sky was not the limit.

Home was out of the question. Mrs. Parnell's place was too close for comfort. So was Elaine's place. By now, the police would have spoken to her. She would be in the position of harbouring a known fugitive if she did anything for me. Extended sick leave notwithstanding, Mombourquette would have to nab me if he was within arresting distance.

On the upside, two of my sisters had arrived back from the cottage, that meant one of them had probably stayed at the cottage. History told me they'd stay in town for dinner at one house or the other. They'd expect me to take the honourable road, turn myself over to the police and let justice take its course. It wouldn't cross their respectable minds a MacPhee could be convicted of anything. But I knew the system. I'd be heaved into a cell until things got sorted out. If P. J. was right, and the warrant was for two murders, the Crown would oppose bail, and any judge I'd pissed off in the past would concur with pleasure. Maybe any judge, period. There were lingering resentments toward me in the Office of the Crown Prosecutor as well as within the police, so they'd all have fun.

But they'd have to find me first.

If I could figure out which sister had stayed at the cottage, I could hide out at her place. Or I could turn to P. J. He might take the risk to help me in return for an exclusive "lawyer on the run" story, but he wasn't answering his phone. Anyway, I had reason to believe he'd recently moved back into his old bedroom at his mom's place.

I needed to sleep for a couple of hours, just long enough to be able to think clearly. But my goal wasn't to remain on the run. My goal was to learn who Laura had really been. I had to ferret out who had killed her and Chelsea. And likely Frances Foxall and Sylvie Dumais. The same person had done an excellent job of framing me. I was awfully glad the police hadn't made the connection between Frances and Sylvie and the other two deaths. I might be on the hook for four murders. Before they did, I needed to track down this Bianca and also to find Jasmine and talk to her, for her own safety as much as anything. Hell, I needed a telephone even more than I needed a bed.

Hotels ask for a credit card before you check in, and I figured the police would have them covered. I was missing something, but what?

It took me long enough to remember I had the keys to Laura's home. The will hadn't been through probate yet, but it would be my property. There was a phone, Tylenol in the bathroom cabinet, and a good bed.

Youssef's cousin, Akbar, when he arrived, was not happy about Gussie.

"Too big," he said. "Not in my cab."

"It's Youssef's cab, and he said it was all right." I opened the door and pushed Gussie in ahead of me. I practically fell in after him and slammed the door closed. "The Glebe please. Third Avenue."

He opened his mouth.

"Don't argue. I'm sick. It's only a ten minute drive. Go. Otherwise you'll have to throw us out."

He took a minute to assess that option. When he finally edged back into the packed traffic in the Market, we passed several cruisers.

"This is hijacking. I could call the police," he said.

"Go right ahead. I'm a lawyer. I love to sue."

"What number Third," he said after a pause.

"I'll know it when I see it."

We cruised down the blocks slowly. My head was full of twinkling sparks, my eyes were swimming. Laura's beautiful little house slowly hove into view. I squinted around. Across the street was a black car with a little red light on top, the telltale sign of the police undercover vehicle.

"Looks like my friend is not home. Head over to Hull."

"Hull? Look, lady, another five minutes with that dog in the car, and I'll be dead. You can sue my widow."

"Point taken. Time to clear the air." I reached into the front and gently dropped forty dollars onto the passenger seat. I didn't mention that the last person I'd bribed was lying in the morgue.

*   *   *

Akbar let me off two blocks from my destination, which suited both of us. Lucky for me, since Alvin locks his doors, he now lives in the basement apartment of a converted house in the old part of Hull. Lucky for me, it has rickety old windows. Gussie and I managed to squeeze in the first window and drop to the floor. Of course, there were good reasons why Alvin's place hadn't been on my list of desirable hideouts. It's always best to brace yourself before you cross his threshhold or fall through his window.

I landed with a thump that gave me a few more stars. Gussie yelped as he followed. I yelped myself when I heard a voice. "Lord thundering Jesus, it's Camilla. What kind of an outfit is that? Canadian Crazy?"

Someone else said, "Very patriotic, Ms. MacPhee."

I lay on the floor and lost consciousness briefly at that point.

I swam back to the sound of Mrs. Parnell saying, "We'll have to get her to the hospital."

"No hospital." I kept my eyes closed.

"Afraid you are *hors de combat*, Ms. MacPhee."

"I'm okay. I think if I can just have a cup of tea." Like most Cape Bretoners, I understand the healing properties of tea, hot and dark, even at the end of summer after a rough day when you are lying on the floor.

"Tea? Splendid," Mrs. Parnell leaned over her walker to look down at me.

I forced my eyes open a bit and regretted it. If the unrelenting blue of the ceiling and walls was supposed to be soothing, it didn't do the trick. Neither did the medieval chant blasting from invisible speakers. Lying on the floor should have helped me feel grounded, but there actually didn't appear to be a floor.

"What is this stuff?" I brushed at the white, fluffy substance surrounding my head and reaching past Alvin's and Mrs. Parnell's ankles. I might also have asked what the harp was doing in the corner.

"Tea coming right up," Alvin said, speeding his bony form toward a door. The door was blue, it should go without saying. His pony tail flicked as he disappeared into the blueness.

"I get it. Don't you think your new landlord will object to having the entire floor covered with cotton batting?" I managed to sit up in the hope that it would feel better. It didn't.

"Glimpse of the future, Ms. MacPhee. Depending on your track record." Mrs. Parnell jammed a Benson & Hedges into her ebony cigarette holder and flicked her silver lighter.

"My track record's just fine, well, at least it used to be. Do you think you should be smoking so close to this flammable material? Keep in mind we are in a badly maintained wooden building in an older part of town with narrow streets."

Alvin emerged from somewhere blue and approached with his grandmother's flowered teapot, two cups and a crystal sherry glass on a tray. "Orange pekoe okay with you, Camilla?"

"The only choice. Look. All this pretense at normality is charming, but there's nowhere to sit."

Of course, once the white stools and table were pointed out to me, I could see them clearly enough, just above the wispy top of the cotton batting clouds.

Alvin bent over the tea service in a way that would have made his grandmother proud.

"Turn off that music, will you, Alvin? It's giving me the creeps."

"But it's *Carmina Burana*," Mrs. Parnell said, shocked.

A trick of the light seemed to ring Alvin and Mrs. Parnell in a special golden glow. Or maybe that was a new symptom.

"What do you think of Young Ferguson's new decor?"

"Unbelieveable." No need to lie here.

Alvin said, "Aw."

"God-given talent," Mrs. Parnell said.

"Hmm. Thanks for the tea, Alvin. Sorry I was late for all the launches. I can't do the next one either. It's a long story."

"No need to worry. We know what a terrible time you've been through."

"You do?"

"Of course. We heard it on the radio."

"Damn. You heard the police were looking for me? It's better if you don't know."

Mrs. Parnell said, "I don't believe we know."

Alvin said. "Know what? Come on, Camilla. Do you think we could let you down?"

"If the cops find out you hid me, you might be able to convince them you did it innocently, but you'll spend time at the station first."

"But where would you go?" Alvin said. "There's a Canada-wide warrant out for you. Not that we know that."

"All for one and one for all," Mrs. Parnell said, pouring her sherry. "We apologize abjectly for putting you under pressure to be at the launches."

I said. "I can't expect you to take chances."

"We are more than fair-weather friends," Mrs. Parnell said. "Something's afoot, and we will assist you to get to the bottom of it."

"Anyway, since when do you mind us taking chances?" Alvin said.

"Okay. You'll be more useful if I can call you when I need you. If I could count on that, it would be great. You won't be any good to anyone if you get arrested."

"She might have a point," Alvin said. "I really hate jail."

"It's nearly five. So head off to your launch and…"

"But…" Alvin said.

"Out of the question," Mrs. Parnell said.

"I'll use the time to make some phone calls. My cellphone was stolen. Did I mention that? I need to track down some people. I also need to get a bit of sleep. I'll figure out where to go next, and I'll keep you in the loop. That way if the police do find me, they won't also find you. Remember, I broke in here."

They looked at each other.

I said. "The sooner you skedaddle, the sooner I get to sleep."

I didn't like the way they hesitated.

"If you want to do the right thing, do what I ask. We'll all be better off. Especially me."

"At least take this," Mrs. Parnell said, handing me her cellphone. "That way you don't have to worry if they bug our land lines. We'll use Young Ferguson's cell."

I was about to say, I didn't think they'd be bugging the phones, since that requires a special warrant. But stranger things were happening.

"Thanks." Mrs. Parnell's phone was state of the art, video included and all. I wasn't surprised.

"Two other things," I said. "When you go home, Mrs. P., things are in a bit of a state. Lester and Pierre broke out."

She chuckled. "I wondered if they might outfox you, the scamps."

So that wasn't too bad. "And I borrowed some of your clothes."

"Glad to be of assistance, Ms. MacPhee. Young Ferguson and I felt we'd let you down. We mustn't get too caught up in our own selfish interests."

"And if it's all right, I might leave Gussie here. He limits my options. And he needs someone to walk and feed him. I'm sure your landlord won't find out, Alvin."

I was proud that I never mentioned the fact that Gussie is actually a Ferguson dog and by rights should have been Alvin's responsibility rather than mine, landlord or no landlord. Considering all the talk of friendship, all for one and one for all, comrades to the end.

"Someone needs to feed your cat, too, Mrs. P."

In the end, I thought they'd never leave.

Twenty-Eight

First things first. Turn off the music. Stop head throbbing. Find Alvin's phone. I didn't want to waste the charge on Mrs. Parnell's. I looked around. Knowing Alvin, the phone would be blue or white to disappear into the decor. Eventually I found a white phone buried in the cotton clouds.

I fished the scrap of paper with Bianca's government number out of my pocket. "You have reached the voice mail of Bianca Celestri. Please leave a message after the beep. *Merci. Bonjour…*" The message was repeated in French as per policy.

I put down the phone and copied down Celestri. So far, so good. Maybe things were looking up.

Jasmine was next. Maybe she knew who Chelsea was supposed to meet.

"Leave me alone," she screamed as soon as I identified myself. "I'm calling the police."

"Why? What good will that do? I didn't hurt anyone. I just need some information from you," I said to the dial tone.

Fine.

I crawled around Alvin's apartment looking for a telephone book. Five minutes later, I found one, covered in blue. I had to ask myself, if Alvin had time to do this, why the hell couldn't he update the goddam mailing lists at Justice for Victims?

There was one Celestri, B. I copied down the street address. It took a while, because my head was spinning, but so far, so good. Next, I needed to check my home messages, in case P. J. had called with something useful. But the spinning head was causing my stomach to turn. I closed my eyes. Sleep might be the answer. Just a little sleep. Right after that, I'd check my messages and pay a surprise visit to Bianca whoosit. I flopped on Alvin's blue and white cloud patterned bedspread and slept long and hard.

I was awakened by nudges and wet kisses. I opened one eye. Gussie was giving me the universal dog symbol for needing a walk. Even if he hadn't been licking my face, a quick sniff of the air would have told me the same thing.

"You've had your last doughnut, buddy," I said. "Before we go, let me check my messages. Maybe the coast is clear, and we can go home, and you can chase the cat."

Gussie regarded me with his head on his paws as I checked the messages. He looked sort of cute, lying on the low cloud cover.

*   *   *

The messages were not so cute. I had seven from my sisters. I deleted them as fast as I could. Plus there were a couple of old ones from Mrs. Parnell and Alvin. P. J. had called, asking me to call him ASAP. Even Mombourquette had left a message. The only surprise call was one from my favourite old client, Bunny Mayhew, wishing me luck. Bless his criminous little heart.

"Wow, Camilla, this is Bunny, saying hi. That is serious stuff you got going down. If I can help you out anyways, let me know, eh. Tonya sends her best wishes. Oh yeah, my phone's the same first three numbers as yours and then, you're really going to laugh, L-I-F-T. Is that cool or what? Tonya thinks I should find a new word now, because I'm going straight, but, it's like a good memento."

There you go, I thought, sentiment takes many different forms.

The last message was from Elaine.

"Listen closely, Camilla. I don't know how to reach you, but this is my one call, so I hope you get it. I have been arrested. If you get this message, can you call Nina Pfeffer. She's the lawyer for WAVE. Her home number is in the book. I would have called her but, as I said, I just get the one call. They keep asking me where you went and what your plans are. I guess it's a good thing I don't know the answers. Excuse me? What do you mean my time's up? My time is not up. Holy moly, I'm just leaving a message for my lawyer. I am not hogging the line. What? Hey…"

Oh, shit.

I looked up Nina Pfeffer in the phone book.

Of course, she wasn't home, it being the Labour Day Weekend and all, but I gamely left a message anyway.

There were a couple of hang-ups just to keep me guessing.

*   *   *

I located my backpack with the supply of plastic bags, dropped the cellphone into it, slapped on the tourist disguise and took Gussie for the overdue walk. There's a strip of parkland in the old section of Hull not too far from Alvin's place. I figured the walk might help settle my head and give me some idea of what to do for Elaine. If anyone could piss off the police and the Crown and get a couple of extra charges laid against her, and maybe me, it would be Elaine.

I had a feeling her family was in Florida, so that wasn't the answer. I didn't even know her mother's new last name. I wasn't sure Elaine did either. I didn't know if her brother, Eddy, still lived in Canada.

I stumbled along after Gussie, thinking my way through the fog. Gussie delivered big-time and efficiently. I guess that was good. I desperately needed to get back to Alvin's apartment.

As we turned the corner, I saw the one thing I didn't want to. Rooflights flashing. City of Gatineau police, rather than Ottawa. But then, that's the thing about a Canada-wide warrant. Everybody gets in on the fun.

Gussie and I turned down the first alley and got as far away as we could. To add to my crimes, I ditched the plastic bag in a nearby dumpster.

Five minutes later, we were blending in with the tourists at the Museum of Civilization. I got Youssef on the phone and asked to be picked up.

"Akbar wasn't all that happy about you," Youssef said.

"What is this, a popularity contest? I suppose he didn't mention the tip. Fine, I'll call someone else."

"Nothing to worry about. Akbar's a bit touchy, but he's off duty now. Now, it's my cousin Faroud."

"Thanks."

He hadn't asked about the dog. Good.

In the five minutes it took Faroud to show up, I had figured out where I was going next. If the cops had arrested Elaine at Maisie's, then the Pathfinder was probably still in the parking lot. I was banking on finding the spare keys.

My nagging worry was, how did the police know to look at Alvin's place? Had one of my family members squealed? I found that hard to believe. Had the police interviewed Alvin and Mrs. P. and broken through their defenses? Maybe Elaine had fingered them; there's often a bit of tension there. I discounted that idea. Elaine would have her fingernails pulled out before she'd give the police any useful information. General principles.

Faroud, when he showed up, didn't blink at Gussie. He had the Holly Cole CD playing. That meant no pesky radio bulletins to give him ideas. It was a short drive back to the market. I was still fishing around in the backpack for my cash when we got there.

"Not that it's my business, miss," he said, "but you should do something about that dog's diet."

"Really? You a vet?"

He didn't like that. I saw him narrow his eyes at me through the rear view mirror. "No, I am not a veterinarian, but I do have a functioning nose."

"Sorry. You're right. It's a problem."

I removed my red sunglasses and kept digging for money. It was a bit hard to locate specific items with all those multiple images. Eventually, I fished out a ten-dollar bill and thrust it at him.

"You need a receipt?" he said.

"No, and keep the change." I said. The sooner I got out of the cab and into the Pathfinder, the better.

He turned around and looked straight at me. "Are you all right?"

"Of course, I'm all right," I said, with remarkable dignity for a person dressed as Captain Canada with the world's stinkiest dog as sidekick.

"One of your pupils is quite dilated. I think you should seek medical attention. Would you like me to drive you to a hospital?"

"You a doctor?"

"Yes, in fact, I am. Maybe not in this country, but with

eight years of training and solid post-grad work too. Good idea to listen to me."

"Thanks. I'll go to the walk-in clinic."

"No. Go straight to Emergency. You probably need a CAT scan. I'll take you if you want. On the house."

"Used to be everyone was a comedian. Now everyone's a doctor."

That didn't go down well. "Perhaps you should show a bit of respect," he said with a flash of anger in his dark eyes.

"With all due respect, I think you should mind your own business."

Okay, so that was rude of me, and the guy was just being a compassionate and competent human being, but hospitals are always crawling with cops, and they'd be on the lookout.

I felt Faroud's black eyes on me as I rounded the corner. I looked back to see if he could see me head into the parking garage. But it looked like the coast was clear.

* * *

What is it about these garages? They're so disorienting. Even without a concussion, how does anyone find their car, figure how to pay the parking and then work their way out of the maze? To make matters worse, the evening light was starting to dim.

Eventually, I spotted the Pathfinder. Dusty as ever. I made a couple of guesses where the spare keys might be. No luck under the driver's door. No luck on the underside of the front bumper. When I tried the rear bumper, I hit the jackpot. That Elaine. Good thing she had insurance.

The next challenge was using the automated payment system to get my exit ticket. Elaine had left the ticket in the Pathfinder, which you're not supposed to do. I blessed her.

Just to be safe, I bent down to the garage floor surface and picked up enough grit and dirt to smear the license plates. Not to be obvious, just enough to obscure the numbers. Paranoia, a person could get used to it.

For a few minutes, I sat in the Pathfinder and tried to concentrate, and to see without all the extra images. I used the time to call Mombourquette. Why should he miss out on all the fun?

"Lennie! I hope I didn't call you in from the garden, but…"

"This is a dangerous game you're playing. Have you lost your mind, Camilla?"

"Why are you yelling? I thought we were buddies now."

"There's a Canada-wide warrant for your arrest, and everyone is worried sick. Your sisters had to take Valium."

"Really? That's probably good for them."

"Can you be serious? They're afraid the shock will kill your father."

That was hitting below the belt. "You tell them, Lennie, to make damn sure he doesn't find out. He's eighty-one years old, and quite deaf, and if they have half a brain in total, they'll leave him at the cottage with a keeper but no radio."

"I think that's what happened. They're afraid he'll find out somehow."

"Maybe they should give him credit for not believing this crap."

"That you're wanted in the killings of Laura Brown and Chelsea O'Keefe?"

"My father will not believe that."

"I hope you're right."

"Do my sisters believe it? Do you believe it?"

"Of course, they don't. And I don't either."

"Well then."

"They're out combing the hospital emergency rooms and looking in ditches in case you have died of your head injury."

"I'm not in the hospital, and I'm not in a ditch, and I didn't kill anyone. How's that for cheerful news?"

I must have been yelling, because the woman getting into the next car jumped. That was all I needed, alarmed witnesses who might tune into the news as soon as they got into their vehicles. I rolled down the window. "Sorry to startle you," I said. "Bad reception in here. Yelling doesn't help." I shook the cellphone.

She slammed her door. All four of her lock buttons went down.

Mombourquette said something.

"What, Leonard? Sorry, I missed that."

"Running away adds to the offense. No one who knows you would believe you killed anyone."

"Maybe someone at the Office of the Crown Prosecutor."

"Even there, they're just going on the current evidence, and I guess it's pretty compelling. But that will get sorted out. Isn't that what you've been telling me? That I'll be vindicated? Now I'm telling you the same thing."

"Compelling evidence? How can it be compelling, if I didn't do it?"

"Apparently, they have witnesses and tips. Conn is working to find out."

"What witnesses? Besides the bartender, there are others? Who?"

"If I did know, I wouldn't tell you, because you'd be on their doorsteps five minutes later, and then you'd get harassment and threatening a witness added to the charges…"

"Look here, Lennie…"

"And, the big thing is, they found Laura Brown's car in the parking lot behind the Department of Justice."

"That's great."

"It's not great. They found your jacket in it."

"They couldn't have."

"Jean jacket with butterflies. Something you were seen to be wearing after Laura died. Which would mean you had her car."

"Someone planted it."

"Of course. When these charges are found to be false, you'll still have to deal with the fleeing arrest."

"Well, how can I flee if I don't know there's a warrant for me?"

"It's all over the media, for God's sake."

"I'm out and about, and I just haven't heard it."

"You just heard it from me."

"You're such a kidder, Lennie, who could believe such a crazy story?"

"Right. They'll laugh you out of bail court. Get a better story."

"Which reminds me, that's why I called. Elaine is being held. She wanted me to call the WAVE lawyer. I couldn't reach her. She could end up spending the night behind bars, because no one knows she's there."

"If you're asking what I think, I'd rather stick pins in my eyes."

"That's too bad, because she thinks the world of you."

"This is just a diversionary tactic on your part, Camilla. I hope you realize that I can see right through it."

"I don't know what you're talking about." In truth, I didn't.

"Tell you what. If I see what can be done to get this woman legal counsel, will you refrain from doing any more stupid things?"

"Sure."

I didn't see anything stupid about finding Bianca Celestri.

Twenty-Nine

The conversation with Mombourquette gave me an adrenaline boost. I felt much better as I eased the Pathfinder out of the parking spot. I adjusted the rearview mirror. How did Elaine ever see out at that angle? In the mirror, I noticed a woman waving her arms and running after me.

Her hair was in disarray, and she appeared to be screaming. She banged on the rear window of the Pathfinder. My job is helping others, and I was not without sympathy for someone with obvious mental problems. But as a fleeing suspected felon, I couldn't do anything for her.

I accelerated away to the exit, slipped my paid ticket in the machine and turned from the garage into the heavy weekend traffic on William Street. Ten feet from the garage exit, a uniform with a cup of Tim Hortons in his hand was walking towards an idling cruiser. He didn't see me, because he was engaged in a lively discussion with a pair of working girls. I figured he'd take care of the deranged woman when he spotted her. That shouldn't take long, because she was running out the exit toward him at that moment.

I rounded the corner and slipped into the flow towards King Edward. I heard sirens in the distance. I turned on the CBC half hour news to see if there were any developments on the me front.

"Police have issued a Canada-wide warrant for Ottawa lawyer Camilla MacPhee in connection with two recent murders. MacPhee is wanted for questioning in connection with the deaths of forty-eight-year-old Laura Lynette Brown and twenty-six-year-old Chelsea O'Keefe. MacPhee is no stranger to the police and was involved at the scene of a fatal shootout during the recent Bluesfest.

"Further charges against MacPhee are expected shortly. She is described as mid-thirties, dark-haired and stocky, and is considered dangerous."

I was so stunned I had to pull the Pathfinder off the road and park until I caught my breath. I didn't know what was worse, stocky or dangerous.

I hoped that Bianca Celestri hadn't been listening.

*   *   *

Bianca lived in a tasteful condo development across the street from the gated grounds of Rideau Hall, the Governor General's residence. To add to the tone, unless I missed my guess, a former Prime Minister resided just down the street.

Cars lined the street, and parking was obviously hard to find. Just as I arrived, a silver Neon pulled out, and I slid the much larger Pathfinder into the spot. I may have bumped the car behind me, I wasn't sure. Give me a small car any time.

The Pathfinder seemed to have heated up again, and I didn't want to take a chance on leaving Gussie. When I rang the buzzer at number two, I told him to be quiet. One good thing, if you were in the entryway at this particular unit, you weren't visible from any of the windows. There were attractive planters filled with large shrubs. It was dark enough that no one could really see you unless they were walking right by. It had the added advantages of being cool and sheltered. I mentioned this to Gussie. He stretched out and laid his head on his paws. He looked at me with big, sad eyes.

"Don't you start," I said. "I have professional guilt inducers in my life, and they're way out of your league."

Bianca Celestri had a shiny black door. I rang the buzzer.

"I'll ask her to give you a bowl of water. Stop with the dramatics."

I stabbed at the door again. No answer. I didn't want to think she might have been away for the weekend. I preferred to believe she was implicated in Laura's death, or she was scared shitless.

Gussie sighed. Pointedly.

I leaned against the peephole to see if someone was peeking out at me. The door swung open with my weight, and I fell forward. I landed on my bruised knees on the marble floor of the entranceway.

"Hello. Your door's open. Hello?" Okay. It sounded crazy, even to my ears.

This time I yelled, "Bianca, I need to speak to you."

It crossed my mind that Bianca might not live alone, and I could encounter some gentleman friend who didn't like strangers falling through the door. But no one appeared. I got to my feet and brushed off my knees. Gussie looked up at me with hope.

When you're wanted for two murders and implicated in two others, why worry about getting the dog a bowl of water? The words "unlawful entering" came to mind, but that seemed like small potatoes.

The tiny but snazzy kitchen was visible from the entrance. I found a lovely blue bowl in a cupboard and filled it for Gussie.

This reminded me to go to the bathroom. When you're on the run, you take opportunities where you find them.

My sisters would have approved of the fashionable powder room. Tuscan colours, nifty sconces, soap from L'Occitane. I was the only discordant element. I stared at myself in the mirror. Scary.

I whipped off the maple leaf baseball cap. That helped, but not much. There I was, in all my dark and stocky glory, with raccoon eyes, looking thoroughly dangerous. And as cool and comfortable as Bianca's house was, I didn't have any business being in it.

"Time to head out," I said to Gussie.

I thought I heard him moan. What the hell had he eaten now? The blue bowl? But Gussie had already dozed off on the cool marble entryway floor.

I heard the moan again. I closed my eyes and listened. It seemed to come from the stairs leading to the lower level.

"Be prepared to get the hell out of here," I said to Gussie.

Stairs had been a problem for me. Was this another trap? Was someone lurking? I figured if anyone tried to sneak up on me, Gussie would bark. Of course, I was dizzy enough to fall without any assistance.

I crept halfway down, keeping my back to the wall, and peered into the dim room. At the foot of the stairs was a crumpled mass. I didn't have to look closely to know it was a woman, dark hair spread around her, one sandal on, the other still on the staircase. This was a fine time to realize I'd left Mrs. Parnell's cellphone in the Pathfinder. I glanced over my shoulder, then scrambled down, gripping the banister.

I knelt beside her. A raw wound gaped on the back of her head. I couldn't see her face, but blood had seeped out around her. She moaned softly again. She was alive, with a weak pulse.

"Bianca. I'm calling 911. They won't take long. You'll be okay."

I pushed the hair from her face. I'm not sure why. But even before that, I knew she was the woman I'd seen lunching with Laura.

The main thing was to call for an ambulance. "Hang in there," I said. I staggered up the stairs and reached for the portable phone I'd seen in the kitchen. I gave the particulars to the 911 operator.

"Who's calling?" she asked.

"A neighbour," I said. "I just came in because her door had been open for a while. I heard moaning, and I found her at the bottom of the stairs. Hurry."

"They're on their way. Stay calm and tell me what happened."

"I don't know. She has a head wound. Should I do something?"

"Don't move her. The paramedics will be there soon."

"Okay." I heard the quaver in my voice. I kept the phone in my hand and wobbled down the stairs again. I put my hand on her back.

"Bianca," I said. "It's going to be all right."

Nothing.

"The paramedics are on their way. They will take care of you. You're going to make it."

"Ma'am?" the dispatcher said.

"Yes?"

"Is she still breathing?"

"Yes, but she keeps making a gurgling sound. What should I do?"

"Just keep calm, ma'am. Help is on its way."

"Please tell me what I can do, because…" I stopped talking, because I heard sirens outside. Then steps in the hallway upstairs and loud barking from Gussie.

"Down here," I yelled. "Hurry."

Two firefighters in rescue gear thundered down the stairs. I knew the fire department and the police often get to a scene before the paramedics.

"What happened?" the first firefighter said.

I said. "I found her here. The front door was open."

"She fell?"

"I think someone attacked her."

I started up the steps, nearly colliding with a couple of police officers. Gussie had decided to block their way.

I grabbed his collar. "Sorry, officers. Can you take a look around? Bianca has a serious wound on the back of her head."

"Who are you?" The first constable had his notebook out. He turned as the paramedics trooped through the door.

"Downstairs. Quick," I said.

"Wait a minute," one of the paramedics said, "don't I know you?"

I put my hand over my mouth. "All that blood, I think I'm going to be sick."

There was a lot of confusion in the entryway. Gussie and I took advantage of it. We slipped out the door and into the Pathfinder in seconds. In hindsight, I should have wiped my fingerprints off the door, the phone, the banister and the bowl Gussie drank from. But I was new at being a fugitive.

*   *   *

Drive first, think later. I hadn't been blocked by the emergency vehicles, so I left without too much trouble, considering my head was swimming. I drove in a random pattern through the neighbourhood streets trying to stay off the main roads, until

I had a plan. At least the cops didn't know what I was wearing, and it might take them a while to connect the attack on Bianca with me. After about ten minutes, I pulled over on a tree-lined street and leaned back. I turned on the radio and caught the nine-thirty news. Might as well know the worst.

According to the announcer, the latest development in my flight from the authorities was shocking: "Police have released video footage of fugitive lawyer Camilla MacPhee following a daring daylight theft of an SUV from a downtown parking garage. Surveillance cameras show MacPhee accompanied by a large mixed-breed dog, believed to be vicious. MacPhee is wearing a Canada baseball cap, T-shirt and large red sunglasses. She is considered dangerous. A reward has been posted for information leading to her arrest."

The story was completed by the owner of the stolen vehicle. "I was terrified. The woman drove like a maniac. She had some kind of a wolf with her. I was lucky to escape with my life."

I argued back. "What are you talking about? You chased me."

Gussie whimpered. "Sorry, Gussie, I got you into this mess with me. So you're going to have to forgive me for what I have to do next."

But the radio wasn't finished. Not by a long shot.

"MacPhee's family and friends are appealing to her to turn herself in."

"Camilla, you get yourself to the nearest police station on the double before there's any more trouble. Do you hear me, Missy?"

Ah, Edwina. In four star general mode.

"Camilla? Please turn yourself in. The police will help get to the bottom of what is going on. Whatever it is."

Sure, Alexa. You can trust the police. You're sleeping with them.

"Ms. MacPhee. I am confident you will do the right thing. And whatever happens, Young Ferguson and I will be at your side."

"Lord thundering Jesus, Camilla. You know we're here for you."

Thanks, guys. Keep up the pretense.

Thirty

I took a minute to ponder the new state of affairs. Laura's murderer was in high gear, and the police were squandering their resources chasing me instead of the real killer. I might have had a concussion or even two, and I was definitely in deep shit, but, even so, I still had the best chance of getting to the bottom of things.

I thought back to the news broadcast. As usual, Mrs. Parnell had been speaking in her own sort of code. All those World War II habits of enigmatic speech were paying off. Her message told me I could count on her, no matter what. And Alvin too, apparently.

But I had a few pressing problems. Number one, finding a way not to look like the lunatic in the news clips. Since my regular description had also been released, being me was not an option. Shopping was out of the question, so was going home to change, or turning up at the homes of any of my friends.

As my father used to say, when the going gets tricky, the tough get trickier. Something like that. He had many sayings that cropped up at tough moments. Some were more useful than others.

I looked around my pilfered Pathfinder. Unfortunately, it didn't contain a complete set of clothing in my size. I spotted a pair of jeans in size sixteen on the backseat. The glove compartment and the cargo space revealed nothing useful, unless I was going to go out disguised as someone's discarded McDonald's lunch.

Under the seat, I found a blue and white flowered silk scarf. I slid out of my shorts and into the jeans. They hung loosely, but so what? I rolled the hems. I turned my T-shirt inside out so the tulip disappeared. I popped the red lenses out of the cheap sunglasses, leaving the black frames. The scarf made a lovely hijab, hiding my hair. The "glasses" gave me a studious look and blended with the raccoon eyes.

I could pass for a graduate student at one of the universities until I came up with something better. I hopped out of the Pathfinder and checked the license plate. Still nicely obscured.

I was feeling quite proud of myself as I headed back to Sandy Hill and Mombourquette's little house. I parked a block away and hustled Gussie along the street to the small gated garden.

I opened the side gate, pushed Gussie in and told him not to eat the beautiful plants. I did my best to look like a grad student and not a fleeing felon as I got the hell out of there.

A couple of miles later, I left him a phone message.

"Leonard, no matter how you are feeling about me, Gussie is an innocent bystander. Please don't let him into your garbage or painting supplies. Absolutely No Doughnuts. Thanks. I'll make it up to you."

*   *   *

Hearing two of my sisters on the nine-thirty news had told me something useful. The third one, Donalda, must have stayed with my father at the cottage. If she'd come into town, I'd have heard her comments too. That meant her house was fair game.

Donalda lived in Alta Vista, much more convenient than Edwina's and Alexa's Nepean homes.

I ditched the Pathfinder in a strip mall on Heron and hobbled onto the bus to Alta Vista. No one gave me a second look. I loved that hijab.

I staggered along to my sister's large bungalow from a strip of green space at the back, feeling worse by the minute. I slid off the scarf and tucked it in the jeans pocket. I wasn't worried about getting in. I know all my sisters' key codes. But at Donalda's, a new keypad had been installed on the back door. The old code didn't work. What word would Donalda choose? I tried MACP but no. Then the first four letters of each of their names. No luck. Donalda's toy poodle. Birthdays. Nope.

I thought hard. My brother-in-law lives to fish. I tried FISH. But then again, Donalda detests fishing. What the hell, I tried fish backwards. HSIF.

I was in.

Donalda's neighbours would know she was at the cottage. If I switched on any lights, the neighbours would spot them. And unless they were comatose, they would know I was on the run. I decided not to give them something to think about.

I headed to my brother-in-law's little kingdom in the basement. It's dark and cavelike, with every comfort you can think of. A great place, if you don't mind mounted pike on the walls. A 54-inch television dominated the only wall without fish. The cave included a microwave, sink, bar fridge, coffee maker, the world's most comfortable sofa and a full bathroom. The basement was cool. Because it's in Donalda's house, everything was spotless.

Unlike me. I was filthy. I felt like a human garbage can. I was sticky and reeked of sweat and dog. I was also exhausted and ravenous.

Unfortunately, I was too dirty to touch food, too hungry to sleep, too wobbly to shower but groggy enough to drown in the tub. Plus I was too addled to figure out a solution to this set of problems.

I sat on the sofa to think and dozed off immediately. When I jerked myself awake, I was still dirty and hungry. I located a source of Tylenol 3 in Donalda's bathroom. I gobbled a bag of potato chips, and I ran the water in the tub. A bath would help get the kinks out. I'd be squeaky clean when I got arrested. I lowered my aching body and a large bar of Zest into the tub. I'd set the clock radio for ten minutes later. No point in having a great hideout and then drowning.

Afterwards, I ferreted out some Old Spice deodorant and my brother-in-law's terrycloth dressing gown. I smelled exactly like one of my old boyfriends before a big date. If there hadn't been a price on my head, I would have been having a hell of a good time. But the police were looking for me, so I needed to think about what to do next.

Luckily, my major legacy of legal aid work was the bag of tricks I'd unintentionally absorbed from clients. How to pass through security undetected. How to disguise yourself. How to steal cars. How to infiltrate locked houses when the owners are sleeping. Bunny Mayhew had been particularly innovative. I'd never needed any of that information, but now it was coming in handy.

A lot of burglars take advantage of an empty house to eat. Once I was clean and rested, potato chips weren't quite enough. I checked the kitchen fridge. I polished off a half-container of orange juice. That felt good. I found a small lasagna in the freezer. I made a salad and set up the TV tray in the basement while the lasagna heated in the microwave. I chose rocky road ice cream for dessert. Donalda would never miss this small amount of food from her vast reserves. I raided the cupboard for a package of double chocolate chip cookies and dropped them into my backpack as emergency rations for the road.

I tidied up my traces. Donalda can sense a shift in the molecules. I settled in downstairs with my tray of food. I turned on the TV, hoping the flicker wouldn't show through the shuttered windows.

My thrilling escapades continued to highlight the news. Local lawyer goes on a murder spree and vanishes into the night. What's not to love? A steely-eyed police spokesperson gave an update. Two women murdered and a third woman in critical condition with head injuries. I had been fingered by my regular paramedic in Bianca's home.

I made plans for an emergency departure in case. Time for a change. Each of my sisters keeps a closet with castoff clothing ready to be sent off to the Salvation Army. I checked out Donalda's and selected a pair of navy blue cotton twill pants. They fit when I cut three inches off the length. I added a long-sleeved blue T-shirt and a pair of grey Keds, slightly too big but better than my broken sandals. I added a khaki fishing hat, a beige nylon windbreaker and a pair of my brother-in-law's golfing gloves. I bet he didn't know Donalda was giving that stuff away.

In the basement, I laid out my new outfit. I stuffed what I'd been wearing under the sofa. I ran my underwear through the washer and dryer. I took the jacket and gloves and folded them, ready to slip into my backpack. Unfortunately, the backpack was stuffed, especially since I'd added the chocolate chip cookies. I emptied it and realized I'd been lugging Laura's book around since I'd left for the park with Gussie. No wonder the damn pack was so heavy. I removed the book and slid it under the sofa with the clothes. It wasn't a night for reading. I unlocked the closest window. I figured I could squeeze through in a pinch. With everything ready for take-off, I curled up on the sofa to get some sleep.

Oddly enough, I felt a bit wired. Maybe it was the chocolate in the ice cream. At the same time, I was rattled, bruised and confused. But I needed to figure out what was going on. Who was killing these people? Why was I being blamed? Who had Laura Brown really been? What did that have to do with her death?

All that thinking gave me a headache. I set the alarm for four-thirty and turned off the lights. Ten minutes later, I turned them back on.

Maybe I did need to read. I wanted something other than *Field and Stream* or *House Beautiful*. I pulled Laura's book out from under the sofa. It wasn't the sort of book that I imagined Laura reading, but then what had I known about her?

I was intrigued immediately, even if my concentration wasn't at its best. Some people can do that: transmit their passion with wit and humanity and still make a decent sentence.

On page eight, I noticed something wrong. Pages stuck together. I couldn't imagine the fastidious Laura eating or drinking while reading a forty-dollar hardcover. I tried to pull the pages apart before I realized that a seam had been fashioned on the top, side and bottom.

I was raised to revere books, so it took nerve to get a pair of scissors and cut off the glued edges, while trying not to damage any of the print. When the pages opened, a pair of newspaper clippings slipped out.

Thirty-One

I stared at the yellowing papers in my hand. Finding hidden clues was no more unlikely than anything else that had happened that weekend. But it felt so very Nancy Drew.

The first clipping was a write-up from an unidentified paper detailing a robbery by a group called the Settlers. The Settlers seemed to be a quasi-wacko urban revolutionary brigade, modelled on The Weathermen or The Symbionese Liberation Movement. They had cut a swath through the American midwest back in the late seventies, robbing banks and bombing cars. They had shot a pregnant bank customer at point blank range and mowed down a teenaged boy in a gas station. Two police officers had been killed during one of their escapes. The body of a young girl, believed to be a Settler, had been found outside the town after the last hold-up. No identification had been found for her.

The second one was an article about Kathleen Soliah facing trial after thirty years as a respectable member of the community. I'd read a lot about her case. What had these clippings meant to Laura? She'd obviously wanted to hide them. But why? These were newspaper articles, hardly secret. I'd seen the Soliah article myself. Had Laura been sending a message? Why would she think I'd find them? The whole idea was crazy. But Laura had planned to have me as her next-of-kin. Because I had been publicly involved in three high-profile investigations in two years? You couldn't read the Ottawa papers and miss them.

Yet she'd never mentioned those incidents when I'd run into her, unlike everyone else. I'd been grateful at the time, but now I asked myself if she'd figured if anything happened to her, I'd find the clippings and investigate. Maybe she'd left other cryptic messages.

There had been nothing at all to do with the law or justice in Laura's home, and yet there in plain view in her bedroom was this book that anyone who knew me even slightly would figure I would reach for. On the other hand, no one on a routine search would find the clippings.

My eyes were getting heavy. I slipped the book back and turned out the light. I had just dozed off when I heard footsteps overhead. What were they doing there in the middle of the night?

Donalda's voice, Queen of the Realm. "How many times have I asked you not to leave glasses in the sink?"

"I didn't." My brother-in-law pathetically protesting innocence.

"Excuse me? Is this not a glass?"

"Yes."

Off with his head. A low mumble from the accused.

"Do I have to tolerate that tone as well?"

Every now and then, I feel sorry for my brothers-in-law.

"Fine," Donalda commanded, "you sleep in the basement."

Damn. Donalda would turn me in to the police in a New York minute. She believes in the justice system. Plus I'd left a glass in the sink.

I grabbed the pile of clothes and the backpack and rushed

for the window. I tripped over the TV table. I could hear Joe slowly descending, too smart to look eager to spend the night with his fish.

I bonked my head on the frame of the window going out and saw galaxies. I crawled across the grass in the backyard, still wearing Joe's bathrobe, dragging the backpack and the pile of clothes. I slithered into the garden shed and lay there, gasping. It was all I could do to stand up. The shimmer was back in a big way.

I slipped into the pants and the T-shirt. I plucked out the glasses frames and put them on. The fishing hat was a nice touch.

I grabbed a fishing rod that I found hanging on the wall. Donalda's ancient one-speed bike was propped in the corner.

I got on the bike and wobbled off into the night.

*   *   *

I biked along Alta Vista, down Pleasant Park to Riverside and then to the bike path. I figured that was one place the cops wouldn't be looking for me. Donalda's bike had no lights. With the cloud cover, there was barely enough moonlight to navigate. Not long after getting on the path, I spotted a thick clump of trees near the river's edge. I saw no sign of homeless campers or partying teens. I tucked myself well out of view and hunkered down to assess my options.

The river glittered in the sliver of moonlight, peaceful and soothing. There wasn't much to do except think. If I'd had a flashlight, I could have rechecked Laura's book, searching for other glued pages or items written in margins, anything to help me understand. But anyway, the book was back under the sofa.

I spent my time planning what to do next before the sun came up and the path filled with runners, walkers, dogs and cops on bikes. It was important to avoid the obvious associates. My former criminal clients showed up at the homes of girlfriends, who immediately turned them in. Or decided to hide them but weren't smart enough to pull it off. Or a buddy ratted them out for a sentencing break. Most of them racked up car thefts, break-ins, robberies, assaults on the run. Those charges stuck, even if the original offence didn't.

Except for the Pathfinder mistake, and running away, I'd avoided indictable offences. But unless I found the guilty party, I'd be serving time in a federal institution for women. I could plead diminished capacity and get myself into a mental institution. Tough choice. No chance of bail for a known flight risk.

All to say, I didn't have much to lose by being on the run. Well, maybe my license to practice law, but that was already in jeopardy. Multiple murder and aggravated assault were my key problems. Everything else was small potatoes.

So.

Rule One for all successful crooks was: Don't get caught.

Rule Two: If you do get caught, have a good lawyer ready.

Rule Three: Pick a lawyer who's wily as a snake, twice as mean, and media savvy.

I decided to check my home phone messages using Mrs. Parnell's cell. I should have done it at Donalda's, but in my muddled state, it hadn't occurred to me. And in retrospect, I wasn't sure if the police could check what number you checked your messages from.

I had lots of messages.

P. J. said, "Don't forget, I get the exclusive interview. Let's do it while you're on the run. Call me."

My sisters had left a flurry of "turn yourself in" messages. Alvin and Mrs. Parnell offered their support, assistance, tea and all the Harvey's Bristol Cream I needed to help me regain my equilibrium.

Three hang-ups

Then Mombourquette.

"Camilla? Leonard here. Pay close attention. You are in deep shit. Your so-called friend, Elaine Ekstein, is not doing you any favours. She is telling police all sorts of strange things. They've let her go. They think she may lead them to you. You cannot trust her. You need to turn yourself in. I want to help. Here's my number, it's easy to remember."

I tried to get my head around Mombourquette's message. Elaine could be unpredictable when dealing with the police. That's Elaine. Elaine had been my friend since university, and I do not turn against my friends.

What had Elaine told the police? Had Mombourquette misconstrued it? I needed to think this through. If I viewed Laura as the centre, which made sense, Elaine fit into the puzzle somehow. If I could sort through the details, I could get a handle on it. And as my father used to tell me when I was stuck on math problems, the devil's in the details. Concentrate on those. Okay, the details. Elaine had known Laura at Carleton. Even though she said she hadn't liked her. Elaine had pictures of people from the Carleton days. She hadn't volunteered that information, I had suggested it. She had trouble finding the right photos, I had fished them out. She had given me some but not all of the photos. She knew I was taking the pictures to try to get identification from the girls at Maisie's. She knew I was in the Market when I was attacked. She knew Frances Foxall and Sylvie Dumais. She knew I was looking for the woman who had lunched with Laura and knew her name was Bianca. She hadn't managed to prevent Norine from calling the police.

Oops. Blinding flash. I had taken the wrong Pathfinder and left behind the replacement photos which I needed to show Jasmine. But I didn't want to get distracted by that. I went back to stewing about Elaine. I wasn't ready to discount my friend, but I couldn't put myself at her mercy either. I decided to follow Rule Two and get myself a lawyer. I called Mombourquette.

To my surprise, he picked up the phone. "Are you okay?"

"Not bad for being on the run. Can you do something for me?"

"Camilla. Turn yourself in before an officer spots you and decides you're resisting arrest. Let the police help."

"Right. Like they're helping so far? I need to find this killer."

"Listen, every officer believes you killed two women and seriously injured another. They're nervous. They think you're armed."

"What?"

"You heard me. Turn yourself in before you get shot."

Thirty-Two

Armed? What could I be armed with? Talk sense, Leonard."

"They got a tip you're carrying a weapon. Might have been Elaine."

"That's just plain nuts. What kind of weapon am I supposed to have?"

"A gun. So some nervous constable thinks he's facing an armed murderer, shoots first and asks questions later. Think about that."

"Come on."

"Or, you get arrested, you kick up a bit of fuss. The officers use reasonable force to subdue you. Your head gets rattled a bit. On top of your concussions, the additional injury leads to brain damage. You want to spend the rest of your days in a rehab centre? You think you got troubles now."

"Holy shit."

"Exactly. So where are you? I'll come and get you and make sure there's medical personnel available as soon as you come in. Conn will show up too. Nothing will happen with us."

"If you want to do something for me, get Sheldon Romanek on the phone. I want him to represent me."

"Romanek? That shithead defence lawyer? I wouldn't talk

to that snake if you did have a gun, and you held it to my head."

"Don't use clichés, Leonard. He's a snake, but he's the best snake."

"I've had cases thrown out because of him."

"I'm not asking you to date him."

"It's not exactly office hours."

"That's pretty lame, Leonard. Romanek has a criminal practice. His clients call when they get arrested. They don't make appointments at convenient times. Please just make the call. I'd do it myself, but I don't have his number."

"You think I have his number?"

"You have a phone book. This cellphone is running out of juice."

"You can't get legal aid. Who'll pay his exorbitant fees?"

"Well, not you, Leonard. So don't worry."

There goes the RRSP, I figured.

"Camilla, listen…"

"And tell Romanek I won't submit to a dehumanizing strip search."

"Be serious. You're a lawyer, you know the rules."

"And I want it in writing. Take it or leave it. Damn. I'm losing power. Don't let me down, Leonard."

*   *   *

I didn't want to squander my cellphone charge arguing with Mombourquette. Plus I had the Elaine problem. Was Mombourquette right? Was Elaine capable of telling the police I had a weapon?

What did I really know about Elaine anyway? She'd moved from the States to go to Carleton. I'd never met any of her family, not even her diabetic brother, Eddy. Estranged from her parents, she'd said. Period.

But Elaine had been my friend through every tough time that had happened to me for the past eighteen years. She'd been part of my elopement plan and a witness at my wedding. Still, I had to be cautious.

I'd been so shocked, I'd forgotten to tell Mombourquette about the clippings. He could have followed up on the Settlers. And I hadn't been able to reach Jasmine. I was counting on her to make connections between Laura and the women at the restaurant. Were there other contacts besides Bianca? Was someone else in danger? Was Jasmine?

Without the photos, I had nothing to show Jasmine. Which brought me back to Elaine. She had gazillions of photos, if I could get my mitts on them. Tricky. The police would have her place staked out. That added an element of challenge.

And police or no police, Elaine's place was like a fortress. How could I get into her second floor apartment? Like they say, when in doubt, ask an expert. I knew just the one. The talented Bunny Mayhew, the best second-storey man ever. The good news: I had his telephone number.

*   *   *

"Wow, Camilla, you are sure in the deep weeds."

"I noticed that myself, Bunny."

"Canada-wide warrant," he said. I detected pride in his voice.

"Can you help me?"

"Name it."

"Okay. You can't talk to the police or the media. And especially your friends." I refrained from saying your shallow-end-of-the-gene-pool friends who always needed information to trade to the cops.

"Hey, you've done a lot for me. I've never even served time. You always got me off, even when I was guilty."

True. If anyone had been primed for the slammer, it was Bunny Mayhew. I couldn't take credit. Female jurors fell in love with him.

"Suppose, speaking hypothetically, I needed to get into someone's house when they were in it, what would be the best way? Not that this would happen or that you would counsel someone to commit a crime."

"Like you said. Hypothetical. They got a security system?"

"Hypothetically, yes."

"It usually means there's alarms on all the ground floor entrances and windows. What kind of system?"

"Don't know. Say an extremely good one."

"Motion detectors?"

"Yes, and a lot of locks."

"No problem. First, you find a place to hide where the cops won't look afterwards, and then you work on the motion detector. You could wave a branch so the shadow triggers the alarm."

"But..."

"A thick tree is a good hiding place. Then when the cops show up four to five minutes later, they check out the house. Okay? That takes maybe fifteen minutes. Ten minutes after that, you wave your branch and set off the alarm again. You go back to your hiding place."

"A tree? I don't know..."

"Cops come, cops check, cops go away again. They don't think you're hanging around in a tree, they think you ran away. Speaking hypothetically. Ten minutes later, you do the same thing. Cops come, cops get a bit pissed off with the resident, cops suggest they'll be charging for all three false alarms. Resident calls the security system and gives them hell. Turns off system. You're in like Flynn."

"Brilliant. But there would be cops outside the house, and they wouldn't think it was a false alarm. They'd think it was me. In this far-fetched scenario."

"Wow. And you're armed and dangerous, eh. They'll just shoot you."

"Ouch."

"You need a better hypothetical plan. Is there a second floor?"

"Yes. That's where I need to be, if this were a real situation."

"Any security there?"

"Motion detectors. Window alarms wouldn't surprise me."

"It's an apartment?"

"Yes. Top two stories of a house."

"Okay. I'll bet you anything there's no security on the third floor."

I closed my eyes again. "I don't know."

"No one ever thinks you can get in on the third floor. But it's a piece of cake. All you need is a ladder."

"I can't carry a ladder around the way I am now. Even if I had one."

"Say you've got a ladder, then you hustle up to the window."

"The window is on the third floor." No point in boring Bunny with my various ailments, such as losing balance and seeing quadruple. I decided to let him finish, then try to find another solution.

"Third floor windows are easy. People leave them open all summer."

"This apartment is air-conditioned."

"Practically impossible to cool off the third floor. Windows will be open."

"Even if a window is open, which I doubt, there will be a screen."

"Nothing to a screen, Camilla."

"For you, maybe. But I would be, hypothetically, up on a ladder, three-stories high, and new to the game."

"Just cut it out."

"I'm merely stating the facts, Bunny."

"I mean just cut out the screen. A box cutter is best."

"It's three in the morning, where's a person going to get a goddam box cutter?"

"So just give the screen a push. That's all it will take. They come away like nothing. Particularly if it's one of those converted places with older windows. You just push it, hard. And either the whole screen, frame and all, comes off or the screen breaks loose from the frame. Either way, you're in."

"If the frame were to fall in, wouldn't it hit the floor and make a lot of racket?"

"Well sure, if you let it fall. You have to be fast. When I was allegedly in this game," Bunny paused, "that's what I would have done."

"I don't think I could pull that off."

"For me, the thing that worked the best was visualization."

"What?"

"You know, mentally rehearsing the outcome, seeing yourself succeed. You never heard of this stuff, Camilla? All the sports guys use it."

"I've heard of visualization, but I just never realized it could be used for…this line of activity." How many times had my father advised me to see the desired outcome in my mind? Of course, he hadn't been thinking about burglary.

The phone beeped, indicating low battery.

"Phone's running down."

"Where's the hypothetical house?"

"Near Spruce."

"Wait half an hour and go to the alley between Spruce and Danton, you'll find a ladder."

One long beep, and the line went dead.

"Thanks, Bunny," I said.

Thirty-Three

I lurched to the rear of Elaine's place on the bike and peered into her Pathfinder. No sign of the photos. That left Bunny's not-so-easy hypothetical plan. In the alley between Spruce and Danton, a lightweight, extendable painter's ladder was propped against a shed. I didn't want to lose Donalda's bike to some other prowler. I slid it into a slim space between two garages. After that, I struggled for a good twenty minutes to drag the ladder to the back of Elaine's house. The less said about how I looked and sounded the better.

First, I groped my way to the front of the house and peered around. I caught the gleam of a dark sedan parked one house down. Not good.

As far as I could tell, only one of Elaine's third floor rear windows was open. I positioned the ladder under it. Grappling with that ladder was the hardest thing I'd ever done. But climbing it turned out to be worse. In my visualizations, I saw myself crumpled on the ground. I felt my neck snap. I heard myself scream. I decided to visualize nice things. Like good Samaritans feeding Mrs. Parnell's cat and Gussie adapting well to Mombourquette's.

The real-world problem was the swaying of the ladder. All the thoughts of the cat and Gussie couldn't override that. By the time I reached the third floor, my heart was beating so loudly, I was surprised the neighbours didn't fling open their windows and tell me to shut up. I realized I should have left my stupid backpack on the ground. My knees shook, my mouth was dry and everything swirled.

The window was in Elaine's office, if my calculations were right. I stared at the screen. I hung on to the ladder with one hand, the window ledge with the other and gave a firm push with my elbow. Technically, that turned my activity from unlawful entry to breaking and entering, a definite notch up on the offence-o-meter.

The screen stood fast. I tried giving it a sharp rap with my palm. What if the cop got out of the car and checked the back of the house? That thought brought a surge of adrenaline, and I whacked the screen. The screen fell in, silently. But in what seemed like slow motion, the ladder swung away from the wall. I visualized a slow arc to the ground, and my life ending in a clatter. I grabbed the window sill and clung. The ladder swayed, stuck on my feet. With every scrap of strength, I pulled myself toward the window. The ladder came forward, hitting the wall with a clunk. After a bit of panting, I disengaged my feet and launched my body into the dark room. At that point, I didn't care if I landed at the feet of the tactical squad.

I should have remembered Bunny's professional history. Specifically the part where his plans go wrong, which is why he always needed a lawyer. If I got out of this spot, I too would go straight.

Lying on the floor, breathing raggedly, I tried to get my bearings. Where was the desk? Where were the photos? Was there a motion detector? I stared around at the walls, but I didn't see a sign of the little green light that would turn red as soon as something, say me, passed in front of it.

But what was that noise? Some kind of alarm system? A guard dog? It took a minute to remember that Elaine snored. I'd landed in her bedroom by mistake. I crawled on my belly past the bed. Elaine's floor was covered with clothing and shoes. No wonder the screen hadn't made any noise. Well, as long as she was snoring, I could keep crawling.

Whenever the gurgle stopped, I froze. A moment later, a thunderous snore would follow. When this was over, I'd insist Elaine see a doctor. Assuming she hadn't shopped me to the police. I slithered across the hall to the office. I had a bad moment when I hit the wastepaper basket, which reverberated. I exhaled when the next snore sounded.

With only the pale sliver of moon to see by, I took ten minutes to hunt through boxes of photos. No luck. I had a vague memory of Elaine pushing some snaps onto a chair. Maybe there had been something in that pile. Would she have gotten rid of them? No, getting rid of stuff was not Elaine's best thing. Would she hide them? Why bother? I was on the run, with the cops ready to shoot me full of holes thanks to false information, maybe from Elaine. So, no need to hide anything.

I found the pile of photos on the seat of one of the chairs. I glanced at the first few. Sure enough, eighties hairdos and sweaters. Groups of people I remembered from Carleton. I couldn't see clearly and I couldn't turn on a light. I stuffed the photos into my backpack and began the return crawl.

As I passed Elaine's desk and saw the blue light of her computer screen, I stopped. Her computer was always on. And she had high-speed internet. I stopped and got on my knees.

This could be the answer to one of my missing bits of information. If I could just remember Jasmine's last name. Norine had called her Ms. What? Thurston? Thingwell? Thurlow! I was easily able to access Canada411. To my surprise, a J. Thurlow was listed. The Lowertown address sounded right. Jasmine would be close to Maisie's and within walking distance of the university when her classes started. I closed down the Canada411 site. I didn't want Elaine knowing what I'd been up to. The phone number was not unlike my birthday, and the address was easy to remember, unless I hit my head again.

I resumed the long crawl back through Elaine's clothing-strewn bedroom. Under normal circumstances, I would have been pleased: she made me look good in comparison, but this time I added it to her transgressions. Thoughtless and messy. False, treacherous friend.

The crawl had its compensations. I picked up a sundress and a light sweater from the floor and stuffed them into the backpack. I snatched one of Elaine's floppy straw sun hats. Every wardrobe change helps.

By the time I reached the bedroom window, I felt optimistic. I checked the ladder and froze. The ladder was still in place, but beams of light flickered. I unfroze and pulled my head in fast.

Who the hell was down there? From the shadows, I squinted down. At the foot of the ladder, a pair of police officers were gesturing. They shone their lights around the yard. I decided they wouldn't climb the ladder. They'd call for back-up, and when it came, they'd surround the building. Then they'd go in. I had no idea if this theory was true, but it made sense.

I picked up a pair of Elaine's shoes. With every bit of strength I had, I heaved the shoes, one at a time, as far as I could, out the window in opposite directions. My aim was pretty bad, but that didn't matter. One shoe landed noisily on the neighbour's barbecue. The other clattered as it hit a shed roof. The officers whirled and inched toward the sounds.

Elaine still snored. I skittered across the bedroom, down the stairs, through the second floor living room and down the final flight to the front door. Out of the corner of my eye, I saw the green motion detector indicator turn red. There's something to be said for adrenaline when you're in a tight spot. I knew the alarm would trigger one minute after I opened the front door. If luck was with me, that would be just enough time to scramble into the middle of the big old blue spruce in the front yard. The door slammed behind me as I made a dash for the tree and wrestled my way into its spiny centre. The thick, dark branches hung almost to the ground. I was counting on my navy blue and beige clothing to blend in.

The alarm was lovely, long and loud. Lights snapped on in nearby houses. By the time the police officers reached the front door, Elaine was standing in her nightie on the doorstep, screaming her head off.

Served her right.

As the officers made their way into the house, I struggled out of the spruce and staggered off around the corner, heading for my bike. I could now add sticky spruce gum on my hands, feet and bum to my list of troubles. Never mind. I jammed on the fishing hat and the glasses and set off like any solid citizen.

Too bad about Bunny's ladder. I hoped he'd wiped off any fingerprints. Otherwise, it could scuttle his plans to go straight.

A couple of squad cars rocketed past as I steered toward the bike path. I would have been toast if I'd been spotted. I needed to lie down, but I reminded myself that you can sleep all you want when you're dead.

My dawn ride down the bike path was a bit easier than navigating by night. Still, by the time I got to the back of the Parliament buildings, my adrenaline boost was depleted. I was ragged. I had trouble biking in a straight line and was getting distracted by some new green flashes in my peripheral vision. It took a while to realize they came from inside my head. I wondered if they were the reason I felt nauseated. Or maybe that was because my painkillers had worn off.

Aside from my balance and nausea issues, I needed to find a place to stop and look at the photos without being recognized. I needed a glass of water to take my pills. I needed a cup of coffee like no one ever before in the history of caffeine. Most of all, I needed a bathroom.

Twenty-four hour cafés are rare in Ottawa. The Second Cups aren't open at five in the morning. There was always Tim Hortons, but they were crawling with cops. I found a small restaurant at the far edge of the Market, not far from Jasmine's address. I took a minute to inspect myself in the window of the shop next door. I brushed off twigs, leaves and dirt from my knees. I ran my sleeve over my face and hoped that if it had been dirty, I hadn't made it worse. I couldn't do much about the spruce gum on my hands.

The diner was warm and smelled of coffee and fresh bread. The breakfast was $2.99. There was a smiling woman behind the counter, and five male customers, wearing baseball caps. None of them looked like police officers.

Someone was hogging the unisex washroom, so I ordered the largest cup of coffee they had, double double, and unbuttered toast to settle my stomach. I sat at a small table with a clear view of the washroom door. I kept my back to the other customers, yet I was close enough to the front door to skedaddle if I had to. At the next table, someone had left behind the *Sun* and the *Citizen*. I scooped them up. No one paid attention.

I was the front page story in both papers, something you never want unless you're representing Canada in the Olympics. The *Citizen* had printed a shot of me entering the court house last year for Elaine's bail hearing. I was in "no comment" mode, holding out my hand to push back cameras. I would not want to run into me in a dark alley.

The headline read: "Rogue Lawyer Armed and Dangerous".

The *Sun* had done even better. They'd found a photo from this summer's showdown at the Bluesfest.

My hair was wild, and my eyes wilder. My mouth was open. I know I was in shock, waiting for the paramedics. But I looked like I'd just busted loose from a facility for the criminally insane after biting a few armed guards.

They hadn't run that photo at the time. I'd been a hero then. What a difference six weeks makes.

The headline read: "On the Run: Body Count Hits Three." And rising. A photo of Chelsea looking innocent and untattooed was included. At least no one was likely to recognize me. I tossed back my painkillers and tried to eat the toast. The washroom was still occupied, so I wasn't ready to start the coffee. I removed the photos from my pack. Before I had time to look at them, a cruiser pulled up outside. Two young police officers sauntered through the front door, looking for a cup of coffee to get them through to the end of their shift. I recognized them right away. Zaccotto and Yee.

The bathroom door swung open, and a guy in a baseball cap swaggered out. I took a sip of the coffee, trying to look calm, shoved the photos in the backpack, and headed toward the bathroom. No one in the restaurant looked up.

I thought I saw a flicker of recognition on Yee's face, even though I tried not to look. The fishing hat must have thrown him off a bit. Inside the room, I jammed the wastepaper basket against the door and took advantage of the facilities. Then I climbed onto the toilet tank and gave the window a shove. I was developing a technique for banging out windows.

At the same time, there was a rap on the door.

"Out in a minute," I said, trying for a slight accent.

"Can you open the door, ma'am?" I think that was Yee.

"Hold your horses," I said. "I waited ten minutes to get in here."

I reached down and gave the toilet a flush with my foot, and with all my strength, heaved myself out and into the alley. My entire body screamed. My head merely reeled.

I didn't wait around to hear if they broke the door in. I careened down the alley beside the restaurant. My bike was back by the front door. No use now.

Within minutes, the APB would be changed to the fishing hat and dark-rimmed glasses. I tossed them into a dumpster as I lumbered past. I stripped off the dark pants and top. There's a first time for everything, including standing in an alley in your underwear. I slipped on Elaine's sundress. I added the sweater and the floppy sun hat.

I got back on to the nearest street and kept my head up, although it felt like it was about to fall off. The inevitable cruisers shot past me, heading for the restaurant. My goal was to get to Jasmine's place without passing out. If there was even a small chance she would recognize someone in those photos, it was worth the risk. There was no chance I could accomplish that if I were in police custody.

I couldn't imagine any kind of happy ending in sight for me. It was a set of circumstances I used to see with my recidivist clients in my legal aid days. Sometimes, it doesn't matter what the hell you do, you're screwed.

Thirty-Four

Jasmine was tousled from sleep when she opened the door of her studio apartment. She blinked nearsightedly at the unfamiliar woman with the sun hat paying her an unexpected visit very early on a holiday Monday.

"Don't scream." I leaned on the door frame to keep from falling over. At this point, what harm could an implied threat do?

She shrank against the wall.

"I'm not going to hurt you, Jasmine. I need your help."

"You killed Chelsea. And she was trying to help you." The grey eyes were huge without the snazzy glasses.

"I didn't kill Chelsea. You have to believe me."

"You killed those other women."

"No."

"And you hurt Bianca. She was one of my customers. She was very kind."

"Listen. Someone else killed them. You have to trust me."

She made a sudden scoot toward the door. I lurched sideways to block her exit. Inside my throbbing head, my good angel squawked about assault.

I said. "I need to sit down. I don't feel well. It's just a matter of time until I'm in police custody, and I need to know what happened. I won't harm you. Please just look at those photos I told you about."

Her body language said she was still ready to bolt.

I continued, "Someone in the photos might have killed Chelsea. The sooner you tell me if you recognize someone, the better."

The grey eyes flickered toward the door.

I said. "The questions I was asking may have precipitated some of these attacks. You are probably in danger. But not from me."

She swallowed. "I'll lose my place in law school if I get caught helping you. It's a criminal offence."

I said. "Tell them I forced you. What the hell. My life is in danger, and the police are after me. I would really appreciate a cup of coffee." My stomach lurched. As much as I wanted it, maybe coffee wasn't the right thing. "Let's make that tea."

Jasmine's hands shook.

I said, "Orange pekoe. If you have it."

"I have it."

I wasn't surprised. It looked like she had everything she needed in her compact, immaculate studio apartment. You could tell she was a practical young woman. I spilled the photos onto her small table and sank into one of two director's chairs.

The kettle shrieked as it came to a boil. I reached and grabbed the handle. "I think I'll pour."

She stared and turned pale. "You don't think I'd scald you with boiling water?"

"Couldn't take a chance."

"That's a horrible thing."

"We agree." I poured boiling water into a brown teapot. "It has to steep for four minutes. In the meantime, I'll tell you what I've learned."

Jasmine slid open a package of cigarettes, took one out and flicked a disposable lighter. Her hands shook. She said, "Look at that. I can't believe I've started this disgusting habit again. After years. It's all this stress. People I know getting killed. Unbelievable."

"There's more," I said. I told her about Laura Brown's false identity. The note about the Settlers, the women who were connected with Laura, the two other deaths and how the women both knew Laura from Carleton days. After I got to the part about finding Bianca, I said, "The whole thing with the Settlers seems so far-fetched."

She shook her head. "Not really. This type of group was in the news a couple of years ago. I took a sociology course, and everyone had to do a presentation on some aspect of those urban terrorists: The Weathermen, The Symbionese Liberation Army. A bunch of European ones. A lot of interesting presentations. One of my classmates did her research on the Settlers. They were similar to the better known groups, a little bit more recent, but the same idea: we're middle-class white students from stable homes, and now we get to shoot and bomb the oppressors because we know what's best for society. Somebody gets killed? That's just the price you have to pay. Too bad, so sad. I did my research on the Kathleen Soliah case. She's probably the best known, if you don't count Patty Hearst. I was starting to think about law school, and I found the issues really interesting. She was like everyone's mom. Nice lady, nice house, nice husband, nice kids, SUV, the whole scene. But she had been living this pleasant life for so many years."

I said, "I know the case. It got a lot of press."

"She thought the authorities should let her go, after all that time. They should look at her life as such a good citizen, you know, part of community groups for progressive change and

271

not charge her with attempted murder or anything else. Water under the bridge. If that's not far-fetched, what is?"

"She stood trial."

"Convicted too. She had plenty of support. Lots of people thought she shouldn't be prosecuted. The same as you get people saying that war crimes are in the past and shouldn't be pursued."

"And what did you think?"

"I took a hard line. The prof thought my paper lacked balance. B minus." She flashed one of her smiles. I relaxed a bit. At least we'd found something in common. I needed her sympathy and understanding. "But anyway, most of the people who have either been caught or who have given themselves up were sentenced to lengthy prison terms, so I guess the courts agree with me."

I said, "Something to worry about if you're a former urban terrorist."

"I don't think they found any of the Settlers. Some of them were killed in a big shoot-out, I think they were mostly young girls, sixteen or seventeen. Some people said they'd been kidnapped. I don't know about that. The leader was a man. Big guy. My classmate showed pictures. Wore a paramilitary uniform."

"Would you recognize him?"

"Hardly. It was one of those grainy shots that some witness took, I think. And it's been a couple of years since the class. I don't think he was ever identified. But I'm not a hundred per cent sure. I could try to call my friend and see if she still has her project notes. But she's probably away for the weekend." She shivered. "It's weird. We were studying these movements like history, like they were a hundred years ago. This is so creepy to think some of these people might have been here in

Ottawa all along. I bet they figured they'd never be discovered here. Nice place to live, no FBI looking for them here."

"Bear with me, Jasmine, I have a theory. I'm thinking if the leader had made a place for himself in society, and someone threatened to expose him, that would be plenty of motive to kill."

She stubbed out her cigarette. "It makes sense. All these women who knew each other and spent time together at Maisie's. And you said, Laura had been using a dead girl's name."

"Classic identity theft. And we don't know if Frances Foxall and Sylvie Dumais were really who they said they were."

"I guess so. I can hardly believe I have a fugitive holed up in my apartment. It's all too bizarre for this time of the morning."

"Yeah, we agree. How about looking at a few snapshots? The night Chelsea was killed, I was attacked, probably because I had a box of photos, which were stolen. It didn't make sense at the time, but now I realize, there must be at least one other person who could be identified."

Jasmine lit another cigarette. "But who knew you had those photos? Was someone stalking you?"

"Those are some of the devilish details I'm puzzling over."

Jasmine reached for the photos. "I guess it can't hurt to look." A moment later, her shoulders started to shake. "What were they thinking?"

"Yeah, yeah, I get the point about the hair and sweaters."

"But what are those shoulder pads about?"

"See anyone you recognize?"

"Besides you, of course. I've seen her." She pointed to Elaine.

"You have? With Laura?"

She pursed her lips and lit another cigarette. "Pretty sure. I wouldn't want to swear to it in court."

"All right." My stomach was heaving.

"But there's someone else. Are you all right, Camilla? You look like you're going to…"

"I'll be okay. You said you saw someone else?"

"Yes, but I don't know her name. She had lunch with Laura too. I'm pretty sure I saw her with Bianca. And she seemed to know Norine."

I sat. "Show me which person."

"This woman." Jasmine pointed with a long, elegant finger.

"My god."

"You know her?"

I nodded. The elegant finger was pointed at Kate Westerlund. Small puzzle pieces clicked in my brain.

Jasmine frowned, "She's older than the others. What's her connection?"

"She is the wife of a prof we all really loved and respected."

"You're kidding. Is she by any chance from the USA?"

I hesitated. "Yes."

"And her husband?"

"Holy crap," I said.

Jasmine said, "Do you think he could be involved?"

"No," I said. "Not Joe."

"But did this guy know all the dead women?"

"Probably, but it couldn't be Joe."

Jasmine shrugged. "Whatever you say. But I saw that woman, Kate, with every one of them. Do you think that's a coincidence?"

"Even Frances Foxall and Sylvie Dumais?"

"Pretty sure. My god, Chelsea would have served her."

It made sense. I just didn't want it to.

Jasmine shook my arm. "You said you loved and respected him. That sounds like a charismatic leader to me. And a prof

274

on top of that. Remember I told you they never found the leader of the Settlers? Is the age right? He'd have to be older than the women."

The age was right. Everything was right. And everything was wrong.

Jasmine leaned back, eyes shining. She inhaled deeply, keen on solving the mystery. Of course, she hadn't cared about Joe Westerlund. She said, "I bet this dude wouldn't be too thrilled to have old murder charges surfacing."

I reeled into the bathroom and was very sick for a long time. When I teetered out, ten minutes later, Jasmine had a glass of water waiting. She said, "You look awful. You can't keep running. You should really give yourself up."

"Not yet. I have something important left to do. Thanks for your help. I'm sorry I frightened you. If something happens to me, tell the police what you told me."

Someone pounded on the door. Jasmine and I jumped.

"Open up, police."

I said. "Stall."

"Coming! I'm getting dressed," Jasmine yelled. She lowered her voice. "You need to scram, Camilla."

"How would they know I was here?"

"Someone must be following you. Shit. I guess that's it for law school."

"Why? I forced my way in. Not your fault. Now how do I get out?"

She pulled open the window and whispered, "Fire escape."

I hate fire escapes more than windows. I hate being arrested more than either. I figured the police would be watching the fire escape unless they were totally incompetent. That was too much to hope for.

At ground level, a nice police officer was checking behind

the dumpster. She was not looking up. I edged along the fire escape, and tried the window of the next apartment. It held firm. I couldn't afford to make noise. I went up instead of down, pressing myself against the building, tiptoeing on the rusty metal steps, hoping by the time the cop looked up again, I'd be gone.

Two floors up, my luck returned. A single window was propped open with a can of Blue. Despite my disintegrating state, I was able to lift the window. I slipped in and lowered the window, gently, carefully and hopefully. I found myself in a tiny, one-room apartment. From the door, I heard thundering steps on stairs. I crawled toward the unmade bed, squeezed under it and positioned myself behind a pile of smelly clothing. I curled into a ball, trying not to gag. I worked to get my breathing under control as the cops banged on the door. I heard the door splinter. In a way, that was good. They couldn't have a warrant for this place, and illegal search and entry can get the best case tossed out of court. Splinter away, boys, I thought. I heard a male and female searching the tiny apartment, pulling on the closet door, scouting out the bathroom. From behind my clothing barrier, I was aware of someone checking under the bed.

"No one there," a male voice said.

"What a pig sty," a female voice said. "You think this guy ever heard of laundry?"

"Maybe she made it to the roof," the male said.

I heard the window open and the clatter of their boots on the fire escape. I felt a whoosh of relief just as everything went pale grey, then black.

Thirty-Five

Goddam concussions, you never know when they'll give you grief. I was dizzy and nauseated as I struggled to my feet. I wasn't sure how long I'd slept. But if the Labatt's wall clock could be believed, I had been out cold for six hours. That was more sleep than I'd had in two nights. I felt a bit better, until I inhaled. There was something important I was trying to remember, but it kept eluding me. What?

I slunk to the window and squinted down. The fire escape obscured my view. I looked around the apartment, which seemed to consist of one attic room, furnished in two-fours of Blue and Ottawa Senators flags. The window must have been propped open to minimize the essence of unwashed socks, sweat pants, overflowing ashtrays and a large selection of running shoes that had seen a lot of running. Nothing like Jasmine's cosy little home. I sniffed something else in the air, a distinctive odour. Was it what I suspected? The question was answered when I located a healthy pot plant thriving under a gro-light in the storage space under the sink. The cops had missed that. Amazing. Probably they didn't think I could fit under the sink.

I peered through the dusty front window. No sign of police. They wouldn't likely hang around for six hours.

So far, so good.

Seemed like the right time to make a couple of important calls.

*   *   *

Alvin sounded breathless when he answered his cellphone. "Lord thundering Jesus, Camilla. What are you trying to do?"

"Thank you, Alvin. That helps to calm me."

"It's not a good time to be calm. Every cop across the country is hunting for you."

"Tell me something I don't know."

"Hang on. Violet wants to talk to you."

"Ms. MacPhee. Don't mind Young Ferguson. He's terribly worried. We're been frantic. Why haven't you been in communication?"

"Your cellphone ran out of juice. And I can't recharge it."

"Ah. Equipment failure. Still, it takes more than that to slow down this band of warriors. We have good news on the legal front."

"What?"

"Sergeant Mombourquette asked us to inform you that he was successful in contacting your preferred legal counsel."

"You mean Sheldon Romanek?"

"Indeed. I spoke to him myself. Mr. Romanek would be honoured to represent you. He is waiting to hear from you."

"Did Romanek give you a private number I can use?"

"Yes. He says you can speak freely on that line."

"Okay, I need the number."

Of course, when someone gives you a number that is not listed anywhere, you want to write it down. That would require a writing implement and a piece of paper. I had neither. I glanced around the apartment. This guy didn't spend a lot of time recording deep thoughts. I did find a chewed-up pencil and a pizza flyer and managed to write down Romanek's number.

"What can we do to assist, Ms. MacPhee?"

"It's risky for anyone caught helping me. I just put this nice girl, Jasmine, in a tough spot."

"We do not abandon our comrades."

"If the police learn you've helped me in any way, you'll be charged, remember?"

"Of course, I remember. I am in full possession of all my faculties, Ms. MacPhee."

"I wish I could say the same about me. The main thing is, you have to keep your distance. Jail is a bad place, Mrs. P. Even for a short time. I guarantee you will not like it. So thanks but no thanks."

"Don't underestimate what we can tolerate."

"You'll just add to my troubles. If they arrest you, that gives them something to manipulate me with."

"You may be pinned down by enemy fire, but your platoon will be there for you. Do not give up the good fight."

I wasn't sure that being stuck in a World War II time warp was consistent with having full use of your faculties. "*You* may not be afraid of jail, but Alvin hates being arrested."

"We don't plan on being arrested. I am eighty years old. Consider the optics."

"That reminds me, speaking of optics. Keep on top of the media reports. I'll try and find a phone and check in every now and then."

"Roger."

"I'd like you to talk to my brother-in-law, Conn. He'll know what's going on. To ensure his personal survival at the hands of my sisters, he won't want his colleagues to shoot me."

"Ms. MacPhee, we can leave Young Ferguson's cellphone for you at a designated spot. That way you will not find yourself at the mercy of payphones."

"Thanks but no thanks. That's aiding a fugitive. But there is something positive you can do. You and Alvin can get every piece of information possible about a group called the Settlers. You can search the computer. Alvin can head over to the library. They love him there."

"The Settlers? You mean that paramilitary outfit? Twenty years back? Females mostly. Bank robberies and bombs. Bad combo. They got a lot of coverage in the media, then they fell off the radar."

I should have known Mrs. P. would be in the loop. "See if you can find anything about their leader and also how they recruited their members. If any of them have been caught. Bundle the information together, and I'll figure out later how to get my hands on it."

"On the double."

"Here's the most important thing. You cannot trust Elaine Ekstein. If she contacts you, don't tell her what you're doing, and don't believe a word she says."

"You mean Ms. Ekstein is a turncoat?"

"I find it hard to believe, but it sure looks that way."

"And she may have some connection with this thuggery? How shocking."

"You're telling me."

*　　*　　*

Romanek picked up his private line. "Romanek."

"This line okay?" I said without saying who I was.

"No problem."

"Good."

"Well, MacPhee. You do have a way of getting media attention. What are you trying to prove?"

"Good question. Originally, I wanted to prove Laura Brown was murdered. Now I'm trying to find out who killed her and who killed these other women before they kill anyone else. And before I get tossed in jail."

"You don't make it easy for a guy to build a credible defence."

"Hold on…"

"This is not a caper movie with a happy ending. It's for real, MacPhee."

"You know me, Sheldon. Do you seriously think I'm killing women?"

"The stuff you've been pulling off, the original charge could be jaywalking, and they could still put you away in a federal institution."

"So you're glad to represent me."

"I can't counsel you to stay on the run. I have to do what's in your best interests."

"I'm your client, you should follow my wishes."

"Where did you go to law school? Within the confines of the law, I can follow your wishes. You want me on your case, start taking advice."

"Any hope of a defence?"

"Diminished responsibility. We'd go for that first."

"That means thirty days for psychiatric assessment right off the bat. And then more time for the hearing."

"Count yourself lucky."

"I'd be locked in the ROH."

"What difference does it make where you're locked up?"

"Good point."

"So you ready to deal?"

"Deal? What do I have to deal with?"

"This is Sheldon Romanek representing you, remember?"

"How could I forget. No strip search. Under any circumstances."

"Your tame cop, Mombourquette, was clear about that. I'll put it on the table."

"Not negotiable. It's like a phobia."

"What's that old line, MacPhee? Can't do the time, don't do the crime?"

"Okay, I haven't committed these crimes. This whole thing is a conspiracy."

"Conspiracy. Great. Crazy talk like that will help our argument. It fits with the head injury, which is the best we got so far."

"Sarcasm is beneath your stature as the city's most effective prosecution-buster. I'll get back to you with details on the conspiracy thing. It has to do with a seventies-style urban terrorist plot."

"We'll reserve your whacko ideas for when we really need them. In the meantime, I'll call a press conference. Give them your demand. I'm calling it a basic human rights issue. Might get national attention. But you'll have to surrender if they agree."

"You get some kind of guarantee we can trust, and I'll consider it."

"Not consider. Do."

"I'll call you."

"MacPhee? Don't hang up."

*   *   *

"Bunny?"

"Wow, Camilla!"

"Yeah, I know."

"Me and Tonya are rooting for you."

"Appreciated. Look, I'm sorry about your ladder. I hope it didn't have your fingerprints all over it."

"Please. I am a pro. Hypothetically."

"I already owe you one, and now I need you to do me a favour."

"Anything."

"I need a book I left at my sister Donalda's place. Just go and say you're a concerned friend or something. Whatever."

"I'll say I'm a grateful client. What's the name of the book?"

"*One Man's Justice* by Thomas R. Berger, and I left it in the rec room, perhaps even under the sofa. She probably doesn't know it's there. The book is mine, so you are not committing a crime by picking it up."

"Anyway, I don't even know you're a fugitive."

"Let's hope you don't have to rely on that in court."

"Tonya says the same thing. She says it's nothing against you personally, but I have to think about us now."

"Smart girl, Tonya."

"Even so, I told her that if it weren't for you, I would have served federal time, and what kind of future would that have meant for our kids. That's true, so she didn't kick up too much of a fuss."

"Interesting reasoning, Bunny."

"Hang on. Tonya's asking why don't I just buy you a copy of the book?"

"It has to be that particular copy. Tell Tonya I think she's right about you staying out of trouble, and I'll find another way to get it."

"That book is going to be by the dumpster in the side alley by Tonya's hair salon, The Cutting Remarque."

"Don't get caught."

"It's a deal. How can I reach you?"

"You can't. My last borrowed cellphone died."

"Bummer. Anything else you need?"

"Not unless you can get me a new identity or an answer to who is killing all these people."

I gave Bunny Donalda's address and crossed my fingers for both of us.

* * *

I needed to eat something. I had nothing in my stomach, and I thought that might be contributing to my lightheadedness. Somehow the place didn't do much for my appetite. Might have been the sweat socks. I settled for a large bag of cheesies which had not previously been opened and a can of root beer. Add a few more crimes to my rap sheet.

I selected a new wardrobe while I was at it: a Sens baseball cap, a Sens T-shirt, baggy jeans, pretty much the only clean clothes in the place. I passed on the footwear. There are limits to desperation. I was about to face the street again, when the door opened.

A young man with a bad brush cut and a sleeveless sweatshirt said, "Hey."

"Just leaving," I said.

He raised his fists. "What are you doing here?"

"Home inspection," I said. "Landlord sent me."

"I don't think so."

"Sorry, my mistake."

He rammed one fist into the other. "You're right there."

"Let's all stay calm," I said.

"Hey, I know who you are. You're that whack job that killed those women. You're worth a lot of money. Cops will be grateful."

"They'll also be impressed with your green thumb."

He narrowed his eyes. "I can get rid of that."

"I don't know. Sufficient quantity to consider you a grow-op."

He wrinkled his brow. This thinking stuff was obviously not as easy as it looked.

I said, "Tell you what. Don't bother calling the cops, because you'll only get arrested, and I will forget about what's in your kitchen. Because if you get that cash, you won't be eligible for legal aid, and you'll have to waste it all paying your lawyer."

The furrows deepened.

I reached into my pocket and pulled out a twenty. "Go get something to eat. When you come back, I'll be gone and your secret will be safe with me."

I waited until he was out of sight but not long enough for him to figure out how to get the reward without jeopardizing the crop. I slipped into my new Sens gear, put on my trusty sunglasses and tried not to fall down the fire escape.

Thirty-Six

I gave Bunny time to take care of business before I grabbed a cab to Merivale Road. I got off a block from The Cutting Remarque and walked. I felt a bit stronger and more awake. My vision was less blurry, things were looking up, if you didn't count the fact I was having memory problems. Five minutes later, I was behind the hair salon. I felt even better when I spotted three bags tucked discreetly out of sight beside the dumpster, looking like overflow garbage. The smallest bag contained *One Man's Justice*, the largest one, proudly bearing the Wal-Mart name, had a black tank top with Pretty Baby on it in sequins, a pink pleather mini-skirt, a woman's jean jacket, extra small, a pair of candy-pink sandals with three-inch heels and a blonde straight wig. A smaller Wal-Mart bag contained a transparent plastic makeup kit plus a mirror. The makeup was still in its packaging. The lipstick was candy pink. The first I'd ever owned. The look included a pair of neon-pink sunglasses. Bunny had even found another cellphone, a slightly clunky older model. I decided not to worry about who owned it. But the real thrill was the box of baby wipes. I used about twenty of them to get the dirt off my face, hands, knees, arms and feet. I could have used a shower, but those baby wipes were better than nothing.

Bunny had come through big-time. I was guessing Tonya had put her stamp on the project too.

I'd adapted to changing in the open. I ducked behind the dumpster and slid out of the baggy jeans and the Sens gear. I squeezed myself into the mini-skirt and the tank top. I could hardly breathe. I promised myself if I stayed out of jail, I'd eat fewer shawarmas. I put on the wig and did my best to adjust it. I added the sunglasses. There was no way I wanted to make eye contact with anyone.

Since I always seemed to need a plan B, C and D, I shoved the jeans and Sens gear into the backpack. Next action: practice not snapping my ankles in those sandals. Except for my bulging backpack, which I didn't plan to leave behind, I didn't resemble any previous version of the dangerous fugitive, Camilla MacPhee.

*   *   *

The thing I hadn't realized about being a fugitive was how hard it is to make good decisions on the run. It's not like you have a comfortable bed or even a bathroom to hide in until you get your act together. You can't sleep properly, and you sure as hell don't follow Canada's Food Guide. Let me tell you, baby wipes only go so far to ensure personal hygiene. Toss the concussion into the mix, and was it any wonder I made a few questionable decisions?

Everything I told myself sounded like the words of a defence lawyer. I thought they might trip off Romanek's expensively forked tongue soon enough. Regardless of future legal implications, which I wasn't keen to dwell on, I had a job to do. So far, I'd made a mess of it. And I was running out of options.

It was time to visit the Westerlunds. I didn't want to screw up there. I needed a safe, comfortable place to plan that visit. Food would help too, since I'd tossed my cookies at Jasmine's many hours earlier. Plus, why not test the new outfit? I flagged a passing cab and sailed off to a small neighbourhood restaurant not far from the Westerlunds. As I got out, I spotted a bevy of brightly coloured balloons drifting lazily in the distance. The driver looked up too.

"Great weekend for it, eh?" he said.

"Should have been," I said.

Inside the restaurant, I slid into the most isolated booth and ignored the two guys giving me the eye. I kept the sunglasses on. I knew I couldn't keep on racing around town like a cartoon character sporting idiotic outfits and thumbing my nose at the law. I was out of time and just about out of brain. My head and vision were getting worse. I needed medical attention. I was being foolish and stubborn. But I needed one more kick at the can. Then, if Romanek got that concession, I'd turn myself in. Once that happened, I wouldn't be choosing from any six-page menu. I kept institutional food in mind as I ordered a deluxe cheeseburger with bacon and mushroom, fries with gravy, a salad, juice, coffee and blueberry pie. The server took a quick glance at the tank top I was spilling out of. She kept one eyebrow raised as she wrote my order. Like I cared. Maintaining a fashionable body image was the least of my troubles. I said, "And I'll have ice cream on that pie. Two scoops, no, make that three."

As I waited, I examined *One Man's Justice*, page by page. Sure enough, pages 149 and 150 were stuck together too. I used my fork to pry them apart. The paper tore a bit, but that was the least of my problems. Inside was a folded sheet of tissue paper with small, precise handwriting.

I felt more irritated than exultant. Secret messages? Glue in books? Not like Laura hadn't had a phone. Why this overly theatrical approach?

Dear Camilla:

If you have this letter, it's because I am dead. My hope is that you will find and read this book and therefore see my message. I have much to regret. I refer specifically to my involvement with the Settlers movement. I have blood on my hands and guilt in my heart. I lack the courage to turn myself in. In recent months, the woman you knew as Frances Foxall attempted to justify our role to the public. For her foolish decision, she is now dead, as is the woman who called herself Sylvie Dumais. I believe that someone is picking off those of us who survived. Bianca Celestri is still alive. I believe you can trust her. Norine Thompson was one of us. I am not so sure about her. I read about your successful investigations and thought you would try to put things right. You'll find information in my safety deposit box, which only you are authorized to open. Please deal with the documents accordingly. I hope they will help you to comprehend our actions and the blight they brought to our lives and the lives of others. I would like you to find my parents and put their minds at rest.

Well, gee, thanks, Laura, wherever your soul is reposing, I appreciate your confidence and this bracing chance to live on the wrong side of the law while people try to kill me.

If Laura had admitted her guilt and taken her lumps, most likely she and Chelsea would be alive, Bianca wouldn't be on life support, and Jasmine wouldn't be in danger. In my frame of mind, I didn't care much what happened to Norine. I found nothing to confirm or dispel my gut instinct that either Joe or Kate Westerlund had played some vile role in the Settlers' rampage.

I examined the rest of the book with care. No more glued papers. No clue as to who might be wiping out the Settlers and why.

The restaurant was soothing, homey and comfortable. I tried to focus my scattered thoughts. My vision was getting worse. I could hardly see in one eye. I foraged through my backpack for a pen and finally located one. But although I had a cool costume collection, I didn't have a pad of paper. The napkins in the chrome dispenser would have to do.

I took four of them. I started by sorting out whom I could count on and whom I couldn't. I could count on my sisters, but only to make things worse, so they went on the napkin marked NOT. I included Conn McCracken with my sisters. Elaine definitely went on NOT. Ray Deveau had a warm heart, cold feet and apparently a short attention span. As a cop, even in Cape Breton, there was no chance he wouldn't have heard about the Canada-wide warrant, yet he hadn't tried to reach me. That made Ray a NOT kind of guy.

Mombourquette would have to call in the cops, but he'd do his best to keep Jasmine safe, once I explained things. He'd help me afterwards, plus Gussie would be in good hands, so he got a separate napkin, labelled "Limited But Necessary". I could count on Sheldon Romanek in court and for any legal jousting before, after, and during. He joined Mombourquette on the "Limited" napkin. P. J. did too. Although his loyalty was always to the story, he'd stick to the right side of the law.

That left Mrs. Parnell and Alvin. Bunny too. They went on the "Count On" napkin. I glanced around the restaurant. The ogling guys had departed, and no one was paying attention to me. My mountain of food arrived. But I had lost my appetite. I ate three fries, then sat staring at the rest. Finally, I pulled out Bunny's phone, at least I was hoping it was Bunny's phone. It had about fifty per cent charge left. I prayed it was enough to do the job. Alvin answered on his cellphone instantly.

"Camilla, where are you? Are you all right? Can we…hang on, Violet wants to talk to you."

"Ms. MacPhee. These news reports are most distressing. Trumped up charges, obviously. We had no idea how to reach you. How may we assist? Shall we meet you in bail court? The hospital?"

"Did you find out anything about the Settlers? Any photos?"

"We have a few print-outs. No photos."

"Are you in the balloon?" Damn that cellphone static.

"Yes, it's the final evening. But we can get down and join you. Just say the word. It's hard to hear you, there's a lot of static."

"Can you get to the Vanier area in thirty minutes or so? River Road near Queen Margaret. I need witnesses. And there's safety in numbers."

"You can count on us," Mrs. Parnell said.

"You're on the right napkin." I gave them the Westerlunds' address and filled them in on what to expect. I repeated everything so the static on the phone didn't screw up my meaning. "You can't miss me, I'm wearing a blonde wig."

"In fact, Ms. MacPhee, the location is excellent. Our balloon is heading south on the Rideau River. We can't control direction, as I imagine you know, but we can control up and down. We'll be there."

I called Bunny and brought him up to speed and told him what I needed. "Wow. I've never been a witness. Cool."

"Thanks for everything, Bunny. You can count on me if you ever need anything." I turned off the phone, in order to conserve power in case I had to call the "Limited But Necessary" list.

I left most of my meal untasted.

At the cash, I turned my attention to the small television set mounted by the coffee makers. The people at the counter were watching with great interest. The local news was on. A reporter stood on a street corner.

"The hunt continues for fugitive Ottawa lawyer, Camilla MacPhee, now considered armed and dangerous. MacPhee is wanted on a Canada-wide warrant in connection with two murders as well as car theft. A third victim, Bianca Celestri, is in critical condition under police guard at the Ottawa General Hospital. In breaking news, MacPhee is believed to have gained access to a weapon from an Ottawa police officer after injuring the officer in a house search. Ottawa police have not yet issued a full statement on this latest development, but we will keep you informed.

Police have increased the reward for information on MacPhee's whereabouts to twenty-five thousand dollars. A special tip line has been set up."

The tip line number flashed below a file shot of me looking deranged. A couple of guys at the counter wrote down the number.

"An officer's weapon?" I blurted. "What the hell was that about?"

"That's something, eh?" the cashier said as she handed me my change. "Apparently, she shot a cop."

"Holy shit."

"They're going to take her down first time they see her."

I said, "And ask questions later."

"Yup. Something's got to be done about people like that. It's got so nobody's safe nowhere."

"You got that right." I headed back to the washroom and lost my three fries.

I did my best to keep my head high as I left.

*   *   *

There wasn't a cab to be found. I whipped out Bunny's phone. The first cab company I called said thirty to forty minutes. The second couldn't commit to a time. What the hell. I called Youssef and said a friend had given me the number, and I needed to be picked up near Montreal Road and the Vanier Parkway. I tried a little French accent just in case. I didn't want him to send the cops. Twenty-five thousand dollars goes a lot further than the average fare. Youssef wasn't on duty. His cousin Faroud could be there shortly.

Faroud didn't recognize me and didn't seem remotely interested in his passenger. That was good, because the tip line reward would probably get him into a program to get his medical accreditation here. Faroud was not in a chatty mood. That wasn't my problem, but I needed his medical knowledge. I said, "I'm visiting a friend with a bad concussion. You ever know anyone with a concussion?"

"Yes," he said.

"She says the symptoms come and go. Did you know that?"

"It can happen."

"She's having trouble with her vision. Did the person you knew have that?"

"I've known people with that problem."

"Sometimes her vision's a bit better, then a bit worse, then a bit better. Can that happen? I mean, in your experience."

He looked back at me in the rearview mirror. I didn't think there was much chance he'd recognize me. Especially without my stinky dog. He said, "In my experience, your friend should get to a hospital fast."

"But my question was, do the symptoms come and go? Get better and then worse and then better? That's what's happening to my friend. Her vision in one eye seems to come and go."

He said, "Concussions are tricky. The symptoms can change rapidly. Seem better, seem worse. But it doesn't matter. If your friend has unstable symptoms, especially vision loss, she has to go to the hospital. She might have bleeding in her brain. Does she live here? I'll take her."

"It's okay," I said. "Just asking."

"No charge to take her," he said. "But maybe 911 is better."

"I'll ask her," I said as we pulled into the Westerlunds'. The meter read five dollars. I dropped ten onto the front seat. "Thanks. Can you come back in fifteen minutes? I'll try to talk my friend into going to the hospital."

I struggled out from the cab and stumbled badly. I had trouble walking. I prayed Faroud thought I'd had too much to drink.

I positioned myself by the side of the Westerlund house, where I couldn't be seen from inside. I watched Faroud drive off. I looked up to see if any balloons were arriving. I could see a small cluster drifting along the river in a lazy formation. I wished that Mrs. Parnell and Alvin, my two most stalwart allies, would hurry, but, of course, arrival by balloon wasn't the most precise. I hoped they would get a move on, since my plan to confront Kate and Joe required reliable witnesses. If my timing was wrong, it was game over.

Patience is not my best thing.

I wandered around the back of the house to check out entrances and exits. There appeared to be a back door from the sunroom where Joe Westerlund spent his life. I ducked past that, in case Kate spotted me. My head was reeling, and I knew there was a good chance, I'd pass out soon. I dug out the cell and called the "Limited But Necessary List".

I had to leave messages for P. J. and Romanek. Thank heavens Mombourquette picked up.

"What?" he shouted.

I shouted back that I was at the Westerlunds'. "I believe Kate Westerlund is dangerous. If I end up in jail, find the connection between them and the Settlers."

"Who the Jesus are the Westerlunds?"

Fine time for the goddam phone to cut out. I had no choice but to go in. A silver Neon was parked in the driveway. My heart jumped. That must be Kate's car. It was just like the one I'd seen in front of Bianca's. The front door of the house stood open. I had a clear view of Kate Westerlund locked in a struggle with another woman. As I ran toward the house, Kate pummelled the other woman's head, knocking her straw hat off. I stumbled close enough to see that the second woman was Jasmine. Her eyes were wide and wild. Why had I left her alone to fend for herself? How had Kate found her? Did she know Jasmine worked with Chelsea and might recognize her? Kate must have systematically tracked her down. I'd screwed up big-time, and I couldn't wait for help. Faroud wasn't back yet. I tried the goddam phone again. My fingers shook as I dialled 911. I could only see out of one eye. The phone crackled. The 911 operator answered. I said, "Emergency. Serious assault in progress."

"You're calling from a cell. We need the address please." Static broke up the operator's voice.

"We're on the River Road in Vanier. The address is…"

"Speak louder, I'm losing you."

I screamed the address into the phone as I raced toward the front door, stumbling on my three-inch heels. The phone died. I stumbled and landed on my knees. When I stood up, Kate and Jasmine had vanished from sight. The front door was now closed. No balloons, no cab, no P. J., no Bunny, and Mombourquette was probably searching for the address. Even Romanek and cops would have been welcome at this point. I lurched up the front steps and grabbed the doorknob. I tumbled into the house and landed chin first on the hall floor.

I dragged myself to my feet and stared around. The good eye had greyed over. Now I could only see dark and light shadows. I put out my hands to keep from bumping into things. Somewhere nearby there was shouting. Was that a shot? Follow the noise. I felt my way along the hallway until I encountered a doorway. I remembered a portable phone in the Westerlunds' hallway. I hoped the dark shape was the table it sat on. Lucky guess. I fumbled the receiver and dialled Alvin's cellphone. I pressed it against my body to muffle his voice. Before he answered, I jumped. I heard shouting from what I thought was the living room.

"Dear God, Kate," I yelled, "don't harm her."

"Way too late for that," Jasmine said.

Thirty-Seven

J asmine, are you all right?" I said, lurching through the door and careening into the nearest wall with its huge soft wall hanging.

"I am now," she said.

I heard soft sobs from the corner. I had a shadowy impression of Kate Westerlund, hunkered down, weeping. She appeared pathetic, but I wasn't fooled.

"Thank God, you're okay, Jasmine," I said.

From the corner, Kate wailed, "No. She killed him."

"What?"

"Joe. She killed Joe. She's insane. What harm could Joe do? He was helpless."

Jasmine said crisply, "But he'd already done plenty of harm in his life, hadn't he? The people your precious Joe killed were just as helpless. But unlike him and unlike you, they were innocent."

Jasmine didn't sound distraught.

Kate said, "He did what he believed in. He always lived by his principles."

"Interesting principles," Jasmine said. "You can shoot innocent people to get enough money to live out your delusions of grandeur. You can complete your education and masquerade as an exemplary citizen."

"Joe lived a good life. He taught at the university. He…"

Jasmine said, "There's the thing. He lived. You see that's the difference between him and his victims. Life. He owned the nice house, had the artwork and the beautiful wife who was just as guilty as he was."

"He gave back to his community. He gave to his students. He made amends."

"How could he make amends? Could he bring back a woman to life? Could he give a mother back to a daughter who never got to know her? Amends? He made me sick, and so do you."

Kate screamed, "You shot him in cold blood. What's the difference between you and him?"

"Here's the difference. I told him why he was going to die, and he understood. He got to think about it and what it meant. My mother never had that chance. She was just a nice young woman with one baby and another on the way who went into the bank to get enough cash to buy a playpen. She never knew why she was cut down. She didn't understand why she had to drown in her own blood."

My knees buckled, and I crumpled to the ground. I slid the cellphone over behind a shadow that I took to be a planter. I couldn't see well enough to tell if either of them saw me do it.

"Joe's dead?" I said, trying to comprehend what I was hearing.

"That's the good news," Jasmine said. "It's working out beautifully. I've got nearly all of them now. They've paid the price for their actions. Kate will be next, then I'll track down Bianca. Of course, they'll let their guard down once they hear you've killed yourself, Camilla. Then I'll finish my job."

"But who else is left besides Bianca?"

"Norine, naturally. Stupid bitch. Where do you think she

got the funding for that restaurant? But then they all had such wonderful false lives, didn't they?"

I was still having a bit of trouble with all this. "You mean they all moved to Ottawa? Isn't that a bit odd?"

Jasmine said, "Not too smart maybe, but you can see why they would. It was Canada, easy to get to, easy to blend in, using dead people's identities, but away from the FBI. And I think Joe Westerlund still had a big hold over them. These women had a shared history. No one else knew what they'd done. I suppose they acted as a vile support group."

"I imagine they'd need to help each other."

"Help each other, my ass. They had everything they wanted. They had money from those robberies. They each got themselves a good education, graduate degrees. Houses, cars, careers. Did you see Laura's portfolio? Do you think I had a wonderful life growing up?"

"I'm sure you didn't," I said.

Jasmine said, "I had a father who never got over his wife's death. He never held a proper job after. Do you think it's easy getting through school on welfare? I can tell you it's a lot harder than buying your way in with blood money and stolen identities."

"You planned this whole thing," I said.

"I planned it wonderfully. But the best part is that I was the last face they saw, the last voice they heard. I made sure they all knew why they died."

"But how did you find the Settlers?"

"Remember all the fuss about Kathleen Soliah? During that time, Frances Foxall wrote an opinion piece in an online forum discussing the beliefs of groups like the Symbionese Liberation Army and the Settlers. She did a great job of justifying her actions. 'Life goes on,' she said. Don't you just love that? She truly believed that she, and all the others, should be left alone because time had passed, enough punishment that she had needed an assumed identity for all these years. I didn't share that view. I'd been reading everything about the Settlers for years. I knew it was just a matter of time until I found one of them."

"But an online forum should be anonymous. How did you find her?"

"It took a bit of work to track her down, but it was worth it. She mentioned her horse farm in her article. She let a few other things slip. It took some digging to find out where her farm was, but then it all paid off. I showed up one day, said I was interested in horses. It wasn't hard to feign interest. She wasn't the least bit suspicious. She had an ego the size of Ontario. I knew she kept in touch with the others. In her article she said 'We are living good lives. We are productive useful citizens.' Wasn't that nice for them? I learned she met a lot of friends in Maisie's. I sweet-talked her into asking Norine to give me a job. Couldn't be simpler. I figured out who was who soon enough."

"The horse," I said loudly. "You frightened the horse. And it threw her."

"That's right. And I made sure she knew why."

"Sylvie Dumais in the canoe. The same thing?"

"It's not hard to put an unobtrusive hole in a canoe. I watched from the shore. I was almost sorry when the hypothermia got her. I had a lot of venting to do."

"I see that."

"Yes. And your precious Laura Brown. That was my best."

"You were her special dinner guest. You wore the straw hat," I said, trying to prop myself up. I hoped like hell Alvin or Mrs. Parnell was hearing this on the phone. "What did you do? Tinker with her insulin?"

"That was a good guess. I put it back afterwards. That's when I ran into you in the night. I'd been searching her house for a couple of hours looking for information on the others. Then you showed up. I'm glad you didn't die then, because you've come in very handy. Now I'm through, and you get to be the guilty party."

"Laura must have liked and trusted you."

"Her actions killed my mother and ruined my life. Then she meets me at Maisie's, and without knowing anything about me, wants to help with my education. Don't you just love it?"

"She obviously liked you very much and trusted you. She didn't bother to hide her code number from you. You didn't want her to die in the house."

"The house would have been fine. A fall down the stairs. But every time I was there, this stupid woman with those miserable wiener dogs would walk by and wave, or else this nosy old geezer next door would be drooling over her. Couldn't take the chance. It turned out for the best, because now we know that people survive falls down the stairs."

By this time, I was on all fours, trying to struggle to my feet.

Jasmine said, "She really didn't want to go over that cliff."

Kate whimpered in the corner.

"How did you get her on the other side of the fence?"

"I had a knife. Knives are persuasive."

"But there were people around."

"Around, but not close enough to see that."

"You wouldn't have used the knife on her, because you wanted all these deaths to look accidental."

"Laura didn't know that. Everything came as a surprise to her. And now, of course, with you in the picture, the deaths don't have to look accidental."

"No. I suppose not."

Kate whimpered in the corner. Not much hope of her getting us out of this trap.

"You seem to understand. It's too bad I need you to be dead."

"Maybe so, but there will be an inquest. Police investigations."

"But at the end of the day, everything will still point firmly to you. I'm just a server in the restaurant. No connection at all, except when you visited me and threatened me."

She had a point.

I said, "I gather you attacked one of the police officers and took his weapon. That was useful to pin on me too."

"Wasn't it?" Jasmine said.

It was a small chance, but I hoped like hell Alvin was on the phone, picking up some of this.

"That reminds me," I said. "Chelsea was your friend. Why kill her?"

"Friend, my ass. Greedy little thing. She figured out I knew them all. She wanted money from me. She became a little more collateral damage."

Jasmine was just a blurred shape. As much as I needed to see, I was glad I didn't have to look at her face. "And I conveniently provided you with props to mislead the police. My jacket. Crashing around making a fool of myself. You hid my cash card."

"Funny, you made me nervous when you came to Maisie's. I just forgot to give the card back to you. Norine must have taken it to get your name. She was quite suspicious about you. It sure came in handy. Helped to make you look guilty."

"Speaking of guilty. That silver Neon of yours. I saw that car outside Bianca's place. Someone else will have seen it too. If she regains consciousness, she'll tell the police."

"I'll make sure she doesn't regain consciousness."

The room was tilting strangely. I felt my head whirling. My

302

stomach heaved. I had to stop Jasmine. But there was no way I could get to her.

"I'm glad you're here, Camilla," she said. "It saves me a lot of trouble."

"You lied about everything," I said, stalling. "You lied about Elaine."

"It doesn't take much to get you to turn on your friends," Jasmine said. "It's surprisingly easy to start a rumour with the police."

"You lied about Kate too. And Joe."

"That was the truth. They were the core of the group. I got that much from Sylvie before she died. Not their new names, though. I had to rely on you for that."

A dim shadow rose slowly behind Jasmine. I did my best to appear to look straight at Jasmine. Anything to distract her. I sensed rather than saw Kate lurch forward. Kate loomed behind Jasmine and slammed into her. Jasmine lurched forward and lost her balance. She staggered, whirled at Kate. A shot reverberated. Without a sound, Kate crumpled to a heap on the floor. The smell of cordite filled the room.

I stood, stunned, unable to react. Even with my limited vision, I could see the stain spread around her, clearly red. Jasmine turned back to me.

"Now look what you've done, Camilla," Jasmine said. "The authorities will not be pleased. Fortunately, I happened along to check on Kate and was able to struggle with you and save myself. It pays to be younger and taller. I was too late for poor Kate, of course. But as Frances Foxall liked to say, life goes on.

I saw the shadow as she raised her arm.

"This is the police," a familiar voice came from behind the door to the dining room. "Put the gun down and step away from it."

Jasmine said, "Thank heavens you're here, officer. I have been able to wrestle the weapon from your fugitive, but I didn't know how much longer I could hold her. Is there an ambulance here? My friend, Kate Westerlund, has been shot by Camilla MacPhee."

If I hadn't been scared shitless, I might have admired her audacity. If it struck her as odd that the police would pussyfoot through the dining room, there was no sign in her voice.

"The game's over. Put the weapon down. And move away from it. Slowly."

If I had one small thing to feel happy about, it was that Jasmine didn't know Bunny Mayhew. She turned slowly.

"Can you come in here, officer?" she said.

Something told me that Bunny hadn't passed the cop test.

Bunny said, "The house is surrounded, Jasmine. Put the gun down."

I was pretty sure the house was not surrounded by anything but wishful thinking. I figured Bunny was about to be dead. What was worse, to shout a warning? Or hope like hell the ruse was working? The decision was taken from me when Jasmine raised her arm and fired the Glock. As far as I could tell, she fired right through the wall. Bunny screamed. Jasmine was more than smart enough to figure out that if the man in the next room didn't come out firing in a Kevlar vest, then he was either out of commission or not a cop. Jasmine edged along the wall in front of me, heading for the door, raising her arm. I had to stop her from killing Bunny.

Across the room, Kate Westerlund gurgled as if her lungs were filling with blood.

"Not dead enough, Kate?" Jasmine said. "We can fix that."

That was my chance. I had nothing to lose. I grabbed the wall hanging and yanked with every bit of strength I had left and hurled it at Jasmine's back. The heavy sheet of fabric came off the wall with a shower of dust. I tumbled after it. The wooden frame behind the hanging hit Jasmine. Something clattered on the floor. I hoped like hell it was the Glock. I fell forward, jarring my head. The grey mist turned black. Now I saw nothing. Where was Bunny? Where was Jasmine?

I yelled, "She dropped the gun. Get help, Bunny. Tell them what you heard."

Kate gurgled again. She was probably dying. I couldn't even find her, let alone help her.

Jasmine spoke, it seemed, from a distance.

"That wasn't at all nice, Camilla. But it gives me another opportunity. Two birds with one stone." She chuckled.

"Someone heard everything you said, Jasmine."

"Someone who didn't mind impersonating a police officer. I don't think I have to worry. Even if anyone believed his story. But here's something more immediate for you and Kate to worry about."

I heard a half dozen small clicks a few seconds apart. A familiar sound, but what was it? Not a gun. I didn't think a Glock would click. I struggled to my feet, reaching out and happy to touch a table to steady myself.

Kate moaned. It sounded like she was just a couple of feet from me. If I guessed right, I had just bumped into the coffee table. Kate must have been by the corner window. I couldn't be sure. My head was buzzing, my thoughts jumbled.

The first whiff of smoke took me by surprise. What was that smell? I inhaled a whiff of acrid smoke, like burning fabric. Seconds later, smoke seared my throat. Everywhere I turned, the smoke seemed thicker. I knew now the clicks were from Jasmine's lighter. Jasmine must have ignited the wall hangings. My eyes streamed.

Vainly hoping someone would hear, I yelled, "Help, fire."

Kate was coughing now. I was confused, disoriented. Where was the door? Where was the window? I tripped over the low table. Something rocked and rattled. I remembered the huge vase with the sunflowers. Vases contain water. I pulled off my tank top and felt around. I tossed out the flowers and soaked the shirt. I put it over my mouth and dropped to the floor, hoping the smoke would rise and I could stay below it. I fumbled around in my pack for another piece of cloth. I dragged out something, the Sens shirt perhaps. I soaked it too. I crawled to where I thought Kate was lying. Even with the wet fabric over my mouth, breathing was difficult. I tried to remember what I'd seen in this room on my previous visit. In the corner, a table, lamp and rug, I thought. I prayed I was going in the right direction and not just deeper into the smoke-filled house. I finally connected with Kate's body. I pressed the cloth to her face. I could feel the small rug on the floor. Coughing and spewing, I rolled her onto the rug. I felt for the edge, got a grip and crawled toward what I hoped was the way out, pulling the rug along with me. I'm pretty sure I couldn't do that on a normal day, let alone blind and concussed. That's the power of fear. I figured the smoke would get us before the fire did.

Was Bunny going to die because of me? The irony was, I might save Kate, who could have saved everyone, and hadn't.

Hacking and gagging, I pulled her toward what I hoped was the front entrance. I said to Kate. "If you have any strength left, push." But Kate had even stopped coughing.

I don't believe in giving up. I didn't plan to die without a fight. But I was too exhausted to move.

Something pulled against me, waking me up. Voices, yelling. Jasmine? I did my best to fight back, connecting fist to face. Someone yelled.

"For Christ's sake, Camilla. Stop fighting."

Mombourquette?

"You have to get Kate," I said, trying to help whoever was pulling me from the building.

"We got her out."

Bunny?

"Don't let the cops shoot me," I said.

Maybe that was a dream.

After That

One last bit of advice. Try not to party in the hospital. The nurses don't like it, and some of those guys are bruisers.

The Labour Day weekend was long gone before I opened my eyes again. Pale institutional green surrounded me. That meant I could see. I sure hoped I was in a hospital and not in hell.

Wherever I was, I must have been expected, because there was the obligatory crowd scene.

From the foot of the bed, a voice said, "Welcome back, Ms. MacPhee. You have been missed."

"Lord thundering Jesus, Camilla," a second voice said, "I guess you'll do anything to stay out of a balloon."

I sat up and grabbed Alvin's wrist, "Listen to me. That girl, Jasmine, she killed all those people. She shot Joe. And Kate. I think she shot Bunny. You have to find Bunny."

My sister Donalda said, "If you mean that young man who picked up your book and helped drag you from the burning house, he's all right. Although the police wanted to talk to him, and he seems to have wandered off."

"You have to tell the police about Jasmine."

"The police know," Mombourquette said.

"Do they believe me now, Leonard?"

"They do."

"That's good. Does that mean you're in the deep weeds for getting involved in the investigation?"

My sister Alexa spoke up. "I think the brass will be overlooking anything Leonard might have done to save your life, since you wouldn't have been in danger if they hadn't been hounding you based on false accusations. That was shocking."

Alvin said, "Your lawyer can't wait to pursue the matter."

"I bet," I said.

Edwina said, "Of course, you could have saved yourself a lot of grief by giving yourself up earlier. You wouldn't have lingered here for five days while we thought you were going to die, Missy."

Time for Mrs. Parnell to speak up again. "Ms. MacPhee did the only correct thing. She waded into battle without regard for her own safety. We will respect that."

I liked the sound of that. So did my father, who had been quiet until now. He leaned over and gave my hand a squeeze.

"Thanks, Daddy," I said. "You were right about the devil."

"Good job, um, Camilla," he said.

Sentimental moment. Always to be avoided with the MacPhees. "What about Kate?" I said.

Mombourquette said. "She's still in critical condition. Between the gunshot and the smoke inhalation and the shock of what happened to her husband, it's touch and go."

Donalda said, "Lucky to be alive. What were the chances that a passing cab driver would turn out to be a doctor?"

"Faroud came back to help?" I said.

"He arrived before the emergency personnel," Mombourquette said. "Damn lucky. If she lives, it's because of him. The papers loved the story, though. Hero doctor can't get a job in Canada."

I smiled. Faroud deserved whatever good breaks he got.

Alvin and Mrs. Parnell exchanged glances. "We are sorry, Ms. MacPhee, that we didn't arrive in time to stop these terrible things. We heard a lot on the cellphone, which of course you intended, but because of the winds, we just couldn't get close enough to land. As soon as we realized your life was in danger, Young Ferguson borrowed another phone from the balloon pilot and called for reinforcements."

"Pretty snippy at 911," Alvin sniffed.

Mombourquette said, "I can just imagine what that story sounded like. But never mind. Police, fire and ambulance all showed up."

"Right after you did," I said. "Thank you, Leonard."

"Hey," he said, "what are friends for."

"What about Jasmine? Did she get away?"

P. J. piped up. "That was the best part of the story, Tiger. Aside from the lawyer on the run and the shoot-out and the burning house."

"What was?"

"Your high-flying friends, Alvin and Mrs. P. here, tracked her in their balloon and kept in touch with the police by phone until they picked her up. What a story that was. You couldn't *make* it up."

"Well, we didn't act alone, of course," Mrs. Parnell said. "Every balloonist on that part of the Rideau kept an eye out for her."

Alvin said, "You gotta love cellphones."

"But she's such a psychopath. She'll concoct a story."

P. J. said, "Her credibility took a dive when she fired at them."

"Ah, yes," I said. "That happens."

P. J. continued, "I think they've managed to figure out who she is. The stuff about University of Ottawa law school was all bullshit, of course. She's been a troubled kid all her life. They're not even sure how she got from the States into Canada. She was putting up a pretty good imitation of a psychotic episode, so that might help her avoid first degree murder charges. Anyway, I've got a feature assignment to track back to the original tragedy and follow her and her family over the years."

"What about Laura Brown and the other girls who were part of the Settlers?"

"I'm trying to track their families too."

"Any luck?"

"Nothing so far. But I bet I'll get a book out of this," P. J. said.

With any luck, there'd be more to add to it when Laura's safety deposit box was opened.

From the back of the crowd, Elaine said, "I'm not quite so happy. I guess we have to talk."

I said, guiltily. "I'll replace your clothes."

She said, "That's not what I mean."

Mombourquette said, "I am afraid I did some damage to your friendship. Jasmine somehow planted those rumours about Elaine. I haven't figured out how yet."

I said, "It was your mysterious appointments that worried me, Elaine."

Elaine said. "I guess Jasmine set everyone up. The mysterious appointments, as you call them, were with a counsellor. When Frances and Laura and Sylvie died, it was a wake-up call for me. I decided to try to reconcile with my family, and I wanted some advice. I found someone I trusted who was willing to give me a couple of sessions on the weekend. I wasn't ready to tell everybody."

Good time to change the subject. "Hey, who are all the flowers from?"

My sister Donalda inspected a weird plant.

"That's from me," said P. J. "Venus fly trap."

"I sent the orange blossoms," Elaine said.

"The snake plant is from your lawyer," Alvin said. "It came with a substantial bill for phone consultation and negotiations."

"The two-dozen roses are from my cousin Ray in Sydney," Mombourquette said. "He's been calling every hour. Crazy with worry."

I snorted. "Crazy with worry, my fat fanny. Now he sends flowers. Where the hell has he been?"

"In hospital himself. Emergency appendectomy when he was on that course. His appendix burst when he was at the training site. It took a couple of hours to get him to a city hospital. They said another half-hour, and he wouldn't have made it. He'll take a couple of months to recover."

I sat up a bit straighter. "Oh. I thought he'd just dropped out of the relationship. Why didn't anyone tell me? You sure he's all right?"

Mombourquette shrugged. "His kids kept trying to call you, but they didn't want to leave an upsetting message informing you that he was in intensive care."

"And they kept hanging up?"

"They're kids. They'd start to cry. By the way, the dog misses you."

"How is Gussie?"

"Aside from an ugly incident with a club sandwich and a Canadian Tire catalogue, pretty good."

"I guess that's one happy ending." I looked around. "Now that this is over, I'm looking forward to going home and spending time with Alvin's dog and Mrs. Parnell's cat."

Silence.

"What? Why are you all looking at each other like that?"

"You can stay with us," my sisters said.

"Thanks. I think I'll just go home."

Mrs. Parnell said. "You can fight it in court. They can't just evict you over that one false alarm."

"Or even the repeated complaints by the neighbour," Alvin said.

I sank back on the pillow and closed my eyes. I felt relieved when the duty nurse said. "Show's over, folks. Patient needs rest. Time to hit the road."

Long after the noisy crowd bickered its way down the hall, I lay there thinking. Maybe Laura's house would come in handy after all.

And roses are always good.

Photo by Giulio Maffini

Mary Jane Maffini is a lapsed librarian, former co-owner of the Prime Crime Mystery Bookstore in Ottawa, author of two mystery series and a double Arthur Ellis winner for short crime fiction.

The books in the Camilla MacPhee series are: *Speak Ill of the Dead*, which was shortlisted for an Arthur for Best First Novel, *The Icing on the Corpse*, *Little Boy Blues* and now *The Devil's in the Details*. In 2003, she launched a new series, the Fiona Silk mysteries, the first of which, *Lament for a Lounge Lizard*, was shortlisted at the 2004 Arthurs for Best Novel.

Mary Jane Maffini resides in Ottawa, Ontario.

Also by Mary Jane Maffini

LAMENT FOR A LOUNGE LIZARD
A Fiona Silk Mystery

As if it weren't bad enough being a failed romance writer with no sex life, poor Fiona Silk has to cope with the spectacularly embarrassing demise of her old lover, the poet, Benedict Kelly. It's exactly the sort of thing people notice in St. Aubaine, Quebec, a picturesque bilingual tourist town of two thousand. Now the police start getting nasty, the media vans stay parked on her lawn and the neighbours' tongues keep wagging in both of Canada's official languages. Worse, someone's bumping off the other suspects. Can Fiona outwit a murderer in the mood for some serious mischief?

"stylish and amusing..."   -Maclean's Magazine

"..as adept at comedy as she is at laying out a tangled crime trail...Maffini surrounds Fiona with memorable—but often annoying—friends... Surviving their needs and obsessions is almost as daunting as solving the murder."
                    -Foreword Magazine

$13.95 CDN, $11.95 U.S.   ISBN 1-894917-02-2   280 pages

The Camilla MacPhee Mysteries

"With its sassy heroine and eccentric but lovable cast of supporting characters, Mary Jane Maffini's Camilla MacPhee mystery series is a bright new addition to the Canadian crime writing scene."
-Lyn Hamilton, author of the Lara McClintoch archaeological mysteries

Speak Ill of the Dead

ISBN 0-929141-65-2
$12.95 in Canada, $10.95 U.S.

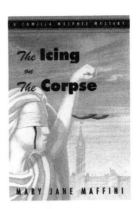

The Icing on the Corpse

ISBN 0-929141-81-4
$12.95 in Canada, $10.95 U.S.

Little Boy Blues

ISBN 0-929141-94-6
$12.95 in Canada, $10.95 U.S.

www.maryjanemaffini.ca
www.rendezvouspress.com